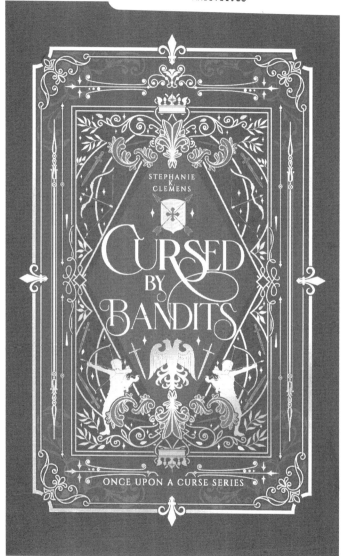

STEPHANIE
K.
CLEMENS

CURSED
BY
BANDITS

ONCE UPON A CURSE SERIES

Alexandria,

Enjoy the adventure!

♡

Stephanie K Clemens

CURSED
BY
BANDITS

STEPHANIE K CLEMENS

ADVENTURES WITH INK

To those who dream of making a difference.

CHAPTER ONE

I landed on my ass with a thud that left me gasping for breath. I scrambled to my knees, desperate to suck in air. For a second, I paused, glaring at my opponent through a curtain of red hair.

"Are you going to do something, or are you going to pose for a painting?" the dark-haired woman asked. She even had the audacity to gesture for me to come get her.

I swiped my hair out of my face and growled as I leapt into action. Using everything I had been taught during my time at the nunnery, I attempted to be cunning like a fox, quick like a cheetah, and strong like a bear. I swung my leg out in a swift kick, but the woman anticipated my move, countering with a well-executed sweep that landed me on the forest floor once again.

It never mattered what I did: I always ended up on the ground, gasping for air.

"Enough, Lady Jane, I can't handle having the wind knocked out of me one more time today," I said as I lay on the ground looking up at the light filtering through the deep green leaves of the forest trees. "One day I will best you in hand-to-hand combat. However, that day is not today. Now help me up off the ground you so kindly laid me out on."

A laugh escaped Lady Jane as she held out her hand. I clasped her proffered hand and practically flew to my feet as she helped me up. I'd been trying to beat Lady Jane in a fight for years now. It didn't help that my friend was at least a head taller than me and built like the warrior nuns my father had sent me to study with six years ago. Lady Jane arrived at the nunnery shortly after I did. It wasn't long before we became friends. A friendship that was forever solidified after the Incident. It was a chapter of our lives I preferred not to revisit, but the event lingered in the bond we shared.

"Maybe one day, but first you'll have to figure out how to take advantage of how you're made and how you think. You're still trying to fight like we're the same instead of using our differences to your advantage." Lady Jane threw her arm around my shoulders as we walked back to the dormitory rooms. "Now, get cleaned up for your birthday feast and our farewell party. You wouldn't want to be late to an event honoring you."

I was finally going home, and I had convinced Lady Jane to come with me. "I can't believe we leave tomorrow for Lockersley. It feels like we just barely got here. And somehow, it also feels like it's been forever."

The brief jaunt through the forest brought me to the stone dormitory building, its sturdy walls and surrounding colorful oak trees stood guard like sentinels, a reminder of how long it had endured there. I opened the door to my home for the past six years. It was simpler than my rooms at the castle, with only a small bed and washbasin, which thankfully was already filled with water. I peeled off my training clothes and washed as best I could with the tepid water and small towel that had been left for me.

I grabbed a fancier version of the uniform I'd worn every day here at the nunnery. The outfit included loose pants that almost looked like a skirt until they cinched at the ankle, something I absolutely adored. The long tunic dress laced up on the sides from under my arms to my hips; there, the fabric split open all the way to the bottom of the tunic. I picked out my favorite color for tonight, a deep teal that made my eyes really shine. I took one last look at myself in the mirror and smiled. I felt pretty as I headed to my farewell party.

"Rowan, you look so pretty tonight. That color on you is magnificent." Lady Jane folded me into a bear hug.

I wrapped my arms around her in return. "Thank you. But you didn't give me a chance to see what you're wearing."

She held me at arm's length. Lady Jane looked stunning in a deep purple outfit that was the same as mine, but hers fit her willowy frame to perfection. It would be easy for me to always look at my friend through jealous eyes. She was tall and beautiful. I was not. In fact, I would describe myself as short and squatty.

Lady Jane grabbed my hand. "Come on, let's go dance." She dragged me to line up with our fellow classmates and the nuns all waiting for the band to play the music for the next dance.

The first notes of the song drifted across the room, sounding like the footsteps of a fairy through a magical forest. As the music built, all the dancers took their first steps, weaving around each other, turning, and promenading until I couldn't help but laugh. The moment was so carefree and happy; I wanted it to continue for as long as possible.

It was hard to believe that my time at the nunnery was at an end. My father had sent me here when I was fifteen. When he told me I needed to learn from nuns, I threw a fit, screeching, stomping, and slamming doors until I threw myself onto my bed sobbing. I hadn't wanted to go and my father sending me away felt like a rejection deep within my soul.

Now that it was time to go home, I had to admit he was right. Studying here was one of the best things that had ever happened to me. I learned more from the nuns than I ever thought possible. When I arrived, I assumed I would only be learning about running a household and the skills related to that task. I should have trusted my father though, because this place was like no school or nunnery I had ever heard of; while I was here, I learned about archery, fighting, battle strategy, and so much more. After being away for so long I was excited to show my father all the skills I had acquired.

"Now is not the time to be deep in thought," Lady Jane said, interrupting my reminiscing.

I shook my head to bring myself back to the present. "You're right. I'm rather thirsty. Let's get a lemonade or maybe something stronger to drink."

Lady Jane laced her arm through mine and together, we weaved through the crowd, smiling and nodding at everyone who acknowledged us.

Jane leaned in. "Do you think the headmistress is going to miss us, or is she secretly doing a happy dance?"

"Did you not see her on the dance floor? There's nothing secret about her celebrating our departure. I'm pretty sure we were both her best and worst students." I pointed to where the headmistress was currently twirling and skipping.

Jane laughed. "You're somehow right. Both of us were quite diligent in our studies, with a tendency to start fires. They really should have stopped trying to teach us how to cook after the Incident."

I shivered dramatically. "No, you must never ever bring that up again. I cannot stand to relive that," I said, shaking my head. Did my friend have no compassion? It might be the basis of our friendship, but it had no place in tonight's festivities.

She poured herself a glass of lemonade and gulped it down as quickly as she had filled it. Then she grabbed my hands and pulled me to the dance floor. "Come on, we must dance all night before our new responsibilities come crashing down on us."

I spun under her arm. "Lockersley could never feel like a burden, or anything like a responsibility. Wait until you see it, you'll understand what I mean in an instant."

CHAPTER TWO

I shuffled back to my dormitory, the only thought in my head that soon, very soon, I would be off my aching feet and asleep, even if it was only for a few hours. The dance had gone into the wee hours of the morning, and I was having too much fun to even contemplate leaving. Which was why I was now looking at a pre-dawn sky, already dreading waking up despite the fact I had yet to go to sleep or even lay down in my bed.

After an interminable amount of time, I was standing in front of my door. I leaned forward, resting my head on the wooden surface and contemplated whether or not I could sleep in this position, but thought better of it and pushed the lever down.

The door whined as it swung open and I stumbled across the threshold. I unlaced my tunic dress and pulled it over my head. Panic set in as I was briefly stuck, arms up as if I was surrendering, the tunic encapsulating my head. I wriggled until I was free and fell into bed, out of breath from all the struggling.

I lay there with thoughts of tomorrow and the trek home drifting through my mind. My eyes fluttered shut, and I fell into a deep slumber.

What felt like moments later, there was pounding. Loud, vicious pounding. I rolled over, covering my head with the pillow, hoping that would make the awful noise go away.

It didn't.

"Rowan! Get your lazy ass out of bed! It's time to go," Jane hollered, her words followed by more banging on the door.

I winced and attempted to force my eyes open. When that didn't work, I rubbed the sleep away. Pushing myself up, I peeked out, squinting when the bright light hit my face. I flopped back onto my bed with a sigh.

Thud!

The door swung open. Jane stood in the doorway, hands on her hips. She reminded me of my nanny growing up. That woman also was annoyed by my inability to get out of bed at a reasonable hour. She constantly told me how I would never be a good wife because I was lazy. I didn't have the heart to tell her becoming a wife was not one of my life goals.

"Okay, Rowan, I have a bucket of water in my hand, and if you don't get out of bed right now, it's going to end up on you."

I didn't hear the slosh of water. Jane was bluffing. There was no way she was going to dump water on my bed and on me. After my perfectly reasonable calculations, I burrowed deeper. I needed more sleep.

Sploosh.

Cold, that's what I felt first, so much cold.

Then wet.

I sat up.

My hair clung to my face.

Water dripped down my forehead, my back, my chest and pooled around my thighs.

I spluttered, only sounds came out of my mouth as I was not coherent enough to put together a complete sentence.

I could hear the dripping of water as it soaked through the mattress and trickled on to the floor.

I stood, trying to get away from the cold and the wet. Water sloshed out of my bed and on to the floor as I shifted my weight.

"I can't believe you did that!" I pushed my hair off my face and the water from my shift and hair caused the puddle on the floor to expand.

"Really? You're surprised? That seems like a 'you' problem since my warning was quite concise." Jane crossed her arms.

"I didn't think you would actually do it." I wrung my hair out and started to braid it. "My bags are packed and I just need to change out of this wet shift."

"I'll meet you by the carriage in five minutes. Do not get back in bed," Jane hollered as she slammed the door to my room.

How could I? The bed was a disaster.

It didn't take me long to throw on my clothes and braid my red hair into two long braids, my wet bangs pinned back because I didn't want to put up with them while sitting in the carriage all day long.

"I was about to get you," Jane said. "I couldn't figure out how you fell asleep in a sopping wet bed. But knowing you, you could probably do just that."

"Ha! There's no way I could fall asleep in a puddle of water." I shuddered. "I don't even enjoy swimming."

Jane chuckled. "Like that would stop you from sleeping."

I looked at her, eyebrow raised, then shrugged. "You're probably right."

The carriage, a resplendent vision of shiny black lacquered wood adorned with elegant gold accents, waited in front of my room, promising a journey in opulence. The luggage was meticulously strapped down, ready for the lengthy trip. Swinging the carriage door open, I hopped in. I stuck my head through the velvet curtains, eager for the journey to begin now that I was awake and not surrounded by the comforts of a bed. "What's taking you so long? We should have left a long time ago."

The look Jane shot me would have caused a lesser woman to take back their words. I, however, couldn't stop myself from throwing back my head with what could only be described as bellowing laughter.

"You're a pain in the ass. You know that, right?" Jane hiked up her heavy skirts to climb up with me, sliding across the red leather seat to settle herself in the corner of the carriage.

I kicked my legs up on to the seat next to her, smirking. "But that's why you love me, right?"

"Do I have a choice?" she asked. Her eyes twinkled mischievously.

"Before the Incident, you might have, but now? You're stuck with me." I lifted my hands behind my head and laced my fingers together, ready for the long day ahead.

At least the carriage was well-appointed, with its padded leather seats and velvet-lined walls. We were travelling in the very definition of luxury. Something neither of us was used to after our stay at the nunnery. I was surprised my father owned such a glitzy carriage. It really didn't seem like his style.

"This is—nice." Her eyes were wide.

Her shock didn't surprise me. I had a tendency to talk—a lot—especially about my father. He was the type of nobility I aspired to be.

"I can't wait to show you around Lockersley. Especially the keep. Just imagine walking down a hundred and sixty steps, which takes you to a beach, then climbing back up a hundred and sixty steps to get to the castle gate. Now you're way above the ocean and you can enjoy watching the waves come and go for hours on end.

"On the top of the cliff is the stone village where I grew up. There's the castle with the great hall and all our bedrooms, but we have so much else there. Not just the castle and church. There's a blacksmith and all our horses, the barracks, the dressmakers, and so much more. On the other side of the stairs are woods and a village with my favorite shopkeeps. You're going to love it." I clapped my hands together, unable to contain my excited, anxious energy. I had been gone for so long I was worried it wasn't going to be anything like I remembered.

"I know, Rowan. You've told me about this paradise you call home so many times I decided to go with you." She nudged my leg with her knee.

"I'm sorry, I can't help it. I've missed it so much." I swayed with the carriage, the motion reminding me of the gentle rocking of a baby's crib. It could send me to sleep. No matter what I tried to do, from watching the scenery parade by, to taking in the splendid transportation, none of it worked. It wasn't long before I started to drift off to dreamland.

The last thing I heard was Jane: "Of course you're falling asleep. Why would I expect anything different?"

The carriage jolted to the side. My feet thudded to the carriage floor and my head collided with the unforgiving side wall. The sudden movement abruptly roused me from my slumber, snapping me back to consciousness. The wheels of the carriage seemed to insist on hitting every bump and rut in the road, causing the vehicle to creak and groan while the clop of the horse's hooves intruded into the space.

My head throbbed to the rhythmic sound of the horses. I rubbed it where it had come into the unwelcome contact with the wall. As I sat, Jane's composed figure greeted me.

"I was wondering if there was anything that would wake you up." Jane smoothed her dress over her knees, and a hint of amusement laced her tone. "I thought you said the roads to Lockersley were well maintained. This feels like we're in for a wild ride."

Sleep clung to me, making it difficult to respond to my friend. I opened the curtain and stuck my head outside. We were in my hometown, but it was nothing like I remembered.

Six years ago, the town vibrated with energy. Everything was well maintained. I had never been anywhere else like it. Now it looked rundown. The once-vibrant homes looked dismal with peeling paint. The straw roofs sagged, and the flower boxes sat empty. The people that were out and about barely glanced at the carriage, focused more on their work. Their slumped shoulders and tired eyes made everyone look so . . . sad. The sadness had weaved its way through everything from the uneven road to the tired buildings and dying gardens. In the center of town, shop signs hung by one ring, their creaking the only reminder of the once-bustling marketplace. I didn't see any food stalls, the general store was empty, and the tavern looked like wild animals inhabited it.

"Stop the carriage." I jumped out before the vehicle came to a complete stop. "This is wrong—so very wrong." A lump formed in my throat as I surveyed the desolation. The lively town of my childhood, the place I had gone on and on about to Jane for six years, was nowhere to be seen. Replaced by something I didn't recognize. What had happened to my home?

Movement out of the corner of my eye caught my attention. A friar walked to the town church. I ran after him as rain pelted the ground, and the smell of water hitting dry dirt filled my nose.

"Friar!" I yelled after him.

He kept his head down and continued on the path to the church.

Catching up with him, I grabbed his arm. "Friar, please, can you take a moment to answer some questions?"

He looked up at me, his brown eyes dejected.

"Tuck?" I couldn't believe my eyes. Everything about my old friend looked tired, from his eyes to his brown skin and gaunt cheeks.

"Rowan?" His only movement was to look at where I held his arm.

I let go immediately. "It's me."

"It's about time you left that fancy school of yours and came home. We can't afford to pay for you to be there for another year." Tuck's tone was as sharp as his words.

I didn't understand. Pay for my schooling? "What do you mean? The nuns never charged anything extra, only what my father paid when he enrolled me." It's why I always helped with dinner and any other chores, including thatching roofs, fixing doors, building furniture, and planting gardens. There was no way the town had paid for my time at the nunnery.

I reached towards my friend again, only for him to take a step back. My arm fell, rejected.

Tuck scoffed. "That's not what your uncle has been telling us."

"My uncle? What does he have to do with any of this?" My eyes were wide with confusion. My father and his brother, Jonathan, never got along. "Why is he saying anything about me or my schooling?"

Tuck looked at me, like really looked at me for the first time. "You don't know?"

"Know what?" Dread caused the blood to drain from my face.

"Your father, he's dead. Some believe he was murdered."

Thoughts jumbled in my brain. Putting together a coherent thought, much less a sentence, was beyond me. I sank to the ground. My father was my hero. How could he be gone, dead—*murdered*? "When—how—why?"

"Rowan, what happened? You're as white as a ghost," Jane asked as she walked up to us.

The hostility I had felt from him before was gone, and Tuck sat next to me on the cold earth. "It was about six months ago. I'm surprised no one told you."

"Six months . . ." I trailed off, clutching my stomach as if that would keep the grief from overcoming me. I turned towards Jane. "Did you know?"

"How would I know? And why would I keep it from you?" Her tone was soft but firm.

"You're right. I don't know what I was thinking." My eyes burned and the dreary town blurred in front of me. "I need to go . . . somewhere . . . not the middle of the road."

Tuck stood, offering me his hand. "I have just the place."

I took his hand and followed him without thought, the sound of crunching gravel the only indication that Jane followed.

CHAPTER THREE

I followed Tuck to a small cottage, the only one in town that still had flowers in the window boxes. It was a bright spot amidst the dull hues of the town. Maybe there lingered someone in Lockersley who still had hope, who hadn't surrendered to whatever forces had reduced my home to the state of decay I saw before me.

"Where are we?" I asked, wiping my wet cheeks with my sleeve.

Jane shook her head. "I have a handkerchief, if you would like one."

I nodded. My sleeves were already damp from wiping away my tears.

"This is William's cottage." Tuck knocked on the door, two short taps, pause, three louder knocks, pause, two short taps.

"Who's William?" Jane asked.

The arched wood door swung open. A blond man stepped forward, the light of the sun illuminating his golden body.

"Will Skarlec?" I questioned, my brain not able to comprehend how the gangly boy had turned into the man standing before me. "Is it really you?" At one point in time, I dreamed about doing naughty things to the mountain of a man in front of me. I almost changed my mind about marriage. But the subject of those dreams changed the day I met Milo.

"Rowan?" He enveloped me in his arms, lifting me from the ground as he hugged me. Once he set me back on my feet, he held me at arm's length. "I can't believe you're here. It's been ages." His eyes roamed over my body, finally reaching my eyes. "What's wrong? Why are you crying?"

"She just found out her father passed away, you big lug." Tuck swatted him with his cap. "Now give her some space before she has to make her way to the castle."

"Damn." He rubbed the back of his neck. "I'm sorry you had to find out like this."

Jane took a step forward. Even as tall as she stood, she only came to Will's chin. "If you don't mind letting us in, Rowan could use a place to compose herself."

"Come in, no need to stand outside," Will said.

Jane rolled her eyes. "We would if you'd move out of the way. I'm sure you know your size is rather imposing and takes up the entire doorway." She didn't wait for him to move, but pushed her way through.

I wanted to laugh at her audacity, but it seemed wrong to find something humorous right after learning of my father's death.

I followed Jane into the cottage. The room gave me all the cozy feelings of fresh baked bread in the oven and apple pies cooling in the window. Much like the home's owner, everything but the actual room was oversized, causing the small area to appear more inviting, despite the lack of space.

"I'm sorry, with the news of . . ." I gulped back tears. "Introductions were forgotten. This is my companion, Lady Jane. And this is Tuck—I guess it's Friar Tuck now—and Will Skarlec." I sat in one of the comfy-looking chairs, tucking my legs underneath me. "What's happened to Lockersley? This"—I gestured towards the outside—"is not what I expected to come home to. I can't believe my father would allow the town to get to such a state."

An uncomfortable silence filled the room. The chair Will sat in groaned as he shifted in his seat, his leg bouncing to a staccato rhythm. Tuck suddenly found a potted plant fascinating. Their actions said more than most words.

"What? There's more about my father, isn't there?" I asked, bracing myself for more pain. "One of you, say something."

"He wasn't well before he died. The few times I was granted access to him, he suffered from hallucinations." Tuck paused. "I don't think he was ill, though. I think he was being drugged."

"It was terrible, Rowan. One day, your uncle shows up for a visit. Then suddenly your father's ill and his mind is going. Your uncle ended up locking him in a tower in the castle." Will stood but seemed to think better of it and sat on the arm of a large chair. "It's right about the time things started going to hell here. Taxes were raised, then raised again. Eventually they were so high none of us could afford them anymore."

"Where's all the money going? It certainly wasn't to pay the nuns," I pondered.

Tuck twisted his cap. "Your uncle said it was to pay for your schooling at the nunnery. That you insisted on staying longer even though he couldn't afford it."

"That's a lie if I ever heard one," Jane chimed in. "We had to earn our keep and our education. The nuns worked us hard."

"It's the truth: I never knew my life would ever involve peeling so many potatoes or washing so many dishes." I gazed into the distance, remembering the day I had said goodbye to my father. I blinked as the room in front of me came into focus. "I was always supposed to come home on my twenty-first birthday. There was never a change of plans or talk of me staying longer. If I had known what was happening here, I would have come home early."

"If any of us had known how to reach you, we would have." Tuck sat. "But your father never said a thing, and your uncle was even worse. It was almost like you didn't exist."

"You know, Rowan, we're going to have to go to the castle at some point. I know you want to stay here, but your uncle is expecting you." Jane stood.

She was right, I didn't want to leave. My time would be better served here, figuring out a way to help the town return to its former glory. How would going to the castle help me do that?

Will stood as well. "Lady Jane is right. Your uncle will want to see you. He might already wonder where you are, and that wouldn't benefit any of us."

"How is going to the castle and being with that man going to help anyone?" I crossed my arms with all the maturity of a sullen teenager.

Tuck rubbed his chin. "We haven't been able to place anyone in the castle. Not that I would ever ask you to spy on your family, but it might be nice to have someone on the inside seeing what's happening."

Jane raised her eyebrows. "Sounds like spying to me. Not that I'm opposed, but maybe we should tread carefully at first."

My ears had perked up at the mention of spying. I could do that. In fact, I could investigate and discover if my uncle had anything to do with my father's death.

"Spying sounds like the start of a plan I can get behind." I leapt up from my seat. "Come on, Jane, we have a lot of walking to do to get to the castle."

CHAPTER FOUR

"You weren't joking when you said we had to walk down one hundred and sixty steps to turn around and walk back up them immediately." Jane held her side, sucking in air as she tried to catch her breath.

"Did you think I was exaggerating?" I looked back at her. She was bent over at the waist, hands on her knees, fighting to breathe. I offered her advice I had been given long ago: "You know, if you breathe in through your nose and out through your mouth, it will help you catch your breath."

"Sure—tell—me—that—now." Each of her words was punctuated by a quick intake of air.

"Try it, and fast. My uncle is coming."

I barely recognized the man approaching me. There were some similarities to my father, like the long nose and square jaw, but the similarities stopped there. In all my memories of my father, he was a jovial man with unruly bright red hair that defied order, sticking out in every conceivable direction. His brother—my uncle—presented a completely different image. His hair, a blend of salt and pepper, accentuated a seriousness about him that I could only characterize as foreboding.

"My niece, Rowan, it's wonderful to see you. Even if it is under these terrible circumstances." He held out his arms like I was supposed to catapult myself into them for a hug.

I curtsied instead. "Uncle Jonathan, it's been too long, I must introduce you to my companion, Lady Jane. I'm sorry, what do you mean terrible circumstances?" I looked around as if I was searching for someone. "Where is my father?"

He paused, staring down at me, his facial muscles shifting until he appeared to be concerned. "You haven't heard."

I took a step back. "Heard what?"

"Oh dear." He pulled on the back of his neck, acting like he didn't want to say anything else. "I'm so sorry. I hate to be the one to do this. But, your father has left this world. I'm shocked the nuns didn't tell you."

I gasped at his words and raised my hands to my face in what I hoped was an appropriate reaction to hearing the news of my father's death for the first time.

As he took my hands in his, I wanted to flinch away but was worried that would make him suspicious. Instead, I looked around the top of the cliff where the keep sat. It was vastly different on this side of the steps. The hustle and bustle around the keep created a convivial atmosphere. The stone buildings stood tall around it, the chapel and great hall competing with each other for which one was the tallest.

The difference in the atmosphere from the town of Lockersley shook me to my core. How could life be so vibrant here in the keep, and so desolate in town? Lockersley had been abandoned by its ruler, left to rot until it no longer existed. But I had been taught from a wee age that the townsfolk were my people. It was my job to look out for them, make choices that benefited them. It was apparent my uncle did not share those beliefs.

But without the town, the keep and its people would eventually dwindle into nothing as well. My father had always emphasized the importance of the people of Lockersley. Out there were the farmers that provided food for the keep, the loggers that chopped and delivered wood to the keep, the list went on and on, from weavers, to seamstresses, to apothecaries. He never exaggerated when he spoke of the importance of the town in keeping the castle up and running. If they were gone, we wouldn't have any of the essentials to survive.

It was clear my uncle did not have the same values. As I walked inside the great hall, I noticed all the new tapestries lining the walls. They were stunning, picturing the lore of the last battle of the dragons, but those must have cost a small fortune. The amount of people they could have fed made my stomach churn.

I clutched my stomach as I wandered through the great hall, my uncle blathering on about something or other, but I couldn't manage to decipher whatever it was he was saying. My mind raced with other thoughts.

"Are you okay?" Concern was apparent in Jane's tone, even though she spoke quieter than a whisper.

I glanced over at her. "This isn't right, the room; it's beyond extravagant while people are starving, unable to make repairs on their homes. Jane, they don't have enough money to run their businesses so the market sits empty. And yet, these tapestries are new and I would guess foreign—the silk threads are not something I've seen used around here."

The more I scanned the great hall, the more the flamboyance of the room revealed itself. The throne, new and resplendent, had been crafted with an unapologetic abundance of gilding. It bore no resemblance to the locally sourced items my father typically favored.

Back in the day, he consistently supported local tradespeople for new furniture or décor for the keep, resulting in a collection characterized by its beauty in simplicity—crafted from trees grown nearby, shaped by the hands of local carpenters. However, within this room, all remnants of that authenticity had vanished. All remnants of my father had vanished. As I took it all in, tears threatened the corners of my eyes. My yearning to return home, once so fervent, now collided with the harsh reality that everything that had once made the keep feel like home was no more.

I turned, ready to run out of the room and go somewhere, anywhere but where I was, but Jane grabbed me before my uncle could even sense my desire to be here was gone.

"You cannot run. Later we can discuss what to do, if anything, about this. But right now you have to remember your uncle is in charge," Jane said, her voice so quiet only I could hear her.

"Well, he shouldn't be. My father sent me to the nunnery because he was going to hand over the throne to me." I gestured around the room. "None of this would be here if I was the one in charge."

"That may have been his intentions, but it doesn't look like he followed through with his edict. If he had, you would have a lot more responsibility," Jane said as she moved through the room, following my uncle.

I huffed and followed. Jane was right; I didn't like it, but I had to agree with her.

The tour of the keep had been nothing short of enlightening. Every nook and cranny had been adorned with items that screamed of extravagance. My uncle showed us his favorite room. He called it his Weapons Room, insisting every great household had one. The space was both ostentatious and foreboding with suits of armor stoically occupying each corner, while an array of weapons—swords, crossbows, maces, and more—hung meticulously from the walls, leaving no inch unclaimed.

My favorite room was the library. It reminded me more of my father than any other room in the keep. The leather chairs were worn, which had me reminiscing of the times I had sat at my father's knee as he read me stories of daring men doing great feats and conquering their enemies.

While I was there, I ran my hand over the leatherbound books on the shelves, dust covering my fingers. It was clear my uncle had done nothing in this room. He didn't even have the servants clean it properly. It was like the only bit of my father left in the keep was being left to rot, to destroy itself over time. Just like what was happening in town.

There was no way I was going to let that happen. I wasn't sure what I was going to do, but I couldn't sit around and do nothing while everything I held dear fell to the ground around me.

The tour of my home ended with just enough time for Jane and me to get ready for dinner.

I stood in my room, the same one I had used before going to the nunnery. At least nothing had changed in here. The four-poster bed was the same I had slept in six years ago, made by the local carpenter out of maple, my favorite wood. My clothes were laid out on the bed by my lady's maid, Winnie. I had sent her to help Jane so I could have a moment to myself. I wasn't used to having someone hover around me anymore, not after the years of learning to be self-sufficient. Glancing at the yellow dress Winnie had left for me, I scrunched my nose. It wasn't the color or style I would have chosen, but I didn't believe my uncle would tolerate any of the things I had brought with me from the nunnery.

Sitting on the bench at the end of my bed, I removed my boots and socks. Feet free, I scrunched my toes into the well-worn carpet that ran the length of the bed and shrugged out of my heavy travel dress. I let it fall to the stone floor as I stood on the rug I had picked out as a child, now barely able to keep the cold of the stone from soaking into my bare feet.

I cast a critical glance at the yellow dress laid out on the bed next to me and couldn't stop my grimace. It would have been charming if it had been a light buttery yellow or even elegant in a rich gold color, but the sickly tinge of green that marred the yellow rendered it almost putrid. I shook my head in undisguised disgust.

I stood, shrugging off my distaste. I pulled it over my head and shimmied until it fell to my feet. Looking down, the top gaped over my less-than-endowed chest, falling off my shoulders, and the sleeves were so long my hands disappeared in them. The only reason the dress didn't pool around my feet and leave me standing in nothing but my undergarments was because it snagged at my hips, pulling at the seams. The putrid fabric hid my feet lying on the floor all around me, a tripping hazard. This was awful: I'd never put on a dress that fit so poorly.

"Jane!" I cried, desperation evident in my bellows.

My friend careened into the room, followed by Winnie, her eyes cast down.

"What's wrong, Rowan?" Jane asked.

I gestured at the catastrophe on my body. "Look at this, I can't go down to dinner in this. I'll trip on the hem, tear it, and end up standing there in nothing but my undergarments."

Jane giggled, and her hand flew to her mouth in an attempt to hide her mirth. It didn't work.

I glared at her. "This is not a laughing matter."

Jane waved her hand in front of her face. "You're right, you can't leave the room in that dress with it looking like that. I'm sure we can figure out something." She tapped her nails on her teeth as she thought.

"Is there anything I can do, miss?" Winnie asked, wringing her hands.

"I can handle this, Winnie, but we might need to re-fit Lady Rowan's other dresses. Why don't you get your dinner." Jane turned back to me. "Where's your belt, the one with the metal disks? Oh, and the chain with the two pins."

In the corner of my room was my trunk. I ran over and dropped to my knees in front of it. After opening it, I scrounged around until I found the accessories Jane had asked for. Standing, I handed them to her.

"First, I'll pin the chain on the back of the dress to hold it together. It'll gape open in the back, but that's better than in the front." Jane pinned the dress just as she had described. "Now put on the belt and we'll use it to pin up the skirt so it only drags behind you. At least we can avoid you tripping on the front."

I looked in the mirror. The color made me look sallow, drawing attention to the dark circles around my eyes, but it looked like it fit. Which was a vast improvement from before.

"Who picked out the color? It really does not suit you." Jane looked at the dress with a critical eye.

I shrugged. It was no use dwelling on how awful it was on me when I couldn't do anything about it. "I don't know, but they clearly don't know anything about me. Hopefully my entire wardrobe isn't like this. Are you ready for dinner?"

"Let's go, see what your uncle has in store for us."

As I descended the stairs, Jane followed me. Again, the overwhelming opulence continued to envelop me, making the once-familiar paths unrecognizable due to their grandeur. I stepped into the banquet hall, and the stark contrast from my memories became even more apparent. A massive, sturdy wooden table stretched before me with enough chairs to seat forty or more people. At the head of the table sat my uncle; to his right sat a man I didn't recognize.

"Rowan, I'm so happy you made it to dinner." He stood, snapping.

Servants laden with food swarmed the room. It looked like a ballet as larders of fish, beef, and lamb were set in front of us, followed by platters of root vegetables, apples, and various forms of squash. The last item to come out was a basket of bread.

Excessive. That was the only word I could think of to describe the amount of food sitting on the table in front of only four people.

"This feast is completely unnecessary, Uncle. Jane and I are used to much simpler fare, aren't we, Jane?" I turned to my friend.

Jane stared at the table, mouth agape. She quickly shut it, realizing I was talking to her. "This is far beyond what we're used to having. The nuns believed the table should never be filled with more than we needed to eat." She demurely sat.

"Nonsense, my niece deserves the best. Now sit, eat." He gestured to the empty chair next to him.

He waited until I took a seat before sitting down again.

"Thank you. There's so much food here, I doubt we'll finish it all. Perhaps we could send what is leftover to the villagers?"

Uncle Jonathan's eyes flashed. "Why would we do that? They're lazy, good for nothings who are unable to pay their taxes, money they owe because they have the privilege of living on this land. We owe them nothing." His tone was a mixture of disapproval and nonchalance, as if he actually believed what he said.

His dismissive tone didn't prevent me from flinching at his harsh words. He didn't see my reaction, he was so intent on the meal placed before him. Jane did see, the slight shake of her head warning me to keep my mouth shut.

He passed me the basket of bread. "We are going to have a ball to celebrate your long-awaited return and your birthday."

I slouched in my chair. After seeing the village today, the last thing I wanted was a ball. "That's not necessary, Uncle."

"Of course it's necessary, we must introduce you to eligible men."

I shifted in my seat, unused to having my wishes so summarily dismissed. "Uncle Jonathan, I wish you would listen to me. I just discovered my father is dead. I would like time to mourn."

"Nonsense, your father wouldn't want you sitting around sulking. Especially considering how important it was to him to see you settled, with a family. Oh, and in that vein . . ." My uncle gestured to the man sitting at his right.

My eyes trailed over to where my uncle pointed. I took in the man sitting there gnawing on a chicken leg. His thin mustache and greasy hair left much to be desired. It took all my willpower not to shudder in disgust when he smacked his glistening chicken-greased lips as he chewed.

"I would like you to meet Jocelin Montfort, the Sheriff of Nottinghamshire."

CHAPTER FIVE

Lost in a thunderstorm of thoughts and emotions, I gazed out the window, where in direct contrast to my inner turmoil, the night was calm. I allowed my tears to flow freely down my cheeks, a silent testament to the pain I carried within. Pain I had no idea I could feel until this afternoon. I made no move to wipe away tears, as if acknowledging their existence might somehow erase the profound ache in my heart. How could my father be gone?

Here I was, back in Lockersley after years of absence, standing in my old bedroom just a few doors down from where my father's presence once was. But he was gone, his absence a cruel blow that shattered the reunion I had longed for in my dreams. Never again would I feel his embrace, his bear hug that could crush the weight of the world, or experience the joy of being lifted off my feet and spun around in his arms.

As I surveyed the town so changed from the place I once knew, I felt the weight of my uncle's unwelcome presence, and it was painfully clear he did not want me here either. What I had yearned for as my homecoming had morphed into a disorienting blend of the foreign and the familiar, leaving me adrift. The void that had been inside me since I left home, something I thought would be filled upon returning, now loomed large and felt impossible to repair.

I hastily brushed my sleeve across my face, attempting to stem the tide of tears, but they continued to flow unabated. My thoughts came back to my father every time it felt like I was done crying, and the river of sorrows started flowing down my cheeks once again. I couldn't bear to be here, to linger in this place that was once my home; the need to escape consumed me, driving me to seek refuge elsewhere, anywhere but here. My resolve hardened, and I wasted no time in shedding the ill-fitting dress I had worn to dinner, exchanging it for one of the more comfortable garments I had brought back from the nunnery—a simple ensemble, entirely black, intended to help me blend into the shadows as I plotted my escape from the keep.

With one last look at the bedroom that no longer belonged to me, I tugged the black hood over my head and climbed out the window. Grateful that my room was situated on the second floor, I braced myself for the descent.

Despite the biting chill of the ocean wind and the relentless mist that soaked my clothes, I knew I could navigate the climb down. It was something I had done many times when I was younger. However as my fingers numbed from the cold and wet, it was difficult to keep my resolve steady.

Finally, as my feet found purchase on solid ground, a wave of relief washed over me, nearly overwhelming in its intensity. My entire body trembled with the release of tension now that I had successfully navigated the treacherous descent from the castle walls.

I brushed myself off and continued on, letting my feet lead the way. I wasn't sure exactly where I was going, only that I needed away from the keep and everyone in it. Which was why I was surprised to find myself standing in front of the old oak tree that had stood like a sentinel in the center of Lockersley long before I could remember. Attached to one branch was a simple swing, nothing more than a plank of wood connected to the tree by two long ropes. I tested the ropes to ensure they were secure before I sat on the wooden plank. Dragging my toe through the soft earth below, I allowed myself to sway gently, the rhythmic motion a soothing balm for my troubled mind.

My father would always bring me here as a child. He would spend hours pushing me as he taught me about the land and my responsibility to the people here. He focused on what it meant to be nobility, how too many of his peers thought it meant they deserved respect and wealth; when in his mind, if he wasn't ensuring that his people were healthy and happy, he deserved nothing from them. The thoughts were so ingrained in my values it was like I could hear his voice talking to me now.

I knew I had to do something to fix what I had come home to. But what?

"What am I supposed to do, Da? It's your brother on the throne. I know you wanted me to be there, but there's no precedent for that. I wish you were here to tell me how to fix all of this. But if you were here, it wouldn't be broken."

The wind whispered through the trees, and for a moment I thought I could hear him. But that couldn't be. He was gone. The leaves rustled, and it was like I felt his presence walk up behind me. I shook my head, but the feeling didn't go away. I could feel him behind me, waiting to push me on the swing and talk through one of his tenants' problems with me, listening to see what solution I would come up with.

With each kick of my legs propelling the swing higher into the air, I allowed myself to drift into a reverie, imagining my father's invisible hand gently pushing me onward, urging me to soar higher. As I swung back and forth, grappling with the weight of my current predicament, a sense of purpose crystallized within me.

The castle, brimming with indulgence and excess, held the key to easing the suffering of my people. It was a realization that seemed to be echoed by the very air around me, whispering its assent to my unspoken resolve. Startled, I turned my head, half-expecting to find my father standing behind me, offering guidance. But he was not there.

However, at that moment, I no longer felt alone. It was as if my father's spirit hovered nearby, a silent presence imbuing me with strength and clarity. With renewed determination, I embraced his unseen guidance, knowing that he was with me, and everything he taught me guided my actions as he watched over me.

With a renewed sense of purpose, I walked back to the keep, down and up the stairs until I stood below the window to my room. My fingers ached from earlier.

Screw it. Picking up a handful of pebbles, I walked over to the window next to mine. I chucked the handful of pebbles towards the opening. Nothing. I grabbed another handful, then another one.

Finally, Jane came to the window.

"Open the door for me," I said, somehow whispering and yelling at the same time.

She rolled her eyes, but nodded before disappearing.

I made my way to the front and waited, my mind whirling. I needed a plan. It's not like I could just start loading up everything from the keep and distribute it around town. It wouldn't be that easy. If it was, my uncle would already have done that instead of amassing the signs of wealth all around the castle. I tapped my lips, deep in thought.

The creak of the door interrupted my thoughts.

"Get in here," Jane hissed. "What were you thinking?"

I shuffled through the door. "I wasn't thinking, I just needed out of the castle. It was enlightening, though."

Jane looked at me, suspicion in her eyes. "What do you mean, enlightening?"

I looked around the corner before making my way up the stairs, keeping to the shadows the entire way. "I mean, I have the beginnings of a plan. Lockersley is going to be the thriving town it was before my uncle took over, and I'm going to make it happen."

CHAPTER SIX

J ane was silent as we climbed the rest of the stairs. I
don't know what I expected from her, but it definitely
wasn't a quiet companion. She had learned early on that
keeping her mouth shut when I was plotting was never
beneficial.

I pulled on the door to my bedroom, its cry loud enough
to wake anyone sleeping in this wing. Closing my eyes, I
breathed a sigh of relief as I leaned against the open door,
thankful my uncle had taken residence in the newer and
less drafty side of the castle. The air stirred in front of me
as Jane walked by. I opened my eyes to see her sit primly
on the edge of my bed. It was obvious she intended for us
to talk about my intentions tonight despite the exhaustion
settling over me.

I yawned loudly.

"Don't. You snuck out. Woke me up. You're going to explain why and what you mean by enlightening." Jane crossed her arms, causing her robe to shift and expose her very prim white nightgown.

I shrugged; it wasn't like I planned on keeping tonight a secret from her. I jumped into my bed and wiggled my way up to the top. Jane just stared at me the entire time. Waiting.

"I couldn't sleep because there were too many feelings to process. So I climbed out the window and went to the oak tree I told you about. The swing is still there." It was actually rather unbelievable that the swing was still there since everything else in Lockersley had fallen into disarray.

She sighed. "I'm so sorry for, well, everything. I can't believe no one sent word about your father." She crawled to the top of the bed until she was sitting beside me. I laid my head on her shoulder as she settled in.

"Jane, it was like he was there, talking me through what my course of action should be. He whispered on the wind as I swung back and forth. It was like I was a kid again and he was guiding me to the resolution he wanted. I can't ignore him."

She took my hand in hers and squeezed it tight. "What do you think he wants you to do?"

I sat up straight but did not let go of her hand. I loved how Jane didn't question any of what I was saying, or try to convince me my father wasn't leading me on this path.

"I'm going to redistribute my uncle's wealth, give it to the townsfolk and tenants." My eyes searched her face, looking for her reaction.

Jane looked at me, her brow furrowed as she rubbed her chin for a moment. She tapped her mouth with the index finger of her free hand, clearly deep in thought. "How do you plan on doing that?"

I shrugged. "That's yet to be determined. I just know it's what my father would have done."

Jane continued to stare at me. "What about the spying? Are you still going to do that for Tuck and Will?"

The plan to spy had slipped my mind as I sat on the swing tonight. However, to find out where my uncle hid his wealth would take work and more importantly, information.

"Spying is essential for my idea to work," I responded absentmindedly as thoughts ran through my head, one after another, some barely connected to my scheming, others very related to the planning. Based on dinner tonight, I doubted my uncle knew much, if anything, about the nunnery. He probably assumed I'd spent my time there learning how to be a lady, a skill my father even thought I needed after coming home with twigs in my hair one too many times.

"How, exactly, do you plan to spy on your uncle?"

"By convincing him I am something that I am very much not." I turned towards her, waiting to see if she knew what I was implying.

Jane raised an eyebrow, and it was clear she didn't know what I was suggesting.

"A lady."

My friend stared for a moment, then blinked. Suddenly, she tossed her head back, laughing so loud I feared she would wake the keep.

"It's not that funny," I muttered.

"Rowan, my dear. We must go over the details of your party."

I kept walking as if I hadn't heard my uncle speak.

Footsteps quickened behind me, leather soles smacking against the stone floor as he hurried to catch up to me. I wanted to speed up, but I didn't want him to know I knew he was there, so I kept to the sedate pace I had set for myself. Walking at a ladylike speed was more of a challenge than I had expected.

A heavy hand fell on my shoulder, halting my sedate pace. My face scrunched up in distaste as I fought the urge to shake off his hand.

"Didn't you hear me calling you?" My uncle pushed on my shoulder until I was facing him.

Forcing my face into a much nicer expression, I giggled—ugh, was this really how I was going to act while I was in the keep? "I'm sorry, Uncle Jonathan, I was lost in my own thoughts and I'm afraid I didn't hear anything." The urge to roll my eyes was overwhelming, but I pasted a smile on my face, glancing down as I did so.

"We need to sit down and go over the plans for your party. I want to go over the guest list. See what you think of the potential suitors I'm planning on inviting." He let go of my shoulder and placed my hand in the crook of his arm, ready to escort me to his chosen destination.

I removed my hand from his arm, clasping my hands behind my back. "Uncle, it's so kind of you to want to celebrate my return. But I don't need a party. I would rather not go to such an expense. It makes me uncomfortable after being at the nunnery for so long."

"That may be, but it is expected. People want to celebrate your return." His hand settled on the small of my back, and it propelled me forward until we stood in front of arched double doors made of solid wood. He removed his hand, and he pulled the doors open. His eyes fell on me.

I could tell he was noticing my all-black outfit, one from the nunnery.

"What on earth are you wearing?" He still stood in the doorway.

I looked down at my clothes, opening my eyes wide as I looked up at him. "Is there something wrong with it? It's the only black clothes I own, and I wanted to pay respects to my father. I know he's been gone for a while, but I didn't know." Tears filled my eyes, the first thing to happen that wasn't an act. "For me, it's like he died yesterday."

His teeth clenched, the tips of his ears turning red. But when he spoke, his words hid whatever emotions he was feeling. "How callous of me, of course you need time. Unfortunately, we can't postpone the party. It's important that people know you are back and ready for a match."

"I . . .," I took a deep breath to stop myself from arguing. I brushed past him into what appeared to be his office. "Of course. Whatever you believe is best."

Any traces of my father had been removed by the man who had taken his place. Which made no sense to me. My father raised me to believe I would take his place one day. He had even shown me his will, where he had put his intentions in writing. How had my uncle taken over my father's role? Was it because I was absent or something worse?

"Please sit." He gestured to a dainty wooden chair. "Here's the list of suitors I intend to invite."

He pushed a parchment across his desk as he took a seat behind the table. Every piece of furniture was daintier than I expected it to be. The level of craftsmanship was instantly recognizable on every piece in the room. But none of it looked like something made near here, which saddened me. All the money spent on this room and none of it helped my people.

I picked up the list in front of me. "Jocelin Montfort? You think the sheriff is a suitable suitor?"

My uncle raised his eyebrow, not happy that I would question him. "He's actually who I would choose for you. He has been very loyal since his appointment. But I did put others on the list."

I scanned the parchment covered in my uncle's spidery scrawl. Most of the names were unfamiliar to me, but there was one name that stood out: Connor Blackwood, the king's eldest son. Marrying me off to the next king was an interesting way to get rid of me, if that was what my uncle wanted to do.

"I'm sorry, Uncle, I cannot make myself care about the guest list. As I said, I would rather not have this party, but since it is expected and proper, I will trust you to invite the right people." I stood, brushing the black fabric of my clothing before walking out of the room.

CHAPTER SEVEN

I tugged my pantaloons up until the waist was directly under my duckies. I tied the drawstring as tight as I could, hoping, this time, they would stay in place. But no, as soon as I moved the unruly undergarments slipped down to rest on my hips, causing the crotch of the garment to take up residence somewhere close to my knees. I tossed my hands up in the air and flopped on to the four-poster bed inhabiting the center of my room. I stared at the corbels, wondering who had spent their time carving the detailed pineapples. These thoughts momentarily eclipsed the plight of my plummeting pantaloons when a knock on the door interrupted my reverie.

"Rowan? Are you ready to head to the banquet?"

I rolled on to my back. "No, and I'm not going!"

The arched wood door opened with an ear-shattering creak. "You have to go: the festivities are in your honor." Jane poked her head into the room. When she found me lying on the bed, her eyes rolled so hard she probably saw the back of her head. She shoved the door open and stalked over to me, crossing her arms as she came to a halt near my feet. "Why are you not dressed? This banquet and all the food involved is for you. How would it look if you didn't show?"

"Like I'm an inconsiderate, spoiled brat, like everyone thinks I am already." I grabbed a pillow and hid my face under it.

My friend snatched the pillow away. "But that's not who you are, and it's time to prove them wrong. Why aren't you dressed? The real reason."

I pushed myself up on my elbows. "Nothing fits. It's all too big. The red one hangs off my shoulders, the blue one makes me look like a child in my mother's clothing, the gold one drags on the floor."

"What about the green one?" Jane held up a long dark-green velvet dress.

I sighed, collapsing back on to the bed. "Too big in the bust and waist."

"Is that it?" she asked as she spread the dress on the bed next to me.

I nodded.

"Good thing I can hear your brain rattle around in there when you nod. If I couldn't, I'd think you were ignoring me." She laughed.

I fumbled around, finding another pillow. I grabbed it and chucked it at her; the soft impact sent me into a fit of giggles as I looked at the incredulous expression on her face.

Jane's hands found her hips as she stood there, ready to scold me like the mother I never knew. "Do you want my help or not?"

I scrambled to sit up, tucking my legs beneath me, my hands held up to illustrate my surrender. "Help, please can you help me, oh wonderful goddess of thread and needle?"

"No need to lay it on that thick. You had me at 'help.'" She searched her pockets for something. "I'm surprised you know the word."

"What are you looking for?" I stared at her quizzically.

Her brow furrowed. "I know I have it here somewhere." She opened the pouch she carried on her belt all the time. "Aha!" She held up a needle and thread like they were a trophy. "Here they are!"

I stared at her, my eyes wide with an incredulous look. "That's a first for me." My tone was serious.

"What are you talking about?" Jane asked.

I held back a giggle. "I've never seen anyone so excited to find a needle and thread."

She put her hands on her hips. "You want my help, right?"

I held my hands up in surrender. "Okay, okay. I'll stop teasing. Help me get this dress fixed."

She grabbed a hair ribbon from my dresser and sewed it on to the back of my dress, creating loops that would allow me to use laces to tighten the dress until it actually fit. She sewed another ribbon parallel to the first. I was amazed at the speed with which she made such tiny delicate stitches. I had been taught how to sew, but the skill was lost on me. Finished, she held out the altered dress for me to wear.

I pushed myself off my cozy bed and grabbed the dress from her. Standing, I attempted to hike up the offending pantaloons yet again. They still refused to stay in place. With a resigned sigh, I left them sagging off my hips and shimmied the dress on over my head. Jane tightened the back, causing the rich fabric to hug my waist and drape over my hips before cascading to the floor in a swirl around my bare feet. I spun, causing the fabric to flare out.

"Where are your shoes? You can't go to the banquet barefoot."

"You take the fun out of everything." I complained as I grabbed my boots.

The banquet hall was decorated for a celebration: candles and torches arrayed the room, and the flickering lights cast frolicking shadows, which escalated the feelings of revelry. The fire roared in the stone fireplace, keeping the room warm while we ate a sumptuous feast for dinner.

Once the plates had been cleared, the celebration moved from eating to dancing. Now the hall, with the scenic tapestries lining the walls, was sweltering as couples twirled and laughter echoed throughout the large room, creating an atmosphere of merrymaking.

I stopped to curtsy as the minstrels played the last notes of a song. It took forever for me to regain my breath after the energetic contradance. I needed a reprieve. I pasted a smile on my face as my eyes darted around the room, looking for an escape. It wasn't going to happen, though. Every direction I looked, eligible gentlemen swarmed me, all requesting the next dance. I wanted to say no, find a place to cool down. But I saw my uncle lounging on the throne at the end of the room, watching everything I did, which meant I couldn't reject a single suitor, especially not the Sheriff of Nottinghamshire.

"Lady Rowan." Montfort bowed, his oily-black hair falling over his eyes. "May I have this dance?"

Montfort was the very definition of swarmy: being near him made me want to bathe. Unfortunately, saying no wasn't an option. I looked back at my uncle as I nodded my assent.

Montfort took my hand in his clammy one. He escorted me to the middle of the floor as the minstrels picked up their instruments and played, filling the room with music. I stood across from the sheriff, waiting for the notes that started the dance.

I went through the steps, offering my hand to my partner when the music called for it, turning away when the dance required, and coming back together as necessary. Every now and then, I would look back and see my uncle's watchful eye following my every move. The sheriff, as repulsive as I thought he was, must be more important to my uncle than the other gentlemen vying for my attention.

With every step of the dance, I felt my body temperature rise until it felt like I was sweating everywhere. The worst sweat was between my thighs; it was slick as my legs rubbed against each other. I cursed the oversized pantaloons that offered no relief. They did nothing to prevent the sweat from forming as the fabric clung to my legs in places that only caused more discomfort as the sweat turned sticky. The seam that had taken up residence somewhere around my knees chafed, threatening to break skin.

Montfort winked at me as he put his hand on my back and spun. I winced with each step as the slick feeling turned sticky; this was the last stage before my thighs burned with the heat of a forest fire, or maybe the sun. Whatever the heat level was, I knew I needed out of this room before the next dance started. The friction of my thighs rubbing together was going to cause me to burst into flames, and starting a fire during my birthday celebration was not on my list of top ten things I wanted to accomplish when I turned twenty-one.

"I'm sorry, I must find a place to rest." I felt like an animal trapped with no means of escape. Montfort's burly body blocked my path to the exit. His resplendent finery looked odd on a man of his size.

He stepped back. I tried to scurry around him, but he still held my hand in his. I looked at it pointedly.

"I'll escort you. I was hoping for another dance, but this is even better. Now we have a chance to talk, get to know each other." He tucked my hand in the crook of his elbow.

I looked towards my uncle, worried he would react if I ran off, but he was distracted for once. "Thanks for the offer, but . . ." I pulled my arm back from where it rested on his and snaked my way through the jovial crowd, praying he wouldn't follow me.

Cool air caressed my heated skin. A sigh of relief escaped my lungs as I pressed my body up against the cool stone wall. The hallway stretched in front of me, a mix of blacks and greys broken up by the flickering of a torch. I was thankful for the draft. But it wasn't enough to stop the thigh rubbing. I made my way down the hall, attempting to walk in a way that kept my legs from touching. This led to a ridiculous cross between a waddle and the steps of someone who was saddle sore.

I fumbled with the first door that I came to, hoping for a refuge. I knew it wasn't a retiring room, but I couldn't remember what it was used for. Hopefully, nothing tonight. I needed a spot just for myself.

I grabbed a candle in its pewter holder and tiptoed into the room, holding the light so it illuminated the dark space. Books lined the walls, and a rug that covered the middle of the floor invited me to lie down there just long enough to cool off. Not one to turn down such a charming invitation, I collapsed on the rug noting the silky-soft texture under my fingertips.

I sat with my back to the door for a moment before I kicked my legs out in front of me. I grabbed my skirts and hiked them up to my waist, or thereabout. I lay down, spread eagle, airing out everything from the waist below. Settling in, I decided I would allow myself to rest for two dances before heading back into the ballroom.

"Excuse me, I wasn't expecting anyone to be in here." A tall, lanky man stood over my prone body. His glasses slid down his nose as he surveyed the scene in front of him.

"Shit. Dammit." I scrambled to cover myself.

The man pushed his glasses up his nose without saying a word, and proffered his hand.

I scoffed at it before pushing myself to my feet. For a moment I stood there, unsure of what to do, when the reality of what he must have seen set in. I felt the blood drain from my face, probably leaving my skin a ghastly shade of white. I was sure my freckles stood out like the inverse of stars in a dark night sky. Heat flooded my cheeks. My face had most definitely turned the color of my hair.

"I have to go." I ran out of my temporary sanctuary.

His voice trailed after me. "Wait, what's your name? I haven't seen you around!"

CHAPTER EIGHT

I scurried out of the library as fast as a rabbit running away from a dog, looking back only briefly to make sure I wasn't being followed. Unfortunately, when I looked back, the lanky man who had discovered me was definitely behind me, his dark curly hair flopping over his forehead with every step he took. He paused his loping pace to push his spectacles up before continuing his chase.

My legs slowed until I was standing in the middle of the hallway staring at the man moving towards me, his every movement bringing back memories of traipsing through the keep and its surrounding grounds while my friend Milo had pointed out every plant, bug, and animal, and told me all about whatever it was we were looking at in that moment. His knowledge was vast for someone so young, which made sense because his curiosity was insatiable.

"Milo?" I choked out, not sure I believed what my eyes were telling me.

He squinted through his glasses as he closed the distance between us. "Rowan? Is it really you?"

The squeal that escaped my body surprised even me. I leapt on him, my arms and legs wrapping around his neck and waist, holding on for dear life. His arms slowly crept around me.

Laughter penetrated my brain, reminding me of where I was and how I should be behaving. I let my legs drop to the floor and took a step back. Milo's hands lingered on my waist, warmth radiating where they rested. Butterflies erupted in my stomach, their riotous fluttering bringing back all of the feelings I had for him as a girl.

"I'll take that as a yes." He chuckled as he took a step back, his arms falling to his side. "I see you're still causing trouble."

I gasped. "What do you mean, trouble? I haven't done anything to disrupt the ball . . . yet."

He threw his head back as he laughed. "You would add the word *yet*. Like you have something in mind to ruin the ball and just haven't acted on it."

I glared at him, arms crossed. "What makes you think you still know me? It's been years since you've seen me."

He glanced towards the library door. "Are you forgetting I just found you lying on the floor?"

"I thought I was by myself. It's not like I thought you or anyone else would walk in on me. The room is the family's library." I huffed, turning my back on him.

I stood there, waiting for Milo to respond. The strains of music from the great hall drifted towards me, a reminder of the celebration I had stepped away from. Time stood still as I continued to wait for Milo to speak. Each moment that passed stretched on for an eternity, and I eventually turned back to see if he was still there.

He was, and he was laughing.

The sound of my leather-soled shoes hitting the stone floor as I stomped my foot wasn't as impactful as I had imagined. "You are so annoying."

"If I remember correctly, that was one of the things you loved about me." He moved towards me, his stride casual, and yet, I felt a bit like I was his prey.

"Who said I loved anything about you?" I cursed at the slight tremble in my voice.

I took a step back, then another, until my backside was firmly pressed up against the cold stone wall. Milo leaned over me, supporting himself with one hand. I looked up into his blue eyes that were made slightly larger by his spectacles. A lock of his dark hair fell across his forehead, forcing me to refrain from pushing the curl out of the way. He leaned down until he was so close I could feel his breath on my lips. Memories flooded my mind as my eyes fluttered shut.

I heard him gasp as the air stirred around me. When I didn't feel his lips on mine, I opened my eyes.

Somehow, Milo had lost his balance. His head hit the wall, causing his glasses to fly off his face. He stumbled backwards, his feet flying out from under him.

I watched as he landed on the ground, his lanky limbs sprawled across the stone floor.

Laughter erupted from me. I didn't even try to stop it. My entire body shook I was laughing so hard. Pushing myself off the wall, I glanced back at his prone position before I walked back into the great hall, leaving him right where he was.

Sweltering heat hit me as I crossed the threshold to the great hall. It was so hot I almost turned around and went to my room. Anything to escape the celebration I hadn't wanted.

I turned to leave but was stopped by a heavy hand on my shoulder. Suppressing a shudder, I turned to see my Uncle Jonathan.

"Going somewhere, Rowan?" His cold eyes stared at me.

I wanted to stare back, but knew I had a character to play if I wanted any of my half-made plans to succeed. Instead, I stared at my hands, clasping them in front of me.

"Of course not. I needed to catch my breath. It's so warm in here I couldn't dance another step." I looked up and back down quickly.

"At least you're back now. There are more suitors for you to meet." Uncle Jonathan took in my appearance before escorting me towards the sheriff.

I wanted to pull my arm out of his and walk right back out of the room. My duty had been performed earlier when I danced with Jocelin Montfort. I had no intention of stepping out on the floor with him again. To do so would be very close to announcing my intentions to let him court me, which I was not about to let happen. My eyes darted around the room, searching for someone I could use to halt our progress. There was no one to aid me in my desperation.

The final notes of the dance filtered through the air, light compared to the stifling air. Amidst the silence a throat was cleared.

"Excuse me, Laird Jonathan, Lady Rowan." A young man who was very easy on the eyes stood there with his hand outstretched. "I believe this is our dance."

I looked at his hand, then over at my uncle, who was glaring at the young man with such animosity I was surprised my rescuer was able to withstand the scrutiny.

"Of course, your highness. I will leave Rowan in your capable hands." Uncle Jonathan bowed before walking off, his posture tense as if he was not happy.

My uncle's disappointment at me dancing with a prince was so ironically funny I couldn't hold the laughter in no matter how hard I tried. At first, I giggled, but the more I thought about how he looked walking away, the louder the escaped laughter was, until I threw back my head and let it out.

The prince stopped. "What do you find so amusing?"

I wiped my eyes with the sleeve of my dress. "Did you see my uncle's face? He was so set on me dancing again with Jocelin Montfort he couldn't hide his disappointment that a prince was going to dance with me instead. I can't thank you enough for rescuing me a moment ago."

"I did what I could: your distress was written all over your face." He took both my hands as the band started to play once again.

I followed as he led me to my spot for the contradance. "Your timing was impeccable, Your Highness."

We turned and walked away from each other as the dance started, skipping around the couple next to us and coming together in the middle for a spin.

Before we broke apart, he leaned over and whispered, "It's Connor. You can call me Connor."

My feet tangled as I turned into the next steps and I felt the tips of my ears burn and my cheeks warm, probably becoming the exact color of my bright red hair. What could I say? I was a sucker for a rescue followed by an intimate moment.

CHAPTER NINE

"How is there this much leftover food from the banquet? There's enough here to feed the entire town for a day or two." My eyes drifted over the heaps of untouched dishes that had lingered in the kitchen, now discarded without ever gracing the tables. Frustration simmered within me, causing my teeth to clench as anger surged. "People are starving, and this was going to be thrown out because my uncle is a tyrant."

Jane placed her hand on my shoulder, giving it a tight squeeze. "But you saved it, and you know it will make a difference."

"Not enough." I drew my hood over my head, concealing the fiery hue of my braided hair. Despite the night's darkness, my locks seemed to glow like a campfire, a stark contrast to the invisibility required for tonight's mission alongside Jane. "Let's hurry and get this packed into the basket, and then I'll lower you down with the food."

My friend stopped, arms full of food. "I'm not getting in that contraption."

It was all I could do not to laugh at the look of horror on her face. "It's perfectly safe. Cows are hauled up in this. And the pulley system distributes the weight so one person can do the work." I didn't add *if necessary* to the last part. She didn't need to know it was normally a two-person job for safety reasons.

"Nope." She tossed the food over the side with a grunt. "I'll walk down. Thank you very much."

"Stop with the grunting and groaning. You're going to wake everyone up," I hissed as she lifted a bag of apples with one arm and another sack of food with the other.

She tossed her armload into the basket. "You know, we would get this done faster if you would calm down and stop criticizing how I'm doing things."

The sharpness of her tone caused me to stop and take a deep breath. She was right, as always: I was on edge and bossing her around in ways that weren't necessary. Not that Jane ever needed to be bossed around. I just couldn't help it.

A branch snapped in the distance, instantly halting our movements. Our eyes locked in a shared moment of apprehension. I pressed a finger to my lips, signaling for silence. Jane responded with a raised eyebrow, accompanied by a playful mouthing of "no kidding."

Peeking cautiously around the stone wall, I caught sight of Milo. His distinctive gait was unmistakable, reminiscent of both a prowling wolf hunting its quarry and a casual stroll through a bustling Saturday market.

"It's just Milo." I leaned up against the stone wall in relief.

Jane's eyes widened. "*The* Milo? The man you went on and on about at the nunnery every single day for years? You didn't tell me he was here."

"There wasn't time. We ran into each other when I was trying to take a break from the ball. He interrupted. It was nothing." I tugged at my braid, drawing it over my shoulder and absentmindedly twirling it around my finger.

"I doubt that." Jane watched Milo as he approached us, assessing his every movement.

He stopped in front of me. "So, this was what you meant when you said you weren't causing any trouble 'yet.' This definitely looks like trouble." He gestured to the food that we hadn't loaded into the basket.

"Feeding people shouldn't be trouble." I turned back to Jane. "Let's get this loaded so we can deliver it all tonight."

His gaze fell on my best friend. "And who might you be?" Milo nodded. "I don't believe we've met."

I stepped between them. "Lady Jane, let me introduce you to my childhood friend, Milo. Lady Jane is my friend and companion."

Milo sidled up beside me, pausing to murmur softly into my ear. "I thought we were more than childhood friends."

I shook off his words. "We have a lot to get done before morning."

The three of us worked together in silence. Each exchange of glances between Jane and me revealed a silent dialogue; her raised eyebrow and subtle shifts of gaze towards Milo conveyed unspoken questions. I merely shook my head in response, focusing on the task at hand, knowing that I would be answering her questions soon. Meanwhile, Milo worked diligently, yet his constant proximity encroached upon my personal space, creating a subtle discomfort as I struggled not to react to his nearness.

"Okay, Jane, we should both get in. Milo can lower us down. It's the quickest way." I grabbed one of the ropes supporting the basket.

Jane looked at the basket, then the ropes, and finally, me. "I told you, there's no way I was getting into that contraption. I will not plummet to my death with a bunch of leftover food. Meet you at the bottom."

She vanished into the night before I turned my attention to Milo. "Seems like you're in charge of lowering me down," I remarked briskly, brushing past him and stepping into the basket. "I've got matters to attend to. Lower away."

As Milo saluted and smoothly lowered me to the ground, a sense of relief washed over me, dispelling the fear that had gnawed at my stomach. It was clear that I would not die on this trip.

The basket hit the ground with a muted thud and I jumped out. The rhythmic sound of hoofbeats reached my ears, causing me to freeze momentarily until I discerned Jane at the reins of the approaching wagon.

I hastily loaded the wagon, driven by the knowledge that there were those in Lockersley that needed nourishment to survive. The pressure of delivering the food to those in need was eating at me, especially since I didn't really know how to get it into the right hands. But when I saw all the leftover food, I couldn't imagine letting it all rot in the keep's kitchen. So here we were, a cart full of food, with only the vaguest idea of a plan.

I put the last bag of apples into the cart. "Now to deliver the food in the dark of night and make it back before Uncle Jonathan knows that I'm gone," I muttered, staring at the darkness, hoping for a plan to enter my head.

"So that's Milo. He's not what I was expecting." Jane raised an eyebrow.

"What's that supposed to mean? Never mind. We don't have time for this now." I shook my head, as if doing so would get rid of the thoughts of Milo that kept intruding while I was trying to think of something else.

"Fine, you know we're just going to talk about him later. You can't keep secrets from me. Especially after I had to hear about him over and over again at school." Jane shrugged before turning towards the horse and checking the straps while she waited for me to take charge.

I didn't say anything as I ran different scenarios through my head. My biggest concern was I would cause more problems when all I wanted to do was to make things better.

"What can I do to help?" Milo's deep voice cut through the silence, startling me out of my reverie.

"Nothing, we have it under control," I said, my words tripping over each other as I spoke.

Milo raised an eyebrow. "Are you sure? I know some people in town that would love to help you."

I crossed my arms. "Did you not hear me? I said we don't need any help."

"I'll be going then." Milo turned and walked away.

Jane glared at me, gesturing for me to go after him.

I sighed and sprinted over to Milo. I reached up to tap him on the shoulder. Hesitating for a moment, my mind questioned if this was really a good idea. The more people involved, the more likely it was I would be found out. But Jane's glare prevailed and I tapped his shoulder. Milo turned immediately, causing my hand to trail down his arm until our fingers caught. I stared at our hands, distracted.

"What do you want, Rowan?"

I pulled my hand back as if I had just touched a hot pan, my body finally registering the heat. My eyes met his before noticing his smirk. "Uh . . . It would actually be nice to have your help. My plan didn't include how to deliver the food in a timely manner."

I twisted the end of my braid around my finger. It didn't sit well, admitting I wasn't prepared, that I really didn't know what I was doing. But here I was doing exactly that.

"Was that so hard?" Milo asked with the raise of an eyebrow. I don't think I had ever seen someone look so smug. It was infuriating.

I crossed my arms and muttered, "You don't even know."

Milo jumped into the cart and grabbed the worn leather reins. "Let's go to Tuck at the church. He'll be able to organize everything."

I nearly smacked my head. It was so obvious, I couldn't believe I never thought of Tuck. "Come on, Jane, we're going to the church."

Milo directed the horses, and I closed my eyes as we made our way through town. It hurt to see the state of the town, and while I resolved to do what was necessary to make things better, it still wasn't easy to see.

The clopping of the horse's hooves stopped. The wagon shifted as Milo dismounted. I opened my eyes to see the church and Jane's eyes boring into me.

Milo disappeared around the side of the church. I followed close behind. Behind the stone building was a small thatched-roof cottage. Milo made his way to the door, banging loudly when he got there.

"Tuck, it's me, Milo. I have Rowan and Jane with me." He paused and listened at the door. "I know you're in there, Tuck. I can hear you moving around. Open up, you'll want to see this."

The door creaked open, and Tuck stuck his bald head out the door. "What are you doing here?"

Milo gestured to the cart. "We have food. For everyone."

Tuck slowly stepped outside to see the cart overflowing with the leftovers from the party thrown in my honor. He stood there for a moment before a smile took over his face.

CHAPTER TEN

As we entered his home, Tuck greeted us with a nod, his eyes immediately fixating on me. Despite the warmth emanating from the roaring fire in the stone fireplace, a chill ran down my spine and settled in my bones. Tuck's scrutiny felt palpable, his gaze assessing my every movement with a keen intensity.

"It seems you've made a decision," Tuck said, his tone neutral but directed at me.

I felt the weight of his judgment, knowing his anger had lessened when he realized I was ignorant of my father's passing. But there was still an unspoken challenge lingering in his gaze, a silent demand for me to prove my commitment to Lockersley and its people. He didn't know I was determined to prove myself, to show just how deeply I cared for the place I called home.

"It's food from the party I didn't want." Despite the urge to fidget under Tuck's gaze, I maintained my composure, refusing to succumb to any of the doubts I was feeling. I reminded myself that my intentions were pure, and I had nothing to hide. With resolve burning through me, I straightened my posture, lifting my chin as I met Tuck's gaze head-on. There was no wavering in my stare, no hint of doubt in my expression. "I need to deliver it all tonight and be back in the keep before dawn and my uncle awakens. I have too much to do to get caught this early on."

My gaze swept across the room until it landed on a spacious armchair tucked away in a corner. Ignoring the less inviting seating options, I skirted around wooden tables and other furniture in my path. Finally reaching my destination, I sank into the plush cushions of the armchair, relief flooding through me as I threw one leg over the armrest. Sitting was an instant relief to the ache in my feet that throbbed from the hours of dancing earlier.

"I see."

That's all Tuck said. His silence made me squirm in the chair. It had me questioning whether my act of confidence was a good idea. Maybe my nonchalant attitude was a step too far.

"Come on, Tuck, I know you've got people in place to make this happen. And you would never turn down the free food for the people in town." Milo leaned against the wall, arms crossed.

Tuck looked from me to Milo, shifting the weight of his unclear expectations away from me.

"This isn't even the first time you've done this. Quit acting like it is," Milo said.

I sat straight up in the chair. "What do you mean, not the first time?"

Milo and Tuck turned towards me and looked at their feet sheepishly.

"You see, Tuck and I . . ."

"Milo has arranged . . ."

Jane held up her hand. Both men stopped talking. "One at a time. Who wants to go first?" She lowered herself down until she was perched on the edge of a chair. "No, since Tuck took Rowan to task when she arrived back, Milo, you can tell us what the two of you have been up to."

Milo cleared his throat. "It's pretty simple. I've made arrangements for food to be delivered to town after one of your uncle's banquets. There's always so much extra. But your uncle refuses to send it to town, even though it's the right thing to do and what all the other lairds do after large parties."

I sunk back into the chair. "So this would have happened without me. I'm not doing anything to help the town. How do you get it all organized?"

Milo ran his hand through his hair, sending his dark curls off in every direction. "It's not that hard. There are quite a few people that work in the kitchen and live in town. They help move the extra food to the side. I load it up and lower it down. Tuck is normally waiting at the bottom with the cart. The two of you beat us to it tonight." He walked towards me, moving as if the furniture in the room didn't exist. He stopped behind the chair I occupied.

I was incredulous. "That's why you were there? I thought you followed me." The words came out of my mouth before I could stop them. Hearing them, I winced. I didn't intend to sound so self-centered.

Milo laughed. "The thought had crossed my mind—if only to see the trouble you were going to get yourself into." He bent over until his lips were next to my ear. "This was a happy accident."

I couldn't suppress the shudder that moved through my body.

Tuck wiped his hand over his bald head as he cleared his throat. "While it's fun to listen to you two, we have other things to get done tonight. Milo, go get Will and Erin. Rowan and I need to talk. Jane, I'm not sure what you would rather do."

"This sounds like plotting." I rubbed my hands together. "Jane stays. She's an asset during any plotting session. Plus, it saves me from having to tell her everything later on."

Milo left with a brief nod, and I couldn't help but watch him go. There was something about the way he moved that captured my attention when I was fifteen. It would seem very little had changed since then.

I turned my gaze back to Tuck as the door closed. "Clearly, food isn't enough to make a difference." I rubbed my hands together. "We need to find something that is."

"I've had an idea for a while, but nobody's in a position to carry it out." Tuck sat across from me, his fingers steepled under his chin.

I twisted my braid around my finger. "That's where I come in. You mentioned some of this earlier. I want to do more than observe, though. I need to do something that will help people now."

"Rowan, you don't have to change everything all at once." Jane clasped her hands in front of her. "Maybe take a moment to settle in, grieve."

"I would rather honor his legacy than grieve his death." My tone was laced with steel.

Tuck nodded. "Your father would be proud."

My eyes welled with tears at his words. It happened so fast I could barely blink them away. "I don't know what to do, though. I just know I have to do something."

"It's the taxes that are causing all the problems. Your uncle has raised them three times in the past six months. He sends the Sheriff of Nottinghamshire, Jocelin Montfort, out every week to collect. Montfort takes any and every bit of coin there is, stating that we are all still in arrears and that he will be back next week."

"That's awful. No one should have to live like that," Jane said.

I stood. "This is why I have to do something." I was feeling twitchy, the need to take action of some sort consuming every part of me.

Even though my attention remained fixed on Tuck, a part of my mind registered Jane's movements. I sensed her rising from her seat, her actions blocked from my view as I remained focused on Tuck.

Tuck watched me, his gaze analyzing every move I made. "Spying on your uncle isn't enough for you?"

As I met Tuck's gaze, his question echoed in my mind, prompting thoughts to tumble through my head, one on top of another.

Was spying truly enough?

The answer came swiftly: no.

But the more important question that continually ran through my head was, why didn't it feel like it was enough? I mulled over the sense of inadequacy that gnawed at me, the feeling that my efforts were too passive, too inconsequential in the face of the challenges ahead.

Despite my resolve to do something, I couldn't shake the sense that it wasn't enough to make a meaningful difference. The thought weighed heavily on my mind, fueling a growing sense of restlessness and discontent. A feeling I wasn't used to and did not like.

My resolve hardened as I stood there. I had already decided to do something, but now I knew it had to be more than bringing extra food to the town. My people needed coin. I refused to remain idle while they suffered under my uncle's rule. It was time to take a more proactive role in shaping the future of Lockersley and helping my people.

"It feels too passive. I need to do something that helps the town now." I felt Jane's hand on my shoulder, pushing me back into the chair.

"You're impetuous, and I love you for it. But if you want things to change here, you need to take a moment. Do the research to determine what we should do first," she whispered into my ear as I sat back down.

I sighed, twisting my hair. Tuck sat back, suddenly relaxed. The intensity I had felt earlier was gone. "Tomorrow, Montfort is collecting. What if it was stolen back?"

"No." Jane stood in an instant. "Come on, Rowan, we're leaving. Stealing is out of the question."

I held up my hand. "Let's hear him out." Jane started to speak, but she stopped when I looked back at her. "There's a plan in the works already. That much is clear."

Turning back, my eyes fell on Tuck. I leaned forward, ready to hear whatever he was going to say.

The friar shifted in his seat, his watchful gaze shifting from judgment to something I couldn't read. "It's not completely worked out. We've been stuck because we need an unknown. Will wanted to be the thief, but his size would give him away. I'm too old. And Milo, well, he can't see without his spectacles, which presented a few problems."

The words leapt out of my mouth before I could stop them. "I'll do it."

"You don't even know what he expects you to do." Jane crossed her arms. "Don't agree to things before you have all the information."

"Jane, you know I have to do something. And my father would have wanted this. I can feel it." I grabbed her hands. "Trust me. This is right."

Jane shook her head but sat back down. She pursed her lips but kept her mouth shut, for now. I knew I was going to hear more about this once we were back at the keep.

"You want me to do this? I need to do things my way." I tapped my foot on the floor. "This means I'll be the one stealing. If I get caught, my uncle's hands will be tied. He's not going to want the world to know his niece felt the need to take from him. Not that I'm going to get caught."

Tuck moved in his chair, opening his mouth to interrupt me, but I wasn't done yet. I shook my head.

"You need to get me schedules and routes. Whatever information you have, I want it and more. I have the skills to take this on, and even a story to explain my actions, but I would prefer not to have to test this theory."

The door swung open. Milo and Will's weary figures appeared framed by the doorway, silhouetted against the darkness behind them. I ignored their interruption and pressed on with determination, addressing Tuck.

"I need to go over all your research and do some more on my own," I declared, my tone resolute and unwavering.

Milo's laughter rang out, breaking through the tense atmosphere. "Are you suggesting preparation before taking action? That doesn't sound like you at all."

Jane's attempt to stifle her laughter with a cough only served to annoy me. I felt the urge to glare at her. I opted to ignore her instead, unwilling to be derailed from my purpose.

Turning my attention back to Milo, I fixed him with a steely glare. "Stop acting like you know me."

Milo turned to Tuck, ignoring me. "Did you tell her Montfort is coming around tomorrow?"

"Of course he did. Why do you think we're talking about this now?" I responded before Tuck could.

Will moved through the cottage, his size overwhelming the small space. He sat in a chair between me and Jane that was too small for his large frame.

"Do you think you can stop the collection tomorrow?" Will grabbed my hands.

I looked into his gaze. Every fiber of my being wanted to say I could do something by tomorrow. But that was only a few hours away. It wasn't enough time, was it?

"Looks like I'm robbing a carriage tomorrow. What do I need to know that you haven't already told me?"

CHAPTER ELEVEN

I hid in the shadows watching the Sheriff of Nottinghamshire go door to door collecting coin the people of Lockersley didn't have to spare. Each person who answered the door was weighed down from the exhaustion of struggling day after day. I wished I could have stopped Montfort from collecting the taxes, but taking the money back was the only way we could figure out how to make this work.

Last night, we'd stayed up late discussing what would happen today. I was to follow Montfort until he finished collecting, then, acting like I'm a highwayman, hold him up in the woods. Will and Milo would be in the woods, ready to back me up if I needed assistance.

It was a hastily put together plan, which happened to be my favorite kind.

Montfort rapped firmly on the door of the last residence Tuck had mentioned. Behind that door lived a mother and her three children left to fend for themselves after the passing of her husband and their father some time ago. Because of the family's hardship, my father had adamantly declined to collect anything from them until the eldest son reached an age suitable for employment. However, Uncle Jonathan held a very different perspective, insisting they repay every last farthing owed.

I stood by the window of the widow's home, eavesdropping.

"Fresh apples." Jocelin grabbed an apple and tossed it in the air before catching it and taking a bite. "How can you claim to have no money when you're buying fresh fruit?"

"We didn't buy it. The food was a gift from the church." The widow's voice quivered as she spoke. "Everyone in town knows we have no money, not even for food. The church makes sure we don't starve. At least someone cares about our well-being."

Jane whistled, soft but persistent, letting me know someone was coming. I cast my gaze down the road and observed my uncle's carriage rumbling steadily towards us. The carriage halted in front of the widow's humble cottage, its tired flower boxes adorned with dried foliage. As the carriage window curtains parted, my uncle's figure emerged, casting a shadow against the dimming light of the day.

"Ride with me, Montfort, bring the gold with you."

I watched as Montfort followed my uncle's orders, weighed down by multiple bags of coin as he climbed into the splendid vehicle.

"Crap," I muttered. This changed everything. I couldn't hold them up now, not when my uncle was in there. But I didn't want to wait for another opportunity. The town needed the money now, not the next time Montfort came around to collect.

I moved with stealth from one house to the next, silently trailing the lumbering vehicle as it made its gradual progress through the town. Its leisurely pace allowed me to easily maintain my pursuit, so it came as no surprise when Jane caught up with me.

"What are you going to do now?" Jane asked through grated teeth.

I glanced back at her. "I'm going to steal the gold, of course. I need to find Milo and you have to stall them."

"I don't think so." Jane shook her head. "We need to wait until next week. There was no plan in place for this situation."

I shrugged. "That's why we need to improvise. I have an idea. It's risky and the probability of success isn't great, but I think I can make it work."

"Rowan, no . . ."

I felt Jane's eyes bore into my back as I ran into the forest.

As the sun dipped below the horizon, casting the forest into a dim twilight, I meticulously scanned the wooded surroundings, searching for any sign of Milo in the dwindling light. The moon's gentle glow filtered through the canopy, casting faint shadows amidst the trees, causing me to strain my senses, determined to locate him.

"Milo . . . Where are you?" I hissed.

With lightning reflexes I reacted to the sudden grasp around my waist. Instinctively seizing my dagger, I countered the attack. With a forceful push, I propelled my assailant backward until they collided with a nearby tree, emitting a startled grunt upon impact. Whirling around, adrenaline coursing through my veins, I leveled my dagger at the individual's throat.

"Rowan, it's me," Milo said with very little movement.

My dagger fell to the dirt. "Don't surprise me like that." The dagger was gone, but I was still pressed up against his body, holding him up against the tree. "I could have killed you."

"I'll take that into consideration next time I attempt to get your attention." Milo's hands settled on my waist. "Do you have any more daggers I should be worried about?"

"Daggers—" I paused, my brain seemed to slow when his hands settled on me. I cleared my throat. "Of course I have more daggers. I always come prepared."

"Maybe you can resist the urge to stab me, at least for a few moments." He raised his hand, his touch gentle as he brushed my bangs aside, his eyes meeting mine.

I chewed on my lower lip as my eyes met his. My gaze filled with questions I knew I didn't have the answers to yet. When he angled his head into a kissing position, panic set in.

I looked away before anything happened. "I could use a tool that could cut a hole into the bottom of a carriage. Got anything like that on you?"

"What are you planning?" Milo searched my face as if that would give him a clue to what I was thinking, feeling. Even if he could sense those things, it wouldn't do him any good this time. My thoughts were cascading one after another, so fast I couldn't keep up with them, and as for my feelings, those were even more jumbled than my thoughts.

"Well . . ." I took a step away from him in an attempt to focus my thoughts. "I was thinking I could stowaway underneath the carriage, cut a hole in the floor, and steal the money through the hole."

Milo pushed himself off the tree and ran his hand through his hair. He stood in front of me, hand on one hip, the other massaging his temple, his exasperation emanating from his body.

"That's not a plan, Rowan—let me rephrase: that's a surefire plan to get caught. It's too dangerous. We need to call the whole thing off."

"Not a chance."

I started to walk away when Milo grabbed my wrist.

"Fine, I might have something that will help you." He knelt on the ground and went through his satchel. He pulled out a few items. "You're going to need a decent distraction, but if you hook these into the doorframe and connect this, it will support you under the carriage so you'll have use of your hands." He dug around some more. "There it is. This should drill through the bottom of the carriage, and this powder can be used to blow the rest of it away."

He held out a corkscrew contraption with a handle and a small sack of powder.

"What do you mean, blow a hole?" I took the items with hesitation.

"It's an explosive. Hopefully, the road noise will be loud enough to hide what you're doing." He looked at me like he expected me to screw up.

I stared back with false bravado. "How am I supposed to light the powder while hanging from the bottom of a carriage?"

"I almost forgot." He pulled a vial out of one of his pockets. "Mix a grain or two of this with the powder. It should do the trick. Too much and you'll blow up every-thing."

"Good to know. Wouldn't want to do anything like that." I stood up on my tiptoes to kiss Milo on the cheek, then ran off to find Jane. I had a heist to carry out.

I sprinted through the trees, my surroundings bathed in the moonlight, which illuminated the forest just enough to guide my path. Trees blurred past as I deftly navigated over roots and around fallen branches.

Suddenly, I skidded to a stop just inches from Jane, narrowly avoiding a collision.

"Follow me. I need you to stop my uncle and the sheriff. Ride back with them. But delay long enough for me to get in position." I grabbed her arm. "How far down the road are they?"

"Not far. If we cut through the forest, it won't take long to overtake them. I've never seen a carriage move so slow. Why is it so slow?" Jane hiked up her skirts and traipsed through the forest.

She pointed to a spot where two roads crossed. I nodded, agreeing with her unspoken words: that's where Jane would distract my uncle.

She brushed her skirts down and unpinned her braid, creating the look of a damsel in distress. The grinding of wooden wheels caused us to look down the road. Jane stepped out and limped towards my uncle's golden transportation with one hand pressed to her back.

I heard the driver stop the horses and Jane's murmurs. The trees blocked me from being seen as I made my way to the carriage sitting and glistening in the pale light. I scurried across the road, ducked down, and rolled under the carriage. I hooked the sling-like item Milo had given me, then using the footman's perch on the back to balance, slid my feet over, and I lifted my weight until my butt settled into the fabric.

The carriage lurched forward, causing me to fumble with my tool. Thankfully, I caught it. I was about to drill the holes when I noticed a latch. This might be easier than I had planned. I unlatched the bottom, peeked through the opening. A rug blocked me from view. I pushed the rug up and felt around, grabbing a foot.

"What was that?" my uncle asked.

I quickly pulled my hand down, so the rug lay flat.

"I'm so sorry, milord. I slipped on that last bump. It was an accident. I would never do anything to intentionally cause you discomfort. Let me just move over to the left so I can prevent it from happening again," Jane said loud enough for me to hear her over the clopping of the horses' hooves and grinding of the wheels on the road.

She said to the left. Was that her left or mine? I ran my fingers along the opening of the carriage under the rug towards my left. A foot stomped on my hand, then pushed it the other way. Jane was directing me. I followed her clues until I felt a burlap sack. My fingers tightened around the sack and dragged it through the opening. I let the bag fall to the ground. I repeated this until Jane nudged my hand again. After grabbing the last bag, I closed the floor hatch and slipped out of the fabric. I rolled out of the road to remain out of sight, not standing until I was in the trees.

I popped up and took off down the street, grabbing the bags as I came across them, and made my way to Tuck's so we could figure out the best way to distribute the coins.

CHAPTER TWELVE

"Where did the money go? It's not like it could walk away on its own!"

I jumped as something crashed inside my uncle's office. Scootching closer to the door, I leaned over to look through the keyhole to decipher who else was in the room. At first the only person who walked within view was my uncle, but it wasn't long until the greasy hair of Jocelin Montfort passed in to view.

"Maybe it was Rowan's companion. That was the only thing different about today."

"And how would she have gotten away with stealing the money?" Uncle Jonathan's tone became deadly quiet. "It's your job as sheriff to collect and protect the taxes. Go do your job and don't make me regret involving you."

I darted away from the door just in time. As it swung open and Jocelin stormed out, he muttered under his breath. I could barely hear him, but managed to capture words that sounded a lot like *no choice*, *death*, and *tyrant*. It made me wonder if the sheriff could, in fact, be turned into an ally. But the thought was lost before I could do anything because another one intruded.

Did my uncle say *collect more taxes*? Was that what the sheriff was off to do? I didn't know if Tuck had passed out the money yet, and even if he had, what was the purpose of stealing it from my uncle only to have him take it back again the very next day? The villagers needed time to spend the money—restock the larder, buy seeds for the garden, find shoes for their children. But right now, the only people that knew about the theft included me, Milo, Jane, Tuck, and Will. No one that needed the money knew about it, at least not until someone handed it out, and now my uncle was talking about collecting the taxes again. If this continued to happen, stealing from him wasn't going to be enough. I was going to have to do more to help my people.

My thoughts continued to race as I walked back to my room. My uncle needed someone to blame for the theft, and it couldn't be the townspeople—

I needed to get a message to Tuck. He needed to hold on to the stolen money until a show could be made of delivering it. Something that would get people talking about the thief delivering money to them. The question was, how was I going to get a message to him before they continued on with the current plan?

I swung open the door to my room and crossed over the threshold. It shut with a thud. I leaned up against it and sank to the floor. I hated knowing I needed to get something done but not knowing how to go about getting it done. It always made me feel helpless.

A knock on the door had me jumping out of my skin.

"I know you're in there, Rowan," Jane said.

I crawled away from the door. "Come in."

Jane's eyes studied my sulking frame. She raised an eyebrow but didn't say a word.

"He's sending Jocelin out to tax them again. They haven't even got the money yet. And if Tuck or Will delivers it, that endangers them even more." I had an idea of what should be done. I needed to stop them and it involved expanding my role in our endeavor.

What I needed was a way to contact them before anything happened. Something that could deliver a message between here and there before the sheriff could collect again.

"Do you think Milo and Tuck already have a way of sending each other messages? They've been working together for a bit." Jane sank to the floor beside me.

I leapt to my feet. Maybe Milo had a way to communicate with Tuck in place. I yanked open the door. "We have to find Milo now."

Jane pushed herself off the floor. "I thought we were sulking on the floor. Make up your mind, Rowan."

Despite everything going on, I laughed. "It's your fault, you have too many good ideas."

I didn't even know where to find him, if he lived in the keep or in town. I wanted it to be here in the keep if only to see if my idea would work.

Grabbing Jane's arm, she had no choice but to run down the hall with me.

"He's in the smaller of the two barracks. I've heard he's turned it in to a laboratory of sorts. Everyone is afraid to live near him, worried he's involved in dark magic." Jane panted behind me.

I changed paths, heading straight for the barracks, still dragging Jane behind me. The stone walls of the castle blurred as I careened around each corner. It was a good thing my uncle presumably was still in his study because there was no way I could explain my behavior if I ran into him.

Jane tugged on my arm until I slowed down.

"What?" Impatience laced my tone as I turned back towards her.

Jane took her arm back and brushed her skirts off. "I tripped."

"I'm so sorry. I didn't mean to pull so hard. Are you okay?" I searched her face, looking for any signs of discomfort.

Jane nodded. "I just needed a moment to compose myself."

We continued to the barracks, which meant leaving the castle proper, crossing over the green, and heading to the left, away from the ocean. I stopped in front of the arched door and stared at the iron holding the wood planks together. With a deep breath, I knocked on the door.

"Milo, answer the door," I yelled.

The door creaked open and there Milo stood. His dark curly hair pointed in every direction and his glasses sat crooked on his nose. He straightened them as he leaned up against the doorframe.

A corner of his mouth quirked upward, creating the lopsided smile I still dreamed about. "What do you need, Rowan?"

"Do you have a way to deliver a message?" I went on to explain my predicament, one he was somewhat involved in.

He put his hands on my shoulders and slid them down to my hands before stopping. "Take a deep breath. I do have a way—pigeons."

"Birds? How will *birds* help us?" I raised an eyebrow, questioning his solution.

He stepped to the side, letting Jane and me enter. "Pigeons, specifically homing pigeons, know where to go. The message gets tied to the top of their feet."

"But how do they know where to go?" The words left my mouth before I realized I had any questions.

Milo's smile was so big, it was as if I offered him a multitude of riches. "I train them. You see, first I—"

Jane stopped him. "We don't have time. Send a message to Tuck to hold on to the coin and that Rowan will explain as soon as she makes the trip to town. You two can talk about training after this mess is straightened out."

"She's right." I turned, about to leave.

Milo grabbed my arm. "What are you planning to do?"

"To start, I need my mask and hood." I shook his hand off me, turned, and ran back to the castle, to my room.

I heard Jane follow me, but her pace must have been much more sedate because the sound of her footsteps disappeared at some point.

I slowed once I entered the castle, unable to see as the dark walls absorbed every ounce of light filtering in through the narrow embrasures. The contrast from the sunlit day was too great. I blinked until my vision adjusted.

Once it had, I raced up to my room and closed the door behind me with a resounding thud.

I fell to my knees in front of the chest at the edge of my bed and rummaged through it, looking for my dark-green hooded tunic and brown leather leggings. I tossed one piece of clothing after another on to every clean surface around me. Before long, the chair, the floor, the bed were all covered with every type of garment I owned.

I used the chest to push myself off the floor, screaming internally as I looked around at the mess, unable to find my leather pants. I couldn't help but stomp my foot.

The creak of the door interrupted my tantrum.

"Is this what you're looking for?" Jane stood in the doorway holding them up. She then plucked a garment off the doorknob.

I leapt over the pile of clothes on the floor and snatched the offending articles out of her hand.

"Since you're here, can you find me a mask? I wore one last night." Stripping off my clothes, I placed one leg into my leggings, then the other, but it got stuck in the twisted leather, which had me hopping around until I stumbled over a yellow garment as it snaked around my ankle. My arms reached out instinctively, grabbing the bedpost before I ended up on the ground. I thrust the cloth off my foot and glared at the offensive garment.

Jane clutched her mouth with one hand while the other held out a green mask. "I believe this is what you're looking for."

"You know it is." I finally pushed my foot through the opening of the leggings. I yanked on the tunic. "Since you're so good at finding things: I still need my belt and boots."

I braided my hair while my friend inexplicably found everything I needed in mere seconds—something that would have taken me much longer to do.

"Will that do, Rowan?" Jane asked. Her tone was prim.

"You were the one laughing at me moments ago." Having put on my boots, I stood to cinch my belt. "No need to act like I'm putting you out now."

"I thought I managed to hide my laughter rather well." Jane shrugged, her smile turning to giggling as she stood there.

I rolled my eyes. "Sure," I said as my lips twitched into a smile, betraying me. "To the stables. I need to get Artie for this." I stopped mid-step. "Wait, I need my bow and quiver."

I maneuvered around the piles of clothes and grabbed my weapons without incident. My mind raced, creating excuses in case my uncle saw me now as I peeked around the corner, hoping to make my escape without him laying eyes on me.

A sigh escaped me as we reached outside, and I could run across the grass to the stables. It was so much better than sneaking around the castle, which had walls that seemed to echo every sound Jane and I had made.

"Did you miss me, Artie?" I whispered into the mane of my horse.

"You know she did," Jane muttered as she laid the saddle blanket over Artie's back.

I hoisted the saddle off the stall, tossing it over Artie.

"Rowan, it's easier if I saddle her since I can reach."

"I'm perfectly capable of saddling my horse." My tone tensed as I tightened the straps.

Jane patted my shoulder. "I know you can," she said with a smile.

I glared at her, tempted to throw something in her direction. Teasing me about my height was one of her favorite things to do.

"Don't you need to go?"

I mounted my horse. "You're right. I'll see you later."

Jane pushed the stall door open as I clicked my tongue, urging Artie forward. I nodded at my friend before urging Artie on, guiding her through the descent from the keep and ascent to town until I arrived on the edges of Lockersley. I dismounted, leading Artie through the maze of streets. My senses heightened as I ensured I was not followed.

My knock on Tuck's door reverberated through the air so much louder than I intended.

"Yes, come in. I got your message and everything is ready." He tugged me into the room, shutting the door behind me with a soft click. "Load your saddle bags with these."

He pointed to the small sacks. I squatted to inspect them further. Each bag had a handful of coins in it, twine that held the back closed, and a secured note that read, *Courtesy of the Hooded Bandit.*

Entering his home, I hugged my friend before stepping back, my hands still on his shoulders. "This is amazing, I love it, and each bag is light enough. I can still use my arrow to deliver it." I brought him in for another hug. "This is the beginning of change. I just know it. Things are going to get better."

We loaded the gold bags, working in harmony for the first time since I'd come home. I gave him a quick peck on his cheek before I mounted Artie and encouraged her to gallop through the streets of town.

From that moment on, it was a blur. I attempted to shoot a bag of gold so it stuck in the door deep enough to stay put until the tenant of the home found it. It took a couple of tries until it worked, but once it did, I passed through the streets multiple times until every house had a bag of gold. The last house I hit was that of the poor widow. My arrow landed with a thud in her door, the paper unfurled in the wind, with my alias emblazoned on the fluttering parchment.

CHAPTER THIRTEEN

Artie and I meandered through Sherewood Forest after our excursion in town. I needed a moment to myself to celebrate before interacting with my uncle again, something I would rather never do again. However, I knew spending time with my uncle was required, but I could at least put it off until dinner.

A whimper interrupted my musings. "Did you hear that, Artie?"

I stroked her neck before giving her a light pat. The horse's ears twitched as a whimper was heard over the rustling of the leaves.

"Yes, there it is again. It seems we have company." I tied Artie to a tree. "Hmm, now where is the sound coming from?"

I followed the whimpers until I saw gold fur mixed in with the red leaves on the ground. I approached slowly, bending down in front of the pile of fur. The animal's head popped up, revealing icy blue eyes outlined in black.

"A dog! What are you doing way out here in the forest?" I held my hand out, letting the dog sniff before I made another move. The canine scooted forward until its ears were under my hand, insisting that I pet it. "You're all fur and bones. I bet you wouldn't say no to a good meal. I think I'll call you Rogue."

I picked up the dog; its legs flared this way and that, making it nearly impossible for me to mount Artie. By some miracle I succeeded and managed to get the furball to lay calmly in my lap as we made our way to the castle.

At the top I glanced to my right to see Jane, skirts hiked above her knees, running towards me at full speed. Milo followed behind her, waving his arms in the air like he was trying to take flight.

I turned to ride over to them, but Jane pointed to the stables. I veered back to my original destination, where I laid a blanket in the stall's corner for the dog and took care of Artie while I waited for Jane and Milo to catch up. The stable door banged open, informing me I would not have to wait very long.

Jane clutched her side as she gasped for air. She held up her other hand, requesting that I give her a moment. "Don't say it. I know . . ." She paused to suck more air into her lungs. "In through the nose, out through the mouth . . . It's not as easy as you make it sound."

"It might not be easy, but it works," I said, stroking the brush across Artie's haunches.

Milo pushed his glasses up on his nose. "Hurry, you have to go change now. Your uncle is looking for you."

"What he said." Jane looked up. "Why do you have a dog with you?"

"Isn't she cute? I found her in the forest. Poor thing is starving." I bent over, picked up the gangly creature, and shoved her into Jane's arms. "Go get her food while I change and find my uncle. Someone keep him distracted until I'm ready."

I left the stall and glanced out the stable door. The square was clear. I darted across the green and through the open door to the keep. I crept up the staircase, straining to hear if anyone else was there. All I heard was my heart pounding in rhythm with my footsteps. Rounding the top of the stairs left only a quick dash down the hall to my door, which I made without incident.

Leaning up against my closed door, I took in a deep breath and looked around my . . . clean room? That's not how I left it. Jane had been busy while I was out delivering the coin.

I smiled at the thought of the townspeople opening their bags. With the even split, every family will be able to put food on their tables, buy essential items for their households.

But was stealing from my uncle really enough? I wasn't doing anything that would cause permanent change. My uncle would need to be gone for things to be different, which I had no idea how to make that happen, especially since killing him wasn't an option for me. Pushing myself off the door, I looked around the room. Where would Jane have put my clothes? The wardrobe made more sense than a trunk sitting at the foot of my bed. I opened the heavy wooden door to find my clothes hanging there, organized by color. I grabbed a pair of billowing gold pants, green overcoat, and white blouse—clothing I wore every day at the nunnery.

Dressed, I walked to my uncle's office, careful to keep my pace sedate, ladylike even.

"There you are, Rowan. I've been looking for you." My uncle's smile did not reach his eyes.

"Uncle Jonathan, I'm sorry I inconvenienced you. It was not my intention." I lowered my eyes to my hands.

He waved away my words. "It is neither here nor there. Come to my office. Let's chat for a bit."

He held the door open for me, ushering me into a room filled with memories of happier times despite the numerous changes he had made that attempted to erase its history and my father. I took a seat in one of the chairs opposite my uncle's desk. I wanted to sink into the chair, but knew a lady would perch on the edge, back straight. And I needed to show my uncle what I assumed he wanted to see.

As he brushed past me, he squeezed my shoulder, causing my muscles to tense as I fought to suppress a visible reaction to his touch. He moved slowly around his desk, deliberately drawing out every movement, making it increasingly difficult for me to maintain my silence. I watched him surreptitiously, my eyes flicking up only occasionally from my lap, determined not to make eye contact or urge him to hasten, no matter what I desired.

"I wanted to talk to you about the masquerade and the potential suitors." His eyes darted to Rogue as she padded in behind me. "What is that?"

"That's Rogue, I found her in the forest. She looked so hungry I had to bring her home." My eyes were wide as I spoke.

The pup curled up at my feet, declaring that she was home.

"I . . . don't think bringing a dog into my home is a good idea," he muttered.

I looked up at my uncle. "I can't just get rid of her. She needs a place to live and we have so much space here."

"Do what you can to keep it away from me." He cleared his throat. "Did any suitor stand out from the others?" He thrummed his fingers on the desk as he leaned back in the chair.

I shifted so my hair fell over my shoulder, providing a curtain for me to hide behind as we spoke. "I'm sorry, Uncle, it was too difficult to focus on something so trivial right after finding out my father was dead." I continued to look down at my hands as I spoke because it was the only way I could continue to look and act demure. What I wanted to do was scream at my uncle for everything he was doing; even pushing me towards marriage made my skin crawl.

"Your future is not trivial. Your father would want me to ensure that you are taken care of. I can't put that off because you're not sure you're ready. The one thing I can do that would have made your father happy is to see you taken care of in life."

The words spilling from my uncle's mouth seemed to make sense. However, if my uncle had truly known my father, he would not be talking to me about making sure I was settled. He would be helping me take my father's place.

"My father wanted me to be so much more than someone's wife," I said under my breath.

"What was that?" my uncle asked, his brow raised imperiously.

My eyes locked with his. "I was taught to want so much more than to be settled. My father wanted me to be happy. He wouldn't want me to rush into marriage."

He planted his hands on the desk and stood, towering over me as I continued to sit in my chair. Instead of straining my neck to maintain eye contact, I let my eyes fall back to my hands.

"I was there at the end. You were not. Your father wanted the peace of mind knowing you were safe and secure in your life. It was all he could talk about in the end." He pressed a hand to his chest as if the thought of my father brought on too much emotion.

"Interesting, it seems like so much changed while I was away," I murmured.

"In fact, your father showed a strong preference for Jocelin, the Sheriff of Nottinghamshire."

Lies! I bit my lip to keep from screaming out loud. There was no way my father would support the suit of the sheriff.

"I found I liked conversing with the prince," I said.

My uncle shook his head. "No, no, that wouldn't do. Your father would never want you to move so far away from Lockersley."

It was obvious my uncle was using my love for my father to manipulate me, inserting his preferences as if they were my father's. I didn't understand why my uncle would invite the prince if he didn't want him to be an actual suitor.

He sat on his desk and leaned towards me. "A lot has changed, especially for you. But you can't stop living your life."

His words should have been comforting. Instead, they sent shivers of dread up my spine. I felt like he was pushing me towards a precipice with the intention of me stumbling over the edge.

"My brother was a very sick man, at the end his mind was failing him. It scared many nurses away. Only one had the fortitude to stay until the very end." He continued on, unaware that I stopped listening momentarily.

"There was a nurse with him at the end? I would love to talk to her." I sat up in my chair, perched so close to the edge that if I moved any farther forward, I would fall off.

My uncle stood, busying himself with rearranging the papers on his table. He slipped a blue leather journal into a drawer and came back with a brown one. "This might have the information you're looking for."

Somehow, I doubted it would. The other journal, though, might hold the answers to everything. I took the proffered book from his hand.

"Thank you, Uncle Jonathan. I will get this back to you soon."

I pounded on Jane's door, willing her to open up so we could go through the journal together.

"What? I'm trying to get ready for dinner," Jane said as she yanked the door open. In one hand, she held the part of her hair that was braided into a coronet in her hand while the rest cascaded down her back in loose curls.

Instead of pushing my way through the doorway, I stopped. "I'm so sorry. I forgot about dinner." I took a step back.

She grabbed me with her free hand, dragging me in to the room. "Don't be a fopdoodle. Hold my hair while you tell me whatever has you so excited."

Her room was almost the mirror image of mine, with each piece of furniture on the opposite side than I expected it to be. Everything was also a little less ornate: her bedposts didn't have any carvings, the tapestries decorating the walls were less detailed, and the enormous wardrobe was somehow less imposing.

I sat on the bed next to Jane, lacing my fingers through her hair to keep the strands separated. It was an awkward way to sit, but Jane's sigh of relief as she dropped her arm by her side let me know it was worth it.

"According to my uncle, my father's illness was so difficult to be around that he had multiple nurses, many who quit. Uncle Jonathan gave me this journal, which he said recorded everything, but he hid another before handing this one over." I slid the journal into her lap. She was the one with two free hands, at least for now.

Jane thumbed through the journal. "Mathilda, Annabeth, Winifred, Elsbeth, Angelique . . . There was a new nurse every three days. The last recorded nurse was Eleanor. But she was there with him for weeks before he died. If the pattern held, he must have seen nine or ten more nurses before he passed."

I clenched my teeth as she spoke. The pain radiating from my shoulder stung like the ache in my heart. "Interesting. We should try to talk with one of the nurses, find out if they thought there was something suspicious happening. And we should find that other notebook. Maybe there's something in it that points to my uncle and a nefarious plot."

Jane bent over the writings, dragging me with her until I was practically sprawled across her back.

"If I could just make out this annotation . . . It might contain something of use," Jane muttered, more to herself than to me.

"Or you could take your hair back and finish it. We can't be late for dinner and raise suspicion." My words sounded sharper than I intended, but I had reached my breaking point on discomfort.

Jane sighed. "Just like you to give me a mystery to solve, then say we have to go do something practical. I think we should try to find Eleanor. As the last nurse listed, she might have the most information." Jane shut the notebook and handed it back to me before lacing her fingers through the strands of hair that made her braid. "You have to get ready for dinner as well unless you plan on wearing that."

She gestured to the tunic and pants set I had put on earlier. It was from the nunnery and so comfortable compared to the ill-fitting garments Uncle Jonathan had left me.

"I wasn't planning on changing." I tossed my hair over my shoulder.

"You know that's going to annoy your uncle."

I smiled. "I do."

CHAPTER FOURTEEN

The sky was painted with streaks of pink and coral as I dragged the straw target across the castle green. Rogue walked beside me as I tromped through the dew-covered grass that glistened as if diamonds had been sprinkled throughout. Rogue and I made our way back across the sparkling field to where I left my bow and quiver full of arrows. When I was at the nunnery on mornings I couldn't sleep, as rare as those were, I would train. So that's what I was doing now, hoping it would help me clear my head.

The routine of putting on my gear was familiar to me, each step was comforting. Once everything was in place, I stood directly across from the target. Rogue curled up like a sticky bun and went back to sleep next to me as I closed my eyes, attempting to find the calm the nuns insisted was necessary to be a superb archer. Releasing my breath, I reached back over my shoulder and grabbed an arrow. I notched and drew the string back along my cheek, keeping my elbow out. Opening my eyes, I focused on the target in front of me and released the string, which slapped against my leather wrist-guard as the arrow whizzed by. The resounding thud of it landing in the target satisfied my spirits. I repeated the motion over and over again, falling into a quick hypnotic rhythm.

"That's quite impressive," Milo said.

Whipping around to face him, I pointed my bow and arrow at him. "It's not wise to startle an armed woman. And you"—I turned towards Rogue—"make a terrible guard dog." I lowered my arms so the arrow pointed towards the ground instead of Milo's heart. "What in the world do you have there?"

He was carrying a bag that was filled with items that jutted out at all sorts of strange angles. I didn't know what to make of it.

His smile was so wide and bright I would've sworn it scared away the last bit of pink sunrise. He pushed his glasses up his nose before reaching in the bag. "I made you something, or rather some things."

It was like the bag had never-ending space as he pulled out quiver after quiver, all filled with arrows.

"There must be over a hundred fresh arrows. Did you spend all night doing this?" I looked on, amazed at the bounty. "That's a lot of tedious work."

"Tell me about it. But these were worth the work." He bent down to grab a quiver. "I made arrows that did different things. Like this one can have a rope attached to it. It should be strong enough that you could swing from it if necessary." He grabbed another one. "If you light this one, it will explode on impact. Oh, and that bow, you can shoot a grappling hook with that one." One word raced out of his mouth after another as he described each of his inventions.

I watched as his dark curls flopped down over his forehead. My hand twitched as I fought the instinct to reach out and push the hair back. His excitement brought me back to when I was fifteen and the two of us would spend time at the beach. He would talk about science and his inventions. I would sit beside him, hanging on his every word as I doodled in the sand. Until, out of nowhere, I would have to move and I would run into the frigid water. Milo would chase after me, eventually carrying me out. That was before I was sent away, back when I thought . . . I shook the thought away. It was no use. Life had changed drastically, and whatever I believed before had no bearing on what my life was now. There were things I needed to accomplish, like helping my people survive and determining how to handle my uncle. Whatever was between us before didn't matter. I didn't have time for it.

"What do you think?"

I looked at him to see his eyebrows raised, his blue eyes eager for my opinion. I set my bow down behind me before looking at each of the things he had made. Each arrow was more impressive than the one before. I didn't know why I needed them or how I would use them. But I wouldn't deny they could be useful.

"It's so thoughtful. I don't know when I'm going to have a need for any of this, but it sure will be nice to have." I gestured at the vast array of pointy weapons in front of me. "At least I'll be prepared for anything. Thank you."

Milo stood. He was so close I could feel his body heat and smell what I could only describe as Milo. It was the same mixture of wood, sawdust, and salt spray from before. As much as things had changed around here, it seemed some things very much stayed the same.

"I would do anything to keep you safe. Make anything for you." He stood there, eyes searching mine for answers to questions I didn't know. He lowered his head as I took a step back. My forgotten bow reminded me of its presence in that moment as my foot tangled with the string, sending my body to the ground. I braced for the impact.

Milo wrapped his arm around me and instead of crashing to the ground, I crashed into his chest. My eyes closed of their own volition. My heart beat so loud, I assumed everyone could hear it and there was nothing I could do to calm it. His arm tightened around me as my world turned upside down. Why would my heart do this to me? I felt so off balance, like I couldn't stand on my own two feet. It had never been quite like this around him.

I opened my eyes seconds before we crashed into the tall, wet grass. Milo took the brunt of the impact as I landed sprawled on top of him. I tried to roll off him, but his arm tightened around me, holding me in place.

"Don't, the grass is wet," he said, implying that I should be concerned about the dew-covered green.

I cared much more about getting caught lying across his body than I cared about getting a little wet. I tried again to roll off him; he reluctantly released me. But our limbs tangled, his boots somehow stuck in my billowy pants, my toe caught the edge of his kilt, which he barely managed to catch before he was exposed.

I felt my cheeks heat at my errant thoughts. Scrambling, I detangled myself without further incident. Milo stood up before I could and offered his hand. I took it. The sharp tingling where our skin touched almost caused me to let go. He pulled me up, and I stood there staring at his chest.

"I have to go," I muttered.

Milo pressed a kiss to my forehead before stepping back and allowing me to gather my things and scurry away.

I thought I heard him call after me, but I decided that it was the wind as I sprinted away. Rogue ran beside me, hopping on me every few feet as if we were playing the most fun game in the world.

Arriving at the keep, I jerked open the heavy wood door. I closed it after I crossed the threshold and took a deep breath in as my puppy sidekick sat in front of me, her eyes eagerly waiting for the next part of our game.

"No more, Rogue, I have to get ready to go into town," I said while patting her head.

For the first time in what felt like forever, I walked sedately to my room. I climbed the stairs, then strolled down the hallway, taking my time the way I imagined a lady would. The steady rhythm of my pace became a game as I tried not to hurry; instead I carefully placed one foot in front of another as if the location of each strike against the floor was significant.

I rounded the corner and saw the door to my room up ahead. It was only then that I realized I didn't have a single set of arrows that Milo had made for me. Crap, I was going to have to go back and get those, and do it quickly if I didn't want to run into my uncle or the sheriff. The questions I would get from them if they saw me with my gear were something I wanted to avoid.

"Rowan, wait." Milo held up a hand. "You forgot all your arrows."

I walked to where he stood in the hall. "Thank you. I was just about to return to get them." I turned to head back to the castle green.

Milo reached out and grabbed my hand before I could leave him standing in the hall alone. "I have them all for you right here." He gestured to his back.

"Thank you," I said and turned my back to him. "Are you coming?"

I heard, rather than saw, him hurrying after me. The sound of our feet hitting the stone floor echoed throughout the hall. It was so loud I expected Uncle Jonathan to stop us at any moment. So I tried to walk softer, which only made me more aware of Milo's footsteps behind me.

"Here we are." I pushed opened the door to my room.

"You're in the same room as before." He leaned forward to peek inside.

I shrugged. "Did you expect me to have a different room?"

"Actually, yes, you're Lady of Lockersley now. And your father sent you away because he wanted you to take his place. Not your uncle. This room is a hovel compared to what you should be in."

"I like my room, thank you very much." I crossed my arms over my chest. "And it's not like the current Laird of Lockersley is going to give up his position. Especially since there's nothing in writing to prove what my father's intentions were. Only what he told me when I left."

The look on Milo's face was comical. "What do you mean, there's nothing in writing? He put it in his will. I saw it."

"What do you mean, you saw it?" Each word left my mouth with precision.

"Before I left to further my studies, he showed me. It's actually when he told me he was going to sponsor me, pay for my studies with the hope I would choose to come back here once I finished." Milo shrugged before he pushed his way into my room and searched for a place to store my arrows.

"What do you mean, sponsor you?" Questions, one after another, flitted through my head so fast I could only verbalize the ones that felt the most pressing, even if they weren't.

"You didn't know? I thought you were the one that made it happen."

He stashed the arrows behind my dressing screen. Was it just me, or was he making himself a little too comfortable in my room?

"I didn't know anything about it. But my father knew of our . . . friendship." I leaned up against a bedpost, watching him move. I had never understood how a professed scientist moved like an athlete. "I was very upset to be sent away for so long, especially because I wouldn't be able to see you."

As the words left my mouth, something in the air changed. The connection I thought we had all those years ago seemed to snap back in place. It was clear I wasn't the only one that felt it. Milo's movements became more deliberate. He walked towards me, his gaze so intense I felt my heart skip a beat.

He placed his hand on the bedpost I was leaning against. I couldn't help but gaze up at him, into his blue eyes.

"You were upset to leave . . . me?" His voice was low, questioning.`

I licked my lips. "I mean . . . Friends . . . Missing years . . . That is. Yes." I couldn't form a coherent thought as they jumbled together in my brain. The most pervasive one was that I wanted to kiss his lips, as an experiment, to see if it was anything like all those years ago.

I pushed up on my tiptoes until I could brush my lips against his. It was the lightest of kisses. Neither one of us moved to embrace the other. But I felt the kiss all the way to my toes.

This did not bode well for avoiding romantic entanglements.

CHAPTER FIFTEEN

"Um . . . You need to go." I looked around the room, searching for an excuse. "I have to . . . go shopping today."

"Shopping?" Milo raised a single eyebrow, taunting me with his knowing gaze.

I shrugged. "A necessary evil. I don't want to end up lying on a rug in the library at the next ball my uncle insists on throwing."

My hands reached for his shoulders in an attempt to push him out of my room. Instead, they landed lower on his chest, leaving me to wonder again why a scientist had such solid muscles. My cheeks burned from embarrassment while warmth pooled somewhat lower. I clenched my thighs together. I was a grown woman. Lust should not overwhelm me because I touched a man's chest.

"I didn't mind the view." He winked at me.

My entire face had to match my hair at this point. "You have to go. Now." I pointed to the door.

He held up his hands in surrender. "I'll go . . ." He grabbed the door, pausing before he pulled it closed behind him. "This time."

The door clicked shut as I threw the closest thing to me at the door. The pillow hit it and fell to the ground. I glared at the offending item as I heard Milo's laughter echo in the hall.

Throwing myself onto my bed, I lay there for some time trying to decipher what had just happened, not to mention the revelations Milo mentioned. My father really had wanted me to take over for him so much that he had written it in his will, at least according to Milo. I knew he wanted me to have choices, but to take over for him was more than I expected, than any young woman would expect. It wasn't the way things were done. And why would he sponsor Milo's education? I had a feeling it had something to do with me. The things I said before I left probably influenced his decision. I had been quite adamant about what I wanted back then. I hadn't thought my father had listened or cared. Turned out, he had done both.

I sat up. Ruminating over anything done or said this morning wasn't going to solve any of the problems in front of me. Not unless I could find proof of my father's wishes, and I wasn't going to do that sitting here in my room. I stood and quickly changed into a deep blue version of the attire I wore at the nunnery. The pant legs were wide enough they might fool my uncle into thinking I wore a dress. Although, it seemed unlikely I would be so lucky: Uncle Jonathan noticed everything.

A soft tap on the door stopped me in my tracks. "Lady Rowan? Laird Lockersley sent me to get you."

I opened the door to see one of the keep's maids standing there. "Thank you. Winnie—I have that right, don't I?"

She bobbed her head and smiled.

I smiled back. "What does Uncle Jonathan want?"

"He said you had a visitor," she said with a curtsy.

My nose scrunched as I thought about who could be visiting me. "Do you know who it is?"

"I'm sorry, miss, he didn't say. But he wanted you down, right quick." She curtsied again. Her entire body looked tense, like she would dart away if only I would give her the permission to do so.

"Thank you. I'm sure my uncle has you very busy. Please, don't let me keep you," I said.

"It's not that, miss. Remember, I'm supposed to be your lady's maid, but you never call on me." Winnie wrung her hands together.

The worry on her face was like a punch to my gut. "I'm so sorry, I'm used to it just being me and Jane. I'll do my best to call you for you more often. You can stay in here, if you're my lady's maid, there's no need for you to get caught up in other tasks."

Winnie smiled before she bobbed up and down in a curtsy. "Thank you, miss."

"I'll leave you to it then." I closed the door behind me, only to pound on Jane's door incessantly.

"I'm coming," she yelled through the door. Her clipped words belied her annoyance. "What is it?"

"So much. But right now I have a visitor and I want you to come with me." I grabbed her hand and pulled her out of her room, not letting go until we were in the great hall.

"You could have at least let me grab a hat," she grumbled as we came to a halt.

In front of us stood my uncle, the sheriff, and Connor Blackwood. At least that answered who the guest was, just not why he was here.

"Ah, Rowan. It seems you have an admirer." Uncle Jonathan turned towards me. His eyes took in my clothing, causing his nose to pinch in his distaste. "He's even agreed to go into town and go shopping with you, as I told him you were desperately in need of new clothes after your education at the nunnery."

I turned towards Connor. The prince was a handsome man, with golden hair and honey-colored eyes. "Thank you, but it's not necessary." I lowered my eyes.

Uncle Jonathan waived my words away. "Don't pay her any heed. She's too obliging."

I heard Jane scoff and attempt to cover it with a cough. Her reaction made me want to laugh. I could feel the giggle trying to escape. So, in an effort to prevent that from happening, I bit my lip so hard it brought tears to my eyes. Connor's eyes darted between the two of us like he knew something was off, but he couldn't put his finger on what. I almost felt sorry for the poor boy.

"Sheriff Montfort, you will go with them and ensure everyone is safe for today. Plus, you have a job you need to finish for me in town." Uncle Jonathan's words weren't harsh, but his tone was sharp as daggers.

"Of course." The sheriff bowed, his obsequence nause-ating.

"We might as well go now, since we are all in attendance at the moment." Lady Jane took charge, linking her arm with mine, letting the men follow in our wake as we left the keep.

Connor walked beside me, his hands clasped behind his back. I opened my mouth to speak but didn't know what to say. This happened a few times before I decided to just walk in silence. If he seemed happy walking in silence, I didn't need to try to fill it.

"Look at the fabrics in that store, Rowan. We have to go in." Jane grabbed my arm and led me into the shop. I wanted to drag my feet because dress shopping was not my favorite, but her excitement was contagious. Instead I found myself running into the shop beside my friend.

A bell tinkled overhead as we entered the dimly lit shop. Fabric lined the walls in a vast array of colors, some vivid and bright, others not so much. I watched as Jane walked around the store, touching everything. After her first lap, she started grabbing rolls of fabric. It wasn't long before my arms were filled with her picks. There were wools in every color she thought would look good on me, from green and blues to oranges and browns. I wasn't sure I agreed with all her choices, but I let her have her way.

"Lady Rowan, let me take those from you." Connor lifted the fabric out of my arms.

I wanted to tell him I didn't need his help, but thought better of it in my attempt to play my part as a demure lady.

"Yes, I can assist you as well," Jocelin said, manhandling a lavender wool Jane had just picked out.

At least he wasn't touching the emerald silk she had slipped into the pile somehow. It was such an extravagance I never would have purchased it. But I rationalized the expense because it would help the shop owner.

I looked around the store. Where was the shopkeeper?

"Excuse me," I called out.

Out of the middle of the rows of material, a head popped up. I squinted at the woman, swearing I recognized her from somewhere.

"Erin, is that you?" I asked, my hesitation at being wrong apparent.

Her eyes focused on me and widened, becoming as large as saucers. "Rowan. It can't be." She squealed as she launched herself over the fabric somehow and threw her arms around me.

I took a step back and looked at her, then around the room. "What are you doing here? Are you still singing?"

"Of course I'm singing. This is one of the few times I don't have a lute in my hands." She pointed to a table towards the back of the shop. Her lute lay there, waiting to be played. "My ma needed me to work the shop. Her health isn't what it used to be. So now I spend my days here, and if I'm lucky, my nights at balls like your party.

If not something like that, I'm at the pub, trying to earn some coin there. Not that anyone really has coin to spare around here."

"I'm so happy to hear you're singing. I didn't know you were at my ball. I wish I had."

She smiled. "You were too busy fending off handsome suitors like this gentleman here." She pointed to Connor. "Nice of you to patron my shop." Her black curls bounced around her heart-shaped face as she curtsied.

"I'm sorry, let me introduce you to everyone." I gestured to Jane. "This is Lady Jane; we became friends during my time at the nunnery after the Incident. Next to her is Prince Connor, the lad you've been flirting with. And I'm sure you know Jocelin Montfort, the sheriff. This is Erin Dale. She used to make up ballads of my grand adventures when we were children."

Jane clapped her hands. "Now these I have to hear. I can only guess what she was like back then, based on the things we did at school."

"Nothing that sounds as exciting as the Incident." Erin looped her arm through Jane's. "I want to hear all about it."

"Excuse me, but we need to pay for all of this." I waved my arm at the two men weighed down by fabric. "Also, Jane and I don't speak of the Incident. It's too painful of a memory." Somehow, I managed not to smile. The

Incident was my best and worst memory of school. I just didn't want to talk about it now.

Jane winked. "We'll talk later. Rowan doesn't want to embarrass herself in front of her suitors."

"That may be true, but we need to be on our way." The sound of Montfort's voice was muffled behind the wall of fabric Jane had stacked in his arms.

Connor came forward. "Let me get this for you."

"My goodness, no. It's too much. Can you not see how much fabric Jane has picked out for me?" I looked at all of it again, spotting a folded dark silver fabric that looked otherworldly. I could only imagine what it would look like on.

"Oh, I insist, it's not a hardship. I promise there's plenty to go around." Connor pulled out a few coins from his purse.

That was the moment I realized Connor could be the solution I was looking for. He had the money to save Lockersley and the power to destroy my uncle. While I hoped to do it myself, right now I didn't see how I would ever be enough to stop my uncle on my own. Milo and Tuck had tried to convince me otherwise by enlisting my help, but the town needed more than I could give them. They needed someone like Connor.

"You didn't need to pay for that. I could have taken care of it on my own," I stated. It annoyed me that he only pretended to ask me if he could pay. His mind had already been made up long before we were at this point.

"I believe aiding damsels is part of my duties as prince." He winked. "It makes me happy, and it adds new coin into the market here. I want to help."

I sighed. How could I be upset at someone who wanted to help, like me? I wished it wasn't so obvious Lockersley needed the assistance. But there was nothing I could do about that right now.

"If that's the case, I think we should stop at the milliner and the silversmith." I smiled. It didn't reach my eyes. But I was trying to feel grateful.

"But first, your fitting. Erin, can we see a pattern book? I don't have time to sew all of this, but I want the silver. I have a design in mind that will be perfection on you, Rowan. Please don't let anyone else take that," Jane chimed in.

"Lady Rowan, your uncle wouldn't approve of someone else paying for clothes. I'm under strict instructions to handle everything for him, of course." Montfort stepped forward as if he was trying to take charge. If that was his goal, he was failing.

Connor clapped him on the back. "Be a good man and take everything to the carriage. There's no use arguing over who's paid for what, as long as Lady Rowan and Lady Jane are happy."

There wasn't much the sheriff could do at that point. He was even thwarted from collecting taxes. I couldn't help but smile as the thought crossed my mind.

CHAPTER SIXTEEN

News of our shopping excursion made its way around town in an instant, drawing out merchants who hadn't planned on opening their shops, much less leave their homes. Before long, Lockersley felt more like the town from my past and less like the place I had come home to. My people wandered through the streets laughing with each other, bringing the place to life. Their happiness almost allowed me to ignore how flower boxes sagged, and shop signs hung by one nail, and paint chipped off every surface.

I wiped away the tears that threatened to fall from my eyes.

Connor leaned over. "Is everything okay?"

"It feels so alive." I smiled up at him.

He took my arm and looped it through his. "Shall we go and make someone else happy today? Maybe get some cock-a-leekie or some cullen skink? And get to know each other a wee bit better."

I looked up at him, his golden hair rippling in the breeze. It didn't feel the same as when I looked at Milo. There were no sparks. My heart didn't race. But he had been kind, not only to me, but to the people I cared about. Maybe he was the solution to my problems. If I did what my uncle wanted and married, marrying him would bring wealth and power and potentially the ability to punish my uncle for the things Tuck believed he had done.

But it would mean moving away from Lockersley. I couldn't be queen and live in my childhood home. The question was, would giving up my home be worth my people's security? And there was only one way to answer that question.

"What made you come calling—unannounced, I might add—today?" I asked, our gait falling into a comfortable rhythm as we walked to the public house.

"You intrigued me the other night. Disappearing at your own ball," he said.

I shrugged. "It was hot. I didn't want to have a party, and I was tired of dancing with men my uncle approved of, so I left to cool off. I didn't think I was gone long enough for anyone to notice."

"I noticed." His words were quiet, almost a whisper. He cleared his throat. "Why didn't you want to have the party?"

I looked at the ground and watched my feet peek out from under my pants with each step. "I just found out my father had passed. For everyone else, it's been six months, but for me, it feels like yesterday. Especially since I was so excited to finally see him again." I looked up and waved my arm towards the town. "It was also an unnecessary expense. The money should have been used here, not on a silly party."

"Events like that bring hope."

"Not when you're starving."

"The town must be happy to see you home." He turned to me, his honey eyes filled with concern.

I looked away. "At the time, they weren't, for reasons that I would rather not share. But hopefully, as time passes, they will see I am the person they remember. Not the one someone told them I was."

"Coming home was nothing like you expected, was it?" He opened the door to the public house and let me enter before him.

I stood there staring up at the prince, unsure of how I felt. This was only our second time meeting, and he was more intuitive than most. It was nice, if not a bit unsettling. His lips quirked into a half smile as I stood there pondering.

"Why don't we go inside and you can tell me everything that's running through your head right now?" He gestured towards the open door.

The room itself was dimly lit despite the rare sunny autumnal day happening outside the public house. The lack of light would have been off-putting if it wasn't for the most heavenly aromas wafting from the kitchen. It brought back memories of food from my childhood. Whenever my father and I came into town, we would always stop for lunch. My father believed that supporting the local businesses was the best way to show the town that the laird and his family believed in them.

My eyes prickled with unshed tears again. Jane handed me a handkerchief. She was a saint, keeping the sheriff occupied while I talked with Connor. I owed her. It would probably take more than my first-born child to pay her back, or maybe I could commission one of those reversible rings she loves.

"Are we going to sit or just stand here lollygagging?" The sheriff's nasally whine interrupted my wayward thoughts.

Jane took his arm, glancing back at me with a grimace. "Of course not. Let's find a table for the four of us."

He stood firm for a moment. "But I'm . . ."

Jane kept drifting towards the tables, away from me and Connor.

"He seems persistent." Connor watched Montfort with a look of distaste.

I studied my nails. "Jocelin Montfort is my uncle's selected suitor to take on the role of husband. I'm not even sure I'm ready to marry, and *that's* who my uncle prefers."

Connor stroked his chin. "Even over me? I am a prince, after all."

"Which means I would have more power than him. That would never do."

Connor departed after lunch, leaving Jane and me with the sheriff. He hadn't done any of the tasks my uncle had set out for him, so we were stuck in town while he collected the taxes I had stolen just the other day.

I turned towards Jane and pointed at something off in the distance. "I'm going to take the money as he collects."

Jane stared at where I was pointing. "Do not do that. You're going to get caught."

"I'm an excellent pickpocket. This is going to be fun." I squeezed her arm before letting go and walking over to the sheriff.

Jane just shook her head and followed me, graceful as ever.

"So, Jocelin, may I call you Jocelin? What do we have left to do in town?" I slipped my arm through his.

He looked down at me, a look of shock and disgust written on his face. "I would prefer not." He removed my arm from his. "And the weekly taxes need to be collected."

I pouted. "Does that really have to happen today? It doesn't sound like much fun."

"Your uncle would be very unhappy if I did not finish this job." His back stiffened, clearly expecting me to put up more of a fight.

"He's scary at times. I would want to stay on his good side, too," I whispered. "Let's go then. I don't want to be the cause of upsetting my uncle."

Tension left Montfort's body as he heard my words. I looked at Jane with a broad smile. She rolled her eyes. But I thought I saw her nod, letting me know he was primed to have his pockets picked.

The three of us walked around the square in silence, while my mind buzzed with ideas about how I was going to carry out this new plan. Taking the gold was not enough. Eventually, Montfort would figure out it was missing by the lack of weight he was carrying around. I needed to cover up the fact the gold was gone by replacing it with something of a similar weight, without him noticing. And for that to happen, I was afraid I needed help. Something my spontaneous mission didn't really allow for.

My eyes scanned the town green looking for someone I recognized. I looked for Tuck, but he was nowhere to be seen, and I was sure Milo was still back at the keep performing some experiment or another. That left Will, someone I had yet to see during my time in town today.

Wait— Was that him in the widow's yard, chopping wood?

I stared at Jane until she looked back at me. Which she did just like I knew she would. I nudged my chin towards where Will was looking handsome wearing his kilt and swinging his ax. Jane rolled her eyes at me and mouthed the word no. I made my eyes as large as saucers and stuck out my lower lip. I even made it quiver. She rolled her eyes and shrugged. I knew I had her when she started browsing the shop stalls while I stayed back with the sheriff.

"I don't remember you living here before I left. What brought you to Lockersley?" I asked.

Montfort's brow furrowed. "I moved here with your uncle."

"Oh, really?" My ears and brain didn't understand the words spoken. Followed my uncle: why would anyone do that?

He stopped in front of me. "He's always been more than decent to me." He paused. "When he offered me the job, I jumped at it. I finally had an opportunity to prove myself."

"But surely you could make a name for yourself another way. Something that helps rather than hurts people." I gestured to the town. The sign at the general store chose that exact moment to give up and fall to the ground with a wooden thud.

"If the people took pride in their town they would make sure it looked nice." Jocelin shrugged. "This isn't about the taxes or your uncle, it's about not caring how they live."

I had to look away. It was that or punch him in the mouth. I didn't even know how to respond. The people in this town cared so much they didn't leave, but kept living here because they thought it would get better. But the way things were going it was never getting any better.

"It's very hard to paint a sign when you don't know if you have enough money to eat." I sped up my steps, wanting nothing more but to run away from here, but now I desperately needed to steal back everything the sheriff took.

Jane was emphatically shaking her head. But Will just held up his hand and walked away, came back with sacks of something, and put them into Jane's hands, who miraculously hid them somewhere. She casually walked back to me and the sheriff right as we approached the first house.

As Jocelin knocked on the door, Jane handed me a bag of rocks. She scampered back to the shops while I waited for the sheriff to finish his business.

My heart skipped a beat when the door slammed behind me. The anger belayed by the action was understandable. I turned back to the door and bumped into Jocelin, freeing the bag of gold coin and replacing it with the rocks in one fluid motion. I held my breath, waiting for him to grab me and accuse me of stealing. But all that happened was a steadying hand on my elbow before he walked towards the next home.

It worked! I hurried to keep up with the sheriff. Jane and I repeated the process at every house. Afterward, I would give her the bag I had stolen and she would take it to Will, who delivered it back to the family. It felt good; I felt good. This might only help for a short time, but at least for a little while, it would help.

CHAPTER SEVENTEEN

As Jane discreetly left the table to send a message to Tuck, arranging for everyone to gather in Sherewood Forest at dawn, I found myself enduring an uncomfortably silent meal with Uncle Jonathan. He sat to my left at the vast expanse of the banquet table, his fingers thrumming a relentless rhythm on the polished wood. His anger cast a dark, foreboding presence over the beautiful room. The tension was palpable, and every attempt I made to initiate a conversation about my father was met with curt, monosyllabic responses. It felt as though I was repeatedly running into a wall, each attempt at dialogue crashing into an unyielding reticence. I assumed he was brooding over the gold his sheriff had failed to collect today.

"Did something bad happen today, Uncle Jonathan?" I asked, carefully modulating my tone to sound concerned but not intrusive.

He looked up, his eyes almost black with intensity. "Nothing you should concern yourself with."

"If it is bothering you, it is of concern to me," I replied, watching as the servants set food in front of us. I signaled for them to leave once the main course was served, ensuring we had privacy.

"I said it was nothing." He slammed his tankard down, the impact reverberating through the table. There was a tense pause as he stared at the liquid left inside. He took a deep breath to regain his composure. "Have you thought any more about your potential suitors? I was surprised the prince called on you."

The sudden shift in topic caught me off guard, but I forced myself to stay calm. "I have thought about it, but I find it hard to focus on such matters with everything that has been happening," I answered honestly, though careful not to provoke him further. "He is nice to be around, and I am considering him. But I had another thought. What about Sir Milo? I wouldn't have to leave Lockersley, and my father sponsored his education so he must have approved of him."

I watched my uncle take in my words. He grimaced when I mentioned Milo, clearly displeased with my suggestion. I looked down at my plate to hide the smile I couldn't stop, relishing how much I was annoying him more and more each day. Especially since I acted sincere in my responses to his questions, like I was taking his insistence on marriage seriously.

"I've told you, your father preferred Montfort for your husband." He took a bite of the sumptuous dinner in front of him.

I picked up my fork so I had something to do with my hands. "That may be, but he does not affect me the way that Milo does. He's also not a prince like Connor. I would think my father would care about those things."

The finger thrumming resumed as my uncle took in my words. "Your father would have wanted you happy." He paused, looking at me with an unsettling intensity. "I know. We'll have a tournament. The winner of the tournament will win a monetary prize and your hand in marriage, since you seem so reluctant to make a decision."

My mind raced at my uncle's suggestion. There wasn't a chance in hell I was going to leave the choice of my future spouse up to whoever wins a sporting event. Multiple scenarios ran through my head, all with questionable outcomes.

One idea stuck out to me, though. I mulled it over in my head, trying to look at it from all the different angles of what could happen before I decided to go through with it. I could enter the tournament myself—disguised, of course. It would be a risky move, but it could give me the opportunity to win my own hand and control my destiny.

"It's unlike you to sit so quietly. Do you not have anything to say about the tournament?" my uncle asked, the expression on his face quizzical.

"I'm not sure what to say, dear uncle. While I am reluctant, as I am mourning my father's death, I do not believe I've been obstinate. I have offered two men as potential suitors that I believe my father would have approved of for various reasons."

The lines that framed his nose deepened as he furrowed his brow. His obsidian eyes glinted back with something akin to hatred as he stared at me. I wanted to shudder under his gaze, but I refused to let my body give into the impulse.

His look reminded me that I wasn't playing the subdued lady very well. Even if his reasons for this announcement were absurd, I should not be questioning him. In fact, arguing further would only hinder my missions, so I swallowed my pride and bit my tongue. "I apologize, Uncle. I should not have spoken so harshly. Please forgive me," I said, forcing the words out as I lowered my gaze in an attempt to appear contrite.

His eyes softened as I acted more like he expected. "Are you opposed to the tournament? Maybe you can convince your potential suitors to enter. See if they have what it takes to win your hand."

"I suppose that is one way to handle it," I finally said, trying to sound reluctant. "If you think the tournament is wise, then that's what should happen." I crossed my hands in my lap. "My only request is that anyone can enter. When do you plan to hold this tournament?"

"In a fortnight," he replied, a satisfied smirk playing at the corners of his mouth. "It will be a grand event, worthy of Lockersley's future."

I nodded, pretending to agree, while inside I was already planning my strategy. This tournament could be the perfect cover for my true intentions. Not only would I have a chance to win my freedom, but it would also give me the opportunity to gather allies and undermine my uncle's plans from within.

As the dinner continued, I remained quiet, letting my uncle believe he had the upper hand. The silence stretched on, the clinking of the silverware the only sound piercing through the heavy quiet. My thoughts raced, searching for a way to end this dinner, but each idea seemed as futile as the last. With a sigh, I resolved to endure the meal, knowing that once it was over, I would have the support of Jane, and in the morning Tuck and the others in Sherewood Forest, to help me find the answers I sought.

Which was why I darted away from the table as soon as my uncle put his napkin next to his plate.

"Thank you for a wonderful meal," I said before I left the room. I paused right outside of the door, contemplating changing into something different, but in the end stayed in the blue wool dress and overdress I wore to dinner.

As I made my way through the dimly lit corridors of the keep, I couldn't help but think about the upcoming tournament, and what my role would be in it. My uncle saw me as nothing more than the prize, the equivalent of an animal at the local fair, but I had another idea. One that was a gamble, but I had to take it because if I succeeded, I would be able to reclaim my home and protect the people of Lockersley.

I stopped outside the library, where I knew Jane would be waiting. She had a knack for finding the quietest corners to read and strategize. When I entered, she looked up from a dusty tome, Rogue curled up by her feet, her eyes curious and expectant.

"How did it go after I left?" she asked, setting the book aside.

"As well as could be expected." I took the seat opposite her, tucking my feet underneath me as I sat. "He's decided to have a tournament in a fortnight. The winner will receive gold and my hand in marriage."

Rogue stood, stretching before walking over and settling under my chair.

Jane's eyes widened. "Your hand in marriage? Are you nothing more than a prize heifer to him? He can't be serious."

"Oh, he is. My uncle is always serious," I said with a bitter laugh. "But I have a plan. I'm going to enter the tournament myself—disguised as a man, of course."

Her shock quickly turned into a sly smile. "Now that sounds like the Rowan I know. But it's risky. What if he finds out?"

"That's why we need to be careful," I said, leaning in. "I'll need your help, Jane. We need to gather information on the competitors if we can, find the best disguise, and train harder than ever. And we'll need everyone else on board, too."

Jane nodded, her mind already working through the logistics. "We can do this as long as we work together. Tuck agreed to meet in the morning."

I smiled, grateful for her unwavering support. "Let's get started now. We don't have much time. I know my uncle will pick sports that Jocelin Montfort is good at. He's insistent that I marry him, even though Prince Connor is interested in me."

Jane pressed her steepled fingers to her lips before she spoke. "I wonder what he has on that man. He obviously thinks he can control Montfort for the foreseeable future."

The night stretched on as we planned, our whispers blending with the rustling of pages and the crackling of the fireplace. There was much to do, but for the first time since returning to Lockersley, I felt more than a glimmer of hope. The tournament would be my chance to take back control, and I intended to seize it with both hands.

CHAPTER EIGHTEEN

The crunching of leaves underneath my feet was one of my favorite sounds, add the sound of a puppy scampering as we walked, and nothing could be more perfect. The joy I felt this morning gave me hope that my plan was actually going to work. Jane was beside me with our notes from last night. We hadn't slept much, but it was worth it to be able to present an actual course of action to Tuck and the others.

Jane looked around. "This is where we agreed to meet."

I wasn't sure how she could tell one flat piece of ground surrounded by trees from another, but it was one of her many talents. Jane and I stopped, sitting on a fallen tree that cut through the middle of the open space. Rogue sniffed around the perimeter, stopping at every single tree.

It wasn't long before Tuck, Will, and Erin joined us, each walking through the trees from a different direction. Rogue went up to each of them and determined that they weren't a threat to me once she had sniffed everyone.

I looked around, wondering why Milo wasn't here yet. Was he coming? Surely Jane included him on the invite. Why wasn't he here yet?

Tuck raised an eyebrow. "Why did you drag us all out of our bed this morning, Rowan? Are you going to enlighten us?"

I nodded. "I'm not sure if you've heard yet, but my uncle has decided to have a tournament where the prize is . . . well, me. Jane and I have devised a plan. I'm going to enter disguised as a male competitor. The goal is to win so I can get the prize money for the town and, of course, my hand in marriage." I couldn't help but laugh at the idea of marrying myself.

Will crossed his arms, skepticism clear on his face. "How do you plan to pull that off?"

"Disguise and preparation," Jane interjected, unfurling the notes she held. "Rowan was one of the best fighters among us at the nunnery. I was the only one she couldn't beat. And if there's an archery contest, she's got that in the bag. No one is better than her. We just need to make sure no one recognizes her."

Erin nodded, though her expression was cautious. "Do you know any of the other competitors?"

"Not yet. We're working on gathering that information," I said, trying to sound more confident than I felt. "But we'll need everyone's help. We need to know their strengths, weaknesses, and strategies."

Tuck seemed to consider this, his gaze thoughtful. "It's a bold move. I worry what will happen if your uncle discovers what you're up to. He's not a very nice man."

Just then, the sound of rustling leaves caught our attention, causing all of us to hold our collective breath, concerned about getting caught before we made it past the planning stages. Milo emerged from the trees, his hair damp after running from the keep. All of us released the breath we were holding when we saw him— Well, everyone but me; mine caught as he ran his fingers through his hair, sending his curls every which way. Rogue ran up to him, her hackles raised at first, but as soon as he got down on her level, letting her sniff him until she was satisfied, she calmed down. In fact, she decided to roll on her back and let him scratch her belly instead of coming back to me.

"Sorry I'm late. What did I miss?" One side of his mouth quirked up in a lopsided smile as he continued to pet my dog.

Jane shot me a knowing look. "Just the beginning of our plan. We're glad you could make it, Milo."

"Where were you?" I asked.

He grinned, his eyes sparkling with interest. "I lost track of time in my lab working on something. But I'm here now and wouldn't miss it for the world. What's the plan?" He came over to stand next to me. He was so close I could feel his body heat emanating from him. Every part of me that was close to him tingled. His fingers brushed against mine . . . Once . . . Twice . . . They started to do it a third time, but instead, he intertwined our fingers and held my hand. He didn't let go until he was caught up on the plan.

His eyes captured mine. "It's a good plan. Risky, but worth trying."

"I hope it's more than worth trying. We have to succeed. I have to succeed. Everyone is counting on me," I whispered so only Milo could hear me.

My eyes looked down at our interlocked fingers. Milo squeezed my hand gently before taking his free hand and tilting my chin until our gazes met, his unwavering. "You will succeed, Rowan. We'll be here for you to lean on as you prepare and compete. Remember, you are not alone in this."

I nodded, his words and the feel of his hand entangled with mine bolstered my confidence in ways the others couldn't. Only Jane was capable of reassuring me as much as Milo was doing now, but in a completely different way.

In that moment, the rest of the world drifted away, and it was just me and Milo together against all the uncertainty of the tournament, and beyond that seemed so distant it didn't matter right this second. My eyes fluttered shut as Milo lowered his head towards mine. This kiss was happening. This was it. I was going to find out what it was like to feel his lips against mine.

Tuck cleared his throat, bringing me back to the present and the fact that we were in Sherewood Forest surrounded by others. It didn't stop me from glaring at the friar. He just shrugged and turned back to those gathered around.

He clapped his hands together. "It's time to start our preparations. We only have a fortnight. It may seem like a lot of time, but the other competitors will start arriving soon so they can settle and practice here beforehand."

Each of our roles assigned, we all sprang into action, eager to get started on the tasks that had been laid out. Jane, Erin, and I would perfect my masculine disguise all the way down to how I moved. Jane and I would practice my combat skills, focusing on my ability to overcome those taller than me, something I struggled with whenever I fought Jane. Tuck and Will would gather information about the other competitors. Milo, with his analytical mind, would help formulate a plan for the fights and potentially create better equipment for the other events.

The day dragged on as we executed the beginning steps of the plan. Jane and Erin fussed over my appearance, yanking my hair this way and that with an excessive amount of enthusiasm.

"Are you interviewing for a job as a local interrogator?" I winced as Jane and Erin pulled my hair in opposite directions. "I'll make sure to give my recommendation."

Next, the two attacked me with kohl, darkening my eyebrows until I looked like a startled owl. They scribbled notes on scraps of parchment about what tortures they had in store for me over the next couple of weeks.

"You need to think about how you move. It needs to be much more like a man. From your stance, to your walk, everything." Erin demonstrated, but she looked more like a strutting rooster than an actual human.

I tried my hand at walking like a man. I imagined the way that Milo moved and attempted to mimic the movement that was burnt into my memory. Instead of copying the fluid movement, I felt stiff and ungainly. I tried to smooth out the motion, but tripped over a rock, stumbled, and flailed my arms until I felt like I was going to stay on my foot. Then my toe came into contact with my heel and I was flying through the air. I landed face-first in the dirt.

I sighed and pushed myself up and sat there with a grimace. Milo ran over to where I had taken up residence on the ground.

"Are you okay?" He knelt in front of me. He ran his hands over my arms and his eyes over my legs.

When he was satisfied I was still in one piece, he stood, grabbed me by the arms, and pulled me up. I crashed into his body. My eyes locked on his, and for a moment, I lost where I was and what I should be doing.

"I'm fine. Embarrassed. But in one piece." Brushing the dirt off me, I looked over at Jane, waiting for her to say something.

"Now that you've learned how not to walk, let's try again." Jane bit her lip in her attempt not to laugh at me. "Right now, when you walk, it brings attention to the curve of your hips. You sway way too much," she instructed.

Milo went back to the edge of the clearing to watch the shenanigans; at least I assumed it looked like shenanigans despite how serious our endeavors actually were. He offered tips and encouragement. "You have to be confident in yourself and your disguise: if you believe, everyone else will."

Eventually, we stopped for the day, and Milo was there beside me. He tapped my shoulder with his and leaned in close, his breath warm against my ear. "This is going to work. I believe in you."

"Thank you," I whispered back, determination surging through me. "It has to work. I can't let the town down."

He smiled, his eyes full of trust and something more, something that made my heart race. "I know you won't."

As we stopped for the day, I looked around at my friends and felt a sense of purpose. Even though the path I had chosen was fraught with danger, I knew we could face whatever challenges came our way. First the tournament and then, together, we would reclaim Lockersley and restore it to its former glory.

CHAPTER NINETEEN

The weeks before the tournament passed in a blink of an eye. I was constantly moving from one character to the next; Lady Rowan with my uncle, Sir Robin during my training, and plain old me when I was with Jane, Milo, and the rest of my friends. Some days I felt lost and constantly on edge, afraid that I would slip into the wrong persona in front of the wrong person, but most days I was just exhausted.

Which was why Jane found me at my desk, head resting on the flat surface with papers filled with notes on the competitors all around me.

"You're supposed to be studying, not sleeping." Jane rushed into the room, picking up parchment as she came to them, destroying my organized chaos.

My head snapped up off the desk, a page of notes stuck to my cheek. I looked at her, eyes wide. "Don't pick those up. I have a system." I threw my hand up, gesturing for her to halt. But it was already too late. She had cleaned up my room.

Her empty hand flew to her mouth. "I did it again. Oh Rowan, I'm sorry. It's so hard for me to see things scattered about and not tidy. Sometimes it even makes my eye twitch, but I really am trying to stop myself." She handed me the stack of papers. "Um, Rowan, you might want to peel off the one stuck to your cheek."

"What?" My hands flew to my face, the crinkling of the paper loud next to my ear as I touched it. "Ugh, I can't believe that was there this entire time."

Jane's laughter bounced off the walls as I peeled the paper off my cheek. The ink was ever so slightly smudged but still legible. "I can't hold it in anymore," she said between giggles. "It's just . . . you look so serious with notes stuck to your face."

I couldn't help but laugh too, the tension easing from my neck and shoulders. "I have to say laughing feels really good. Everything has been so intense lately." I shrugged. "It's been a lot."

Jane's smile softened as she reached over and squeezed my shoulder. "I know. Saving a town is a lot, but you're not alone. We're all here to support you, remember?"

I nodded as I fought the overwhelming urge to cry, taking a deep breath. "I know. Thank you." I looked at the mess in front of me. "I just need to win this tournament. Once I do, everything will start to fall into place."

Jane nodded. "I almost forgot why I actually came to see you. Connor is here for the tournament. He requested to see you."

The mention of Prince Connor brought me back to the present, instead of the future where my thoughts had been drifting off to once again, bringing with it the crushing weight of my own expectations, not to mention those of others. "Connor? He's here? And he's entering the tournament. I haven't seen any notes on him. Why would he do this to me?"

Jane nodded. "Yes, he arrived this morning. Your uncle tried to brush him off, but you know Connor. He's persistent. As for why he's entering the tournament . . . He likes you. I believe he's trying to pursue you. But you are oblivious and your uncle doesn't want you to have more power than him."

A smile tugged at my lips. Prince Connor had been a friend since I had come back home, even though he was . . . officious at times. But it's hard to turn off the need to be a hero when it's so deeply ingrained in who you are as a person, so I couldn't hold it against him too much. His arrival was a welcome surprise. I didn't like that he was also joining the competition, but I assumed it was a way he felt that he could save me from my situation here.

"I should go down and welcome him to the keep and the tournament," I said, standing up and smoothing out my dress. "We haven't seen each other since our shopping excursion."

Jane nearly shoved me out of the room. "I'll organize the notes so you can study them. Say hi to the prince for me."

I threw my arms around her in a tight hug. Words weren't enough to express how much I appreciated her and all that she did for me. I left her to it, feeling somewhat lighter than I had felt in days. I navigated the familiar halls of the castle, my feet carrying me to the green where Connor was waiting.

As I stepped outside, the cool breeze ruffled my bangs, which tickled my nose, causing me to sneeze almost immediately. Wiping my eyes caused my vision to blur momentarily, but when it cleared, I spotted Connor leaning against a rock wall of the keep, his princely bearing and golden hair unmistakable. He looked up as I approached, a wide grin spreading across his face, causing wrinkles by his honey-colored eyes. I waited for my stomach to flip-flop like it did around Milo, but it didn't.

"Lady Rowan! It's so good to see you." He stopped in front of me with his hands clasped behind his back and bowed his head.

A wave of guilt washed over me as I watched his courtier manner. "There is no need for such formality." I looped my arm through his. "After all, we have gone shopping together."

"Right you are. It's a hard habit to break after spending the last few weeks in foreign courts." He placed his hand over mine. "Being here is a welcome change."

"It's good to see you, Connor," I said, smiling up at him. "I'm surprised you're here. How did you manage to get past my uncle?"

Connor's laugh seemed to echo off the stone walls surrounding us before it drifted off with the breeze. "I have my ways. Besides, I couldn't miss the chance to compete in the tournament. I wouldn't want you to be forced to marry anyone, not even me if I won. Which seems unlikely based on the rumors of someone training extensively in Lockersley."

Panic coursed through my body, telling me I should run. Did he know I was entering the tournament? My cheeks warmed as I tried to decipher at what he was hinting. "Oh really? I haven't heard about anyone local entering other than the sheriff."

"You know that isn't true. I believe the scientist is entering, and so is this mysterious lad who's been training night and day."

Milo had entered? I would potentially compete against him. Why would he do such a thing?

Connor stopped as the view of the ocean stretched before us. "We should stop here. It's a beautiful place to sit and enjoy the view."

Connor and I spent the next hour catching up. He expounded on his travels, telling me all about each court he visited in astounding detail. While I tried to tell him how I had spent my time the last few weeks, I couldn't because it would mean divulging my entire plan to him.

"I do so enjoy hearing about your travels, Connor," I said, trying to steer the conversation away from my secret activities. "I've only ever been here and the nunnery."

He smiled as he leaned onto his forearm, more than a hint of wistfulness in his eyes. "I have, but none of it compares to our land, whether it's Lockersley or the country I will one day rule over. There's something about it that calls to me. Every time I leave, my father is desperate for me to find a match outside of our boundaries. All I want to do is come home. I want to marry someone who feels that as deeply as I do." His eyes searched mine before turning to look at the sea.

His words touched me because I understood the way he felt about his homeland, and I couldn't help but feel a pang of guilt for not being entirely honest with him. Connor had become a good friend, but my heart was entangled in the complexities of my mission and my feelings for Milo.

I wanted to tell him that the person he was looking for wasn't me. But I couldn't, not yet. I still needed him to be an option. I was determined to win the tournament, but what if I didn't? I needed another suitable candidate for a husband. Someone other than Montfort. My uncle would want to deny a marriage to the prince, but he never would. Connor could be the only way for me to save my town.

I followed his gaze, watching the waves come in one after another. It was selfish of me to even contemplate using this man that cared so deeply for everyone. But I had to leave it open as an option. I wasn't sure I was going to be enough to accomplish what needed to be done. I wasn't even confident winning the tournament would be enough. Maybe the masked bandit needed to ride again during the tournament, while my uncle was distracted with all the incoming visitors.

CHAPTER TWENTY

"Let me in, Rowan. I have something to show you."

Rogue nudged me awake before jumping off the bed. My eyes followed her path to the window as I searched my room, trying to determine where Milo's whisper was coming from. Was he outside my window? Is that why Rogue was standing there whining? And if that's where he was, why was he out there?

"I could really use some help getting inside with all my new gadgets."

Throwing my blankets off, I rushed to the window and peered out into the moonless night. Below me was Milo perched precariously on the narrow ledge, a mischievous grin on his face and a bag slung over his shoulder.

"Milo, why are you standing on a ledge outside my window?" I whispered, my tone a combination of annoyance and amusement.

"I have something to show you," he said. His eyes twinkled in the light of my candle. There was no hiding his excitement. "Take this." He held the bag up for me to grab.

It was impossible to resist his enthusiasm. It brought back more memories of before. Of all the times when he would sneak into my room with some new gadget he'd made. All of them nonsensical, but adorable. My favorite was a wind-up dog. I would always go to my father's study first thing in the morning to show him my new things, never realizing how inappropriate it was for Milo to be in my bedroom. I found myself blinking back tears again at the reminder that I would never be able to show my father a Milo invention ever again.

"Hold on," I said, reaching out to grab the bag. I hoisted it through the window and set it on the floor next to me before helping him climb through the window. It took a bit of effort and a lot of noise. Why was he so loud? Milo managed to haul himself through.

As soon as he was inside, he gave me a quick, grateful smile so bright it lit up the room and sent my heart racing. "Thanks. I was worried I'd have to spend the night out there."

"I was asleep. You know that thing people do when it's dark outside?" I poked him in the chest as I spoke.

He backed up until he was against the wall, me glaring up at him. He stared down at me, still smiling.

He held up his hands in surrender. "I was teasing you. I would have climbed back down if you hadn't come to the window. Just like I used to do when I wanted to show you inventions and you didn't want to wake up."

"What's so important that you had to climb up to my window in the middle of the night?" I asked, trying to keep my voice low, but I was a hair past exasperated so it sounded shrill and so very loud. The last thing we needed was someone running into my room to find us here together. It would probably just hurry along my uncle's plans to marry me to Montfort.

Milo's mouth twitched in one corner as the half smile I love took over his face right before he opened the bag and pulled out an array of strange-looking devices. "I've been working on some new inventions. I think they could really help the next time you go looking for gold."

Curiosity piqued, I sat on the floor beside him, inspecting everything. There were grappling hooks, small crossbows, and something with two handles and a wheel. I had no idea what it was for.

"You've been busy," I said, impressed.

"Only because I've been inspired." Milo paused, his eyes locked with mine, and as he handed me one of the crossbows, our fingers brushed. "I know there is a lot weighing on you, Rowan. I wanted to do something to make at least some of your plans a bit easier, and potentially a lot safer."

I stared at his work laid out in front of me, the physical evidence of his concern for my well-being, as his words echoed in my head. "Thank you, Milo. I don't have the words to express how much this means to me . . ." I wanted to say more, tell him how much he meant to me, but didn't know how to say what I was feeling or if now was the right time to say it.

He shrugged, his attempt to play it off as if it didn't really matter, but I knew he'd spent hours if not days working on these tools. The truth shone through his eyes. "I would do anything for you, Rowan. Now, let me show you how these work."

The two of us sat on the floor of my room for the next hour with our heads together. Milo was meticulous in demonstrating how each device worked, explaining what it could be used for and his thoughts on how it would make future heists easier. It wasn't long before I found myself caught up in his excitement, admiring his ingenuity.

"This one," he said, holding up a small, compact grappling hook attached to what looked like a crossbow, "is designed to be lightweight and easy to carry. It should help you get in and out of tight spots quickly."

"And this?" I asked, pointing to the thing with the wheel and handles.

"It's for an emergency escape," Milo explained. "You can shoot the grappling hook; fingers crossed, it hooks on something, then you would secure your end of the rope. Place the wheel—see where the wheel is concave—put that part on the rope, hold on to the handles and jump. You should glide down on the rope until you hit something."

By the time he finished I was itching to get outside and actually use some of the new gadgets. "You've outdone yourself. I can see how each of these could be used in different scenarios. It's impressive."

His cheeks turned a soft pink.

"Are you blushing?" I nudged his arm with my elbow.

He shrugged, concentrating on putting everything back into the bag. "I'm glad you think these will make a difference. The things I know you'll do to make everything better here means the rest of us need to step up and help. I want to make sure you are as safe as possible without hindering your actions."

I don't know what came over me, but something about his words, what his goal was, shifted something deep inside me. Next thing I knew, I launched myself towards him—not an easy task since we were both on the floor—and threw my arms around his neck. My lips searched for his until they pressed up against his. It wasn't enough—I pushed my hand into his hair at the nape of his neck, curls twining their way around my fingers. His tongue swept across my lips. I gasped at the sensations running through my body as heat pooled in my center. I pressed my body closer to his, my chest up against his, my legs straddling his as the kiss deepened and our tongues tangled together.

It was too much, too fast. I pushed away. Both of us breathing heavily as we stared at each other. I glanced down, fully comprehending where I was, and moved off Milo faster than I had ever moved before.

I reached up and touched my mouth. "I'm sorry, I don't know . . ."

He stopped me from saying more with a raised eyebrow followed by his goofy grin. I waited for him to say something but he just continued to pack up the gadgets. We hid them away in a silence that was somehow both tense and comfortable.

He turned to the window, ready to leave me so I could sleep. Not that I would, how could I after that kiss?

"Thank you again, Milo," I said softly as he prepared to leave. "For everything."

He paused, looking at me with an intensity that made my heart skip a beat. "I'll always be here for you, Rowan. No matter what."

He wrapped his arm around my waist and pulled me until our bodies touched. He bent his head down and lightly pressed his lips to mine. The kiss was over before it really started and he was climbing back out the window.

He stood in the window, the moon shining behind him. "Goodnight, Rowan. Until next time." He jumped out of sight.

I heard rather than saw his boots hit the ledge below. Part of me thought about running to the window to watch him climb down. But that would ruin his perfect exit. Instead, I climbed into bed knowing my dreams would be filled with new images of the boy I left behind and the man he had become.

I pointed down the hall towards the exit, letting Jane know where I expected her to go. It's not like she didn't already know the plan for tonight, but it made me feel better to point her in the correct direction. Especially since she was less than happy with my planned heist. It was the most dangerous idea I had come up with, but it would be the most profitable if it worked.

A few days ago, we had learned that my uncle stashed bags of gold not in the treasury under lock and key, but in his room, with only him guarding it. I had wanted to take it during the day, but every day he kept me occupied not only with participants but spectators arriving for the tournament. It was maddening. Tonight I was going to steal the gold and tomorrow it would be in the hands of the people. My uncle couldn't get it back because he was busy with the tournament, which he had insisted the sheriff enter, making them both too busy to collect taxes.

Jane rolled her eyes before she nodded, her expression a mix of worry and determination. "You better be careful, Rowan. I need you, we all do." Her arms wrapped around me and squeezed me tight.

"I'll be fine," I assured her. "Ignore the pounding of my heart. Meet me at the old oak tree once you have the gold. Milo is setting up the zip line right now. At least he should be."

With one last look, Jane silently ran, disappearing down the hall. I was alone in the dimly lit corridor. I took a deep breath, squaring my shoulders to prepare myself for what lay ahead. Quietly, I tiptoed towards my uncle's quarters, every creak of the floor making me wince, afraid I was going to be caught before I really began.

The massive double doors that opened to my uncle's chambers towered above me. I stood, pressed up against the wall, listening for any sounds from within. Hearing nothing, I slowly pushed a door open and slipped inside, keeping to the shadows. The room was dark, but the faint moonlight streaming through the window provided just enough illumination for me to see the outlines of furniture and the large chest at the foot of the bed.

My uncle rolled over. "It isn't fair, it's never fair," he muttered before his breathing returned to the rhythm of sleep.

Once I was satisfied he was asleep, I moved quickly, knowing that every second counted. I tied the rope to the iron hook that held back the heavy velvet drapes lining the windows of the room. Once it was as tight as I could get it, I turned back towards the bed, slinking across the floor as silent as I could be. Stopping at the foot, I opened the chest and found it filled with heavy bags of gold, just as expected. My heart leapt with excitement, but I forced myself to stay focused. One by one, I lifted the bags, secured them to one of Milo's gadgets, and sent them careening down to the waterfall across the inlet.

As I was about to leave, a floorboard creaked behind me. I ducked behind the curtain, my heart in my throat, and peeked around the fabric but saw nothing. I waited there, breathing in the musty smell of velvet that needed to be cleaned, straining to hear any further sounds. The room remained silent. Taking a deep breath, I moved away from the curtain.

A hand covered my mouth and pulled me to the floor. "It's me. You left this in your room." He held up an invention of his crucial to my escape plan.

I glared at Milo, angry at him for frightening me even as my heart seemed to miss a beat at the sight of him. Then I swiped the wheel out of his hands. The sound the metal made as I took it sounded like a thunderclap in the silent room. I ducked down, waiting to be discovered.

My uncle stirred in his bed.

I looked back at Milo, my eyes wide. I couldn't get caught now, it would ruin everything.

I moved as quickly and quietly as I could, my ears straining for any sign that my uncle was awake.

"Who's there?" Sleep tinged my uncle's voice.

"Shit," I whispered, handing the last sack of gold to Milo. "You're going to need to hold on."

Milo nodded. He clipped the gold to his belt while I grabbed the wheel device.

Without waiting for a response, I tossed the device over the rope and grabbed the zip line handle. Milo wrapped his arms around my shoulders as I jumped from the window.

"Halt," Uncle Jonathan yelled. "I said stop."

The weight of both of us and the gold was no joke. I was thankful for all the training I had been doing. It's the only reason I was able to hold on and not drop us into the waves below.

The rush of wind in my face and the thrill of the descent almost made me forget the danger we were in. Almost. As we neared the hole in the cliffside, I watched until we passed the waterfall and were close enough to the ground not to be injured before I let go of Milo's invention.

We hit the ground and rolled. Limbs seemed to be everywhere. I wasn't sure which arms and legs were mine as we flipped over each other. I lay on the ground next to Milo, panting. When I finally stood, my legs slightly wobbled from the adrenaline.

"Do you think he saw us?" I asked, looking around nervously.

"No," Milo said. His eyes scanned the area until he found the rope and cut it, destroying the only thing that pointed to our location. "But we need to hide. Quickly."

I didn't wait to be told twice. Together, we ran behind the waterfall, the stolen gold securely in the possession of Jane and the others. All but the one bag tied to Milo's waist.

CHAPTER
TWENTY-ONE

I held Milo's hand as we ran to hide behind the water-fall. The walls glistened in the moonlight, light reflecting off each droplet of water. I felt like I was surrounded by diamonds and fireflies. The sight took my breath away as the magic of it enveloped me. However, this form of magic meant it wasn't long before the mist soaked our clothes and hair, making us as wet as everything around us.

I turned towards Milo as soon as we were out of sight. "What do you think you were doing showing up like that. You almost got us caught."

He at least had the decency to look contrite. "I don't know. I was worried about you . . . so I checked your room, and you were missing this." He held up his invention. "I knew it was your plan to use it to escape."

"I would have figured it out. Please don't do it again. I can't be worried about you getting us caught or worse. Promise me it won't happen again."

He opened his mouth, clearly wanting to say something more, but thought better of it and nodded his acquiescence to my words.

"This way," I whispered, taking the lead and guiding him deeper into the cave. The roar of the water was nature's cover for our illicit activity. It masked our movements and voices. We were both drenched, our clothes clinging to us, but we didn't stop. The urgency of what we were doing pushed us forward.

It wasn't long before we reached a small alcove, almost completely hidden from view and shielded from the worst of the mist. I leaned against the damp stone, trying to catch my breath as I watched the waterfall from above. Milo stood close, his presence a comforting warmth despite the cold water dripping from us.

"That was close, too close." His voice was barely audible over the waterfall's roar. His eyes met mine, filled with a mixture of excitement and concern. "Are you okay?"

I nodded, squeezing his hand. "Just a bit wet." I threw my head back and laughed, the sound almost lost in the cacophony around us. "It actually worked, Milo. The gold is out of my uncle's hands and on its way to Lockersley and my people."

I couldn't sit still as adrenaline and something else coursed through me. We had succeeded in a way I wasn't sure was possible. My uncle had almost caught us, and we had leapt from a building and flew to safety. It had felt like we were going to die more than once, but here we were, safe, together. Leaping to my feet, I spun and spun until I fell, dizzy, into Milo's arms.

He smiled down at me. Relief and pride flickered across his face. "I'm so glad you made it out of there." He pulled my body in closer until I was sitting in his lap. "You're the bravest person I have ever met."

I looked at him, feeling a rush of emotions come over me. I was thankful and something more, something deeper. It had been growing between us over these past weeks, as much as I hadn't wanted it to. I wasn't even sure if I could pursue this, not with Lockersley still hurting, not if I wasn't enough to save it on my own. "Thank you, Milo. For believing in me. For being here by my side."

He reached up, brushing a wet strand of hair from my face. "I wouldn't want to be anywhere else." His fingers lingered on my cheek, brushing across my lips, and for a moment, the world outside the waterfall ceased to exist. It was just us, standing in the moonlit cave, the sound of the water creating a cocoon of privacy.

"Milo," I began, but whatever I was going to say was lost as he closed the distance between us. His lips were on mine, soft and warm despite the cold droplets all around us. I melted into the kiss, the world spinning away until there was only the sensation of his mouth on mine, the warmth of his body against mine.

When we finally separated, I was breathless, my heart pounding in my chest. "We should move," I whispered, my mouth mere inches away from his, though part of me wanted to stay in this moment forever.

He nodded, his eyes never leaving mine. "We should." But he didn't move immediately, but instead he took a moment to rest his forehead against mine. "I will always be here, supporting you, Rowan. If you let me."

I closed the distance between us, my lips crushing his, opening my mouth, and our tongues twisted around each other, exploring, sparring. I heard myself whimper as Milo moved away from my mouth and trailed kisses down my neck, moving my wet clothing out of the way as he did so.

Shivering, I reached out, my hands running up his chest, the wet fabric incapable of hiding his muscles that were beneath it. I couldn't stop my hands from wandering over his abdomen, finding the hem of the shirt and lifting it over his head and tossing it aside.

My hands touched his bare skin. It was hot under my icy fingertips. Milo watched my hand travel from his chest down to the ridges of his muscles, slowly caressing each one. His hand covered mine, placed it behind his neck, and lowered his head until our lips met again.

"It seems unfair for my shirt to be gone, but you are still wearing yours." Milo's breath was hot against my neck.

My cheeks grew hot as I thought about his words. "Is there something you would like me to do about it?" My words sounded much more confident than the voice in my head.

He reached for the laces on my leather bodice. His eyes met mine. "Is this okay?"

I nodded without hesitation. In the back of my mind, the thought this wasn't the right time to do this lingered, but I couldn't stop what was happening.

Not that I wanted to.

Milo's fingers made fast work of the laces and slipped the bodice off my shoulders. The sound it made as it hit the ground was drowned out by the roar of the waterfall.

My blouse was plastered to my body, clinging to my skin in a way that showed more than hid. Milo untucked the shirt. His fingers grazed the hem that now rested against my thighs, sending shivers of desire through my body. I held my breath, waiting to see what he would do next.

It wasn't long before I found out. He grasped the bottom of the shirt and pulled it over my head. Instinct caused me to cover my small chest, but when my eyes met Milo's, all I saw was desire and it made me brazen and my arms dropped to my sides, allowing him to look as much as he wanted to. I let my eyes wander over his body, watching the way water ran down his chest and slowed over the ridges of his abdomen.

I bit my lower lip as I debated whether I should reach out and touch him or lean forward and kiss him, letting our bare bodies press against each other. The decision was made for me when he took my hand in his and tugged me towards him. Our lips met, melding together as our bare skin touched for the first time. The heat of our bodies, slick from the water all around us, pressed together overwhelmed my senses. I didn't have any words to describe every nuanced sensation I felt, not that I needed any words. Which was good because the only coherent thought I had was I wanted more. More of what I was feeling right now, more heat, more tingles, more of everything.

I whimpered when Milo moved his mouth away from mine until his lips rested on my neck and he kissed and nibbled his way down and across my collarbone and then farther down, until he was cupping my breasts and switching between sucking on my nipple and lathing it with his tongue, starting a fire inside me that would not abate. I fumbled with the metal holding his kilt closed, my normally nimble fingers stiff with cold.

"Here, let me help with that," he whispered against my ear.

His hands closed over mine and worked the item out of the fabric until it fell away from his body, leaving him in nothing but a pair of leather boots. My eyes widened at what I saw, his muscular, lean, lanky body completely exposed in front of me. I would be trying to cover myself, but he stood there unashamed of what I saw—or what my eyes devoured as I allowed them to graze over every inch of him.

Milo reached for me, his arms encircling me, as we were lost in each other's kisses. I felt his hands at the waistband of my leggings, tugging them down as far as he could without having to take his lips off mine.

I pulled away, taking his kilt and laying it on the ground before I sat. My fingers fumbled as I rushed to take off my boots. Once again, he came to the rescue. He moved slow and deliberate, taking my foot into his lap and untying the laces before slipping the brown leather off, followed quickly by the leather of my pants. I was about to protest when his fingers grazed my calf and up my thigh. Any thought of speaking vanished as I watched his hand. He went back to removing my other boot. Momentarily, my thoughts wandered to how wide my thighs looked at the moment. But the thought was brushed away by the way Milo's hands swept over them, not to mention the desire in his eyes as they took in my naked body.

Once again his mouth was on mine, then it moved, raining kisses all over my body. I ran my hands through his hair and over his wet skin, placing my lips on whatever bare skin I could reach. Wanting more, I pulled him until I could kiss him again, so I could run my lips down his neck and nibble on his ear like he'd done earlier. My control did not last long though as his hands ran along my hot skin, one finding its way between my legs. He caressed me there, sending jolts of lightning down my limbs, at least those were the only words I could find to describe it. My toes curled as everything intensified. I could feel one finger slide into me. I pressed my eyes closed, not knowing exactly how to react to such intimacy. But as his hand started to move, I felt more and more that was unexpected. I barely registered the use of his second finger other than everything feeling inside and around me becoming more intense. When there was nowhere else for the sensations to go, it was like a burst into a million pieces of pleasure.

"That was . . ." I paused, not knowing what to say.

Milo rolled us over so I was atop him. His cock felt like silken heat as I slid my hand up it. He stopped me.

"Not this time."

My eyebrows raised, not knowing what he wanted. He lifted me up, showing me what to do. I took it in my hand and lowered myself on to him. The stretching was both pleasant and not. At least at first, but as I sank farther down, everything I felt before rushed back. His hands grabbed my ass, kneading it as he directed me to ride him. He let me control the rhythm as I slid up and down on him, slowly at first, reveling in his reaction, the power, my body coming alive. But then it wasn't enough. I needed more. I wanted faster, so I moved faster and harder until I shattered again. My body clenched around him, his moans of my name letting me know he felt the same thing.

CHAPTER TWENTY-TWO

For a moment we lay there watching the water dance around us, listening to the other breathe. But staying here longer wasn't an option, as much as I would have loved to escape from the world with him forever. At least that's how I felt in the moment.

It didn't take long for my responsibilities to come crashing down on me. I hastily grabbed my clothes, trying, and failing, to put on the wet leather leggings that were suddenly too small for me. After hopping around trying to get them on like I was a court jester, I gave up. My blouse was long enough, I supposed. It did almost cover my knees.

I looked up to see Milo watching me, a goofy grin plastered on his face.

"We have to go," I said, urgency lacing every word.

"I know. I have to get my kilt on, it will take but a moment." He laid out the fabric like he had done this a thousand times, which I'm sure he actually had. And it wasn't long before he was fully dressed; damp, but dressed.

I wasn't fully dressed and I was soaked to the bone. He grabbed my hand and, with a last squeeze, we moved deeper into the cave, searching for the exit we had found six years ago during all of our exploring. The night wasn't over, and our mission was far from complete, but at that moment, standing together behind the waterfall, I felt stronger than ever. But was it enough? Was I enough to make the changes Lockersley so desperately needed, or did I need someone with more power by my side?

As we emerged from the other side of the cave, the moonlight cast long shadows across the forest floor.

"What took you so long?" Jane hissed from behind the trees. "And where are your pants?"

I glanced down at my bare legs and shrugged. "The leggings were too wet to get back on."

Jane rolled her eyes but didn't press further. "Sounds like a story when we have more time. But now we need to move. The guards are looking for us."

The three of us clambered up into the wagon ladened with my uncle's gold, or I should say, with the gold of the people of Lockersley.

The horses trotted through the forest, with Jane leading us to the others; long shadows stretched in front of us. The moon was to set soon, and morning would be upon us. My mind raced with the events of the night, most of them exhilarating, and everything that was left for us to accomplish, leaping back and forth between the two like a child over a babbling brook.

We rolled up to the designated meeting spot where Tuck, Will, and Erin were waiting. Their anxious pacing turned into relieved smiles as they greeted us. Briefly, their eyes flicked to my unconventional attire, but not a single one of them said a word about it.

"Did you get it?" Tuck asked.

Milo nodded, patting the side of the wagon. "Every last coin."

"Good," Tuck said, a satisfied gleam in his eye. "Now, let's distribute it before the sun rises. The people need to know the hooded bandit is here for them."

"I'm going to need another pair of pants if I'm delivering tonight." I stood there in just my wet blouse, waiting for a response.

"Are you missing your pants? I hadn't noticed." Erin's words were stiff as she turned towards Tuck. "Do you have anything she can use? If not, I'm pretty sure I do."

Tuck shook his head. "Go get them . . . Hurry!"

Erin ran out of our meeting spot. My eyes followed her, hoping she would have something for me, even though I doubted she had made anything that would fit my hips and thighs.

"Shouldn't we hide some of the gold? Keep it back until it's needed. That way, my uncle cannot get it back in one fell swoop of the sheriff coming to town to collect taxes."

Tuck nodded thoughtfully. "That's a good idea. We'll keep a portion well hidden in the old abbey. It's been abandoned for some time."

Milo stepped closer, his arm brushing against mine. "Allow me to take care of that. I still use the area for some of my more explosive experiments. I know a few good hiding spots in the abbey."

I glanced at him, grateful for his support, wondering if the physical contact was intentional. "Thank you, Milo. And you too, Tuck. I couldn't do this without you."

"Don't start getting sentimental now. There's a lot of work that needs to be done and we need to be strategic about it." Tuck ran his hand over his bald head.

Erin returned with a pair of pants that looked like they could have belonged to me. She looked away as she handed them to me. The fabric was a green wool that was softer than anything I had ever felt in my life. I pulled them on, amazed at how perfectly they fit around my waist and through my hips before they loosened around my thighs, and tied under my knees, right below the top of my boots, allowing me to tuck them in. I looked at Erin, wondering how she had such a perfect pair of pants for me.

"I used your dress measurements. I thought you might need some clothing for your after-hours activities." She blushed, then stared at her shuffling feet.

I threw my arms around her. "Oh, Erin, I love them. I've never worn anything that's fit so perfectly."

"Let's divide the gold," Tuck said, motioning for everyone to gather around. "Rowan can distribute most of it tonight. We can pass out the rest in different ways as it's needed."

We worked quickly, dividing the gold into smaller bags. Artie was brought around and her saddle bags were filled with as much gold as she could carry. Milo and Jane took the rest and carefully stashed it in a secure spot in the old abbey, just as we had planned.

As I set off into the night, the weight of the gold felt lighter than the burden of the responsibility I carried. I moved silently through the forest, using my bow and arrows to deliver the gold to those who needed it most. Each time my arrow landed with a bag attached, a grateful villager would peek outside and signal their thanks. After each delivery, I felt a little more of my father's legacy living on through my actions, through all our actions.

After the last bag was gone, I made my way back to our meeting spot. Milo and Jane were there waiting for me. The others had gone to their homes to sleep, some before the town was overrun by those arriving for the tournament. Exhausted but exhilarated, the three of us gathered by the wagon as the first light of dawn was beginning to break.

"We did it," Jane said, a tear running down her cheek.

I watched, surprised that she felt this moment as deeply as I did. But why shouldn't she? Her actions were making as much of a difference as mine. Together we were changing people's lives.

"Yes, we did," I agreed, looking around at my friends. "This is only the beginning. The road ahead of us is long and filled with danger. My uncle will not go down without a fight."

Milo squeezed my hand, reminding me I wasn't alone in this fight. "And we'll walk it together."

As we set off towards the castle, I felt a surge of confidence. We were making a difference, a little bit at a time. With renewed determination, I looked towards the horizon. Lockersley needed change, and right now, in this moment, I was ready to lead that change, one step at a time, with my friends by my side.

Yes, the road ahead was long and fraught with danger, but together, we were unstoppable.

I stood outside my uncle's study, listening to him throw things. Glass shattered and fell to the floor, followed by the dull thud of heavy objects hitting the floor. It sounded like a battle was raging in the room, one in which my uncle's things were on the losing end. His anger echoed through the halls, a stark contrast to the silent determination that had guided my actions last night.

I took a deep breath, squaring my shoulders before knocking softly on the door. "Uncle Jonathan, may I come in?"

Silence was the immediate answer to my request, but eventually, the strained voice of my uncle could be heard. "Enter."

I pushed open the door and stood on the threshold, surveying the damage before me. The room was a disaster; books and papers were scattered everywhere but on his desk; broken glass glinted on the floor, reminding me of morning light caressing dew-covered grass. My uncle was surrounded by the chaos, his face red with fury.

"What is it you want, Lady Rowan?" he demanded, his voice a low growl.

I plastered a look of concern on my face as I cast my eyes down, trying to sound calm and concerned despite my heart pounding like thunder in my chest. "I heard the commotion and wanted to make sure you were okay."

"Okay?" His laugh was brittle. "Nothing is okay! My gold is gone, stolen from me as I slept!"

I feigned surprise. "Stolen? How could that have happened? Don't you keep the gold in your room?"

His eyes narrowed, suspicion flickering in their depths. "That's what I intend to find out. The thief leapt from my window in the middle of the night. But hear me now, I will find whoever did this and make them pay."

I nodded, keeping my face calm as my palms started to sweat. "That's terrible, Uncle. If there's anything I can do to help, please let me know."

He waved his hand dismissively. "Just stay out of my way, Rowan. Figuring this out will require actual skills, not whatever they taught you at the nunnery."

I closed the door to the study quietly behind me before I grimaced. *"Require actual skills."* If only my uncle realized what I was capable of, he wouldn't be in his current predicament. My lips turned up in just a hint of a smile as I walked away, my sense of satisfaction overcoming my fear of getting caught. The gold was safely hidden thanks to Milo and Jane, and my uncle was too busy with his fit to suspect me, at least for the moment.

Jane was waiting for me at the end of the hall. She appeared calm, poised even. "How did it go?" she asked.

I shook my head, nodding to my room. Jane nodded back. We made our way to my room and away from any prying eyes and curious ears.

I swung open the door, letting Jane enter first. Closing the door, I leaned against it.

"He's furious, but he doesn't suspect anything yet." I pushed myself off the door to walk around the room.

"Good," she said, relief in her voice. "With the tournament and the theft, it's going to be difficult to stay ahead of him, but we have to."

"We will," I promised. "If he finds out we're behind this, I'm not even sure what he would do. He's killed before. What's to stop him from doing it again?"

Jane gulped, her eyes wide. "I hate that I have to agree with you. What's next?"

"We keep the charade going around my uncle and the sheriff. This was the plan from the beginning. Nothing has changed," I said. "We can't afford to do anything different and bring attention to ourselves."

Jane looked around, making sure we were alone. "What should we tell the others?"

I nodded. "I think everyone needs to continue on as if our nighttime activities weren't happening. Shops need to open, especially with the tournament. There's no way anyone here would pass up the opportunity to make money this week."

Jane tapped her lips, deep in thought. "And the gold? Where should we distribute it first? I'm not sure it's going to stay safely hidden if your uncle really sends people to search for it."

I took a deep breath. "We start with the families who need it the most. We'll spread it out gradually to avoid raising suspicion. I was thinking Tuck could distribute some on Sunday."

Jane rested her hand on my shoulder. "You've got this, Rowan. Your father would be proud of you."

My breath caught as a lump formed in my throat from her words, but I swallowed it down, stopping the tears that I didn't have time to shed right now. "Thank you, Jane." I placed my hand over hers. "Let's go find the others and let them know how my uncle reacted this morning."

We made our way through the castle, keeping our heads down and avoiding any unnecessary attention.

My uncle's tyranny had to end. His reaction today confirmed what I already knew: he was not the right person to lead. I wished I felt confident enough to know I was the right person. I feared I was too impetuous, not organized or focused enough, and in the end, no matter what I did wouldn't be enough. But for now, I would focus on what I could do instead of what I feared I couldn't.

I glanced at Jane as we approached the hidden entrance to our meeting place for the day. "Are you ready?"

She locked eyes with mine, her smile filled with determination. "Always. If we survived the Incident, we can survive anything that comes our way."

Together, we pushed open the door and stepped inside, ready to face whatever challenges lay ahead.

CHAPTER TWENTY-THREE

T he first light of day made its way through my window to shine directly in my eyes. Most days, I would have thrown the covers over my head, buried myself under the inordinate number of pillows around me, and ignored the fact that people were waking up and starting their day. At the very least, I would have pulled the bed curtains tight in an effort to block out the offending light. Instead of doing any part of my normal morning routine, I sat up and threw off the covers. Today was the first day of the tournament and I had been awake for hours, potentially all night, nervous about what the day would bring.

I slipped out of bed, careful not to wake the snoring body sleeping next to me. Jane had stayed the night with me in her attempt to calm my nerves. It had been fun giggling late into the night like we had at the nunnery. Unfortunately, I couldn't keep my mind from running every single scenario that could possibly happen during the tournament over and over again. She didn't need to know that I had been unable to sleep, which was why I was trying to get ready as quietly as possible.

My heart's pounding echoed in my ears as I wrapped the binding around me to flatten my chest, wincing at the discomfort it caused. Erin insisted I use it, but I didn't think it was necessary because my chest was practically flat anyway. But it was better to take every precaution. I would hate to have skipped this one step and it to be the reason I'm discovered.

Once I was done with that bit of unpleasantness, I stepped into a pair of pants that did nothing to flatter my curves. It was intentional, but that didn't stop me from making a face in the mirror. The pants were so large at the waist I had to use a rope as a belt to hold them in place.

The tunic was even worse. They hung from my frame, disguising every part of my body that identified me as female.

The last thing I had to do was hide my hair. I tucked it into a cap and secured it with pins to keep any stray strands from escaping, giving my identity away.

I looked at myself in the mirror and adjusted my stance in an attempt to mimic Milo and Connor. They both stood and moved differently. I felt like I was trying on different personas and none fit quite right. So I kept trying different stances until I found something that I could maintain and I didn't think would have anyone questioning my identity. I practiced a few phrases, deepening my voice until it sounded almost natural. It wasn't perfect, but it was the best the transformation was going to get.

Grabbing my boots, I snuck out of the room. Once in the hallway, I quickly pulled them on and made my way to the stables. I needed a horse for today and it couldn't be Artie.

The stable boy, Thomas, stared at me as I approached.

He squinted as if he was trying to bring something into focus that wasn't quite clear. In response I attempted to make my stride look masculine, only to trip over my own feet. A curse, or two, slipped out before I was able to regain my balance and composure.

"Lady Rowan?" he asked, confusion lacing his words.

"It's Robin today," I whispered with a wink. It was unfortunate he had recognized me. I hoped he would keep my secret to himself. "I'll need a fast horse, one that is not recognizable to the laird."

Thomas nodded, a smile tugging at the corner of his lips. "As you wish, Master Robin."

He brought out a chestnut mare; her coat was a rich warm brown in the morning light. I mounted her in one fluid movement and felt a rush of excitement as I took the reins into my hands. This disguise hadn't passed its first test, but it had to work if I was going to participate in the tournament and avoid all suspicion.

"Thank you, Thomas. She's lovely."

He nodded as he waved farewell.

I urged the horse forward, her hooves thudding softly against the ground as we made our way towards Shere-wood Forest. It seemed silly to leave the keep only to return, but it was necessary to maintain my disguise. So here I was, riding out as the sun was just beginning to peek over the horizon, casting a golden hue over the landscape. The icy cold air of morning filled my lungs as I took a deep breath. Autumn wasn't going to be around much longer if the current chill in the air was any indication. I shivered as the mare continued along the path, covered in the colorful carpet of fallen leaves.

This was it—the true test of all the planning, plotting, and practicing. Soon I would be in front of my uncle, convincing him I was Master Robin, and not the woman that had sat across from him at dinner for the last few weeks.

I directed the mare through the maze of tents set up by all the competitors, vendors, and different artisans. The area was quiet as it slowly came to life. It was like the entire place was drowsy and rubbing its eyes, trying to wake up. But that shifted as I approached the edge of the town square. The marketplace was bustling with merchants setting up their wares on the street. The aroma of breakfast drifted through town on the breeze, reminding me I needed food before the competition.

I followed my nose and the smell of meaty, smoky goodness. I tied my horse to a post near the public house and made my way into the throng of people sitting around and eating. My eyes scanned the crowd for any familiar faces, but I saw none. I needed to find Milo and the others and make sure our plan was still on track.

But first I needed to eat. Now that I was standing in the room, there was no way I was going to walk out without getting some of the delicious smelling food. I weaved my way through the scattered tables and chairs, most occupied by patrons, concentrating on not swaying my hips as I walked. Everything Jane and Erin had said about how I needed to move ran through my head. It took a moment before my movements smoothed out and my boots striking the wood floor sounded even, and I felt myself slipping into the role I set out to play. I took a seat at an empty table in the corner of the pub.

That's when I spotted Milo walking into the building. His eyes skimmed over the crowd but didn't rest on anyone, including me. I hoped this meant he didn't recognize me in my disguise as Robin. The chair screeched as I pushed away from the table to make my way over to him, careful to keep the timbre of my voice low.

"Milo, it's me," I whispered, tugging at his sleeve.

He turned, his gaze going straight over my head before he looked down at me. His eyes widened before a smile broke out across his face. "Row . . . bin! You look—different," he said as he took in my disguise.

"Do I pass?" My voice wavered as nerves took hold of me.

"I didn't even recognize you at first. If I wasn't expecting you to be dressed like this, I'm not sure I would have recognized you at all." He paused, and his blue eyes clouded with emotion. "I've entered the tournament as well. I'll be there, with you, every step of the way." He clapped a hand on my shoulder. "Are you ready to go win this thing?"

I nodded slowly at first, my conversation with Connor flashing through my mind, and then worry knotted my stomach. Milo was built, but he'd never been interested in athletics, and as far as I knew, he hadn't trained. He could get seriously hurt.

"Why?" I couldn't stop myself from blurting out the question.

He glanced over at me. "To help. I want to be there for you. If you need me."

It was an answer. I wasn't sure if it was the entire one, but it was something. I was going to ask something else, but the questions about Milo and the tournament flitted away as I straightened my spine, faking confidence I did not have. "Let's do this. But first, food."

Back at the keep, the green was filled with vendors getting their stalls ready for an influx of people excited to see their wares. There were colorful banners that fluttered in the breeze, and the sounds of laughter and music reached my ears, filling me with happiness. The joy I felt coursing through me as I surveyed the field was overwhelming. It was the buzz of excitement from everyone here. As much as I disapproved of the idea behind the tournament—I was not a prize to be won—the event was doing more good for the town than I could on my own.

I pulled the brim of my cap lower, trying to blend in with the growing crowd.

Today my uncle would welcome all the competitors. This afternoon the competition started in earnest.

I meandered through all the stalls, taking in everything around me, the smell of roasting meats and freshly baked bread that wafted through the air and mingled with the scent of flowers from a nearby vendor. If I wasn't so nervous about the tournament, my mouth would be watering instead, but right now my stomach gurgled with distaste. Near me children ran and played, waving flags in different colors to support their favorite contestants. Their faces were even painted with vibrant colors. The energy was infectious, and despite my reservations about the tournament, I felt the smile on my face, unable to stop it from spreading. I could admit when I was wrong, especially since it didn't happen very often.

As I continued to wander, slowly making my way towards the grandstand, I spotted Jane examining a delicate necklace with a stone pendant at a jewelry vendor's stall, her eyes alight with interest. I took a mental note. It could be an excellent way to thank her for all her help, especially the time she had spent with the sheriff.

I approached her, careful to walk in character. "Jane," I whispered, "it's me, Rowan."

She quickly covered her surprise with a wide smile. "Robin, you mean," she said with a wink. "You look convincing—short, but still convincing."

"Thank you." I took in the crowd in an attempt to ensure no one was paying us any extra attention. "Have you seen Milo or the others?"

"Not yet." She handed a coin to the vendor and tucked the necklace into her pouch. "But they'll be here. Everyone's excited about the tournament. Even Tuck couldn't stop smiling last night and the friar is one grumpy man.

It's too bad the reason behind it is a bit . . . unconventional. Better than being auctioned off, I suppose."

"Is it, though?" I was on high alert, attempting to watch what everyone was doing near me. "Not that now is a good time to debate if it's better or worse to be a prize at a tournament or auctioned off to the highest bidder. We need to stay on our guard. If my uncle suspects anything, this will all fall apart."

Jane grabbed my hand and squeezed it. "Stop being so serious. I know you love a good caper, and this is definitely a caper."

I thought about Jane's words as we continued to weave through the crowd, making our way towards the grand-stand where my uncle would soon make his appearance. She was right. I needed to let go of the pressure I was feeling and have some fun with what I was doing. Things always seemed to work themselves out when I was doing something I loved. This tournament, competing in it, was something that I would normally love doing. I would see it as a bit of a lark. I was doing this for much more serious reasons, but that didn't mean I couldn't enjoy myself while doing it.

We finally made our way through the crowd to the grandstand. The dais was decorated with rich tapestries and garlands of pine and berries. It was a stark contrast to the poverty that still plagued Lockersley and a reminder of why I was here that somehow both boosted my confidence and caused me to break out in a nervous sweat.

My eyes darted around the area as the nerves refused to settle. I spotted Milo talking with a group of competitors. His eyes connected with mine and he excused himself from the men he was talking to, then made his way over to us. A grin spread as he looked me over again.

"Robin," he said, clapping me on the shoulder in that way men always did when they interacted with each other. "You made it. I'm happy to see you don't look any worse for wear from your travels. Are you ready for this?"

"As ready as I'll ever be," I replied, trying to keep my voice steady. "I'm hoping for some easy matches early in the tournament."

"That would be nice," Milo said, his expression serious. "Let's find Tuck and the others. Confirm each of us know where we need to be and when."

I nodded. We made our way through the throngs of people, finding Tuck, Will, and Erin near a weapons stall. They greeted us with slight nods and tight smiles, and we huddled together to review our strategy.

"Remember," Tuck said, his voice low, "once the tournament begins, we'll have a better idea of what we're up against. Well, what Robin is up against."

I nodded, wiping my palms down the front of my pants. This was it, the moment we had been preparing for. I rolled my shoulders back, reminding myself of why we were all here. For Lockersley. For my father. For a future without my uncle. Reclaiming what my father wanted to be mine.

We broke apart and moved to our respective positions. As I watched the people around me committed to this, to me, I couldn't help but feel a surge of hope. Despite the risks, despite the dangers, we had a chance to make a change for the better. And I was determined to see it through, no matter what it took.

With one last glance at my friends, I pulled the brim of my cap lower and melted into the crowd, ready to face my uncle and whatever challenges lie ahead.

Winnie came to a screeching halt in front of me. "Lady Rowan, your uncle . . . He's looking for you. You're going to be discovered if you don't attend the opening ceremonies," she whispered as she dragged me back to my room.

"How did you know?" It was the only thing I could think of to say.

Winnie's eyes darted around nervously. "I have my ways. I always listen to anything being said about you. Now hurry, you need to change."

She shoved me into my room with zero regard for my status, something I appreciated at the moment. I stripped out of my men's clothes, tripping over myself, my clothes, and my boots. Jane steadied me, stopping me from tumbling to the ground. Winnie must have warned her as well, and now Jane was here with my silver gown, the one she had been working on late into the night.

"Here, put this on," Jane said, her voice urgent but calm. "We don't have much time."

I slipped into the silver gown. I felt the whisper of Jane's fingers move up my back as she helped me fasten the dress. The shimmering fabric felt heavier than it had earlier, weighed down by the urgency of the situation. If I didn't get out there in time, I will have failed before I had even started.

"What did Uncle Jonathan say?" I asked as Jane adjusted my crown. The combination of silver and emeralds matched the dress and complemented my hair.

"He's been asking everyone where you are. He doesn't think you're taking the tournament or the opening ceremonies seriously," Winnie said, her eyes wide with concern.

I took a deep breath and rolled my shoulders back. "Okay, let's do this."

Once again, I hurried down the hallway, the sound of Jane's footsteps behind me echoing off the stone walls. As we approached the grandstand, I could hear my uncle's voice, tense with impatience.

"Where is Lady Rowan?" he demanded, his voice carrying over the crowd.

CHAPTER TWENTY-FOUR

The crown weighed heavily on my head as I stood outside the grandstand and took a deep breath. This was the first time I was going to be Lady Rowan in public. I didn't count my birthday ball because at the time I was still reeling from everything I learned upon my arrival and wasn't really playing the part of the young woman my uncle expected. Now, it was different. In a way, presenting myself here, today, was showing my people how I intended to show up for them every day.

Gathering the shimmering silver fabric that Jane had insisted on making for me and taking a deep breath, I walked towards the grandstand. With each step, I felt the weight of the crown and the responsibility it symbolized. My heart pounded in my chest, but I kept my head high and my pace steady. This was my moment to show my people that I was ready to lead, ready to fight for them.

I stepped into view of my uncle and the crowd, raising my hand in greeting, my head held high, attempting to look as regal as my father had been, like the nuns attempted to teach me to be.

"I'm here, Uncle," I called out, my voice quiet but steady.

Our eyes locked for a moment. He nodded his head in acknowledgment. I couldn't help but quirk an eyebrow up, a challenge and a question rolled into one barely perceptible expression.

His eyes narrowed as he took me in, his smile forced. "Ah, there you are. We were beginning to worry." He held his hands out.

"I apologize for causing any concern." I took his hands. I'm sure this looked like a meaningful family moment. "The tournament is so important I wanted to make sure everything was perfect."

He nodded, but I could see the suspicion in his eyes. "Very well. Let's proceed."

My uncle turned, raising our hands over our heads. "Ladies and gentlemen, it is my great honor to introduce

Lady Rowan of Lockersley!" His voice boomed across the green, and a wave of applause followed.

I stepped forward, releasing my uncle's hand. I waved to welcome everyone. The crowd's applause grew louder, and I felt a swell of emotion. These were my people, and they were looking to me for guidance and hope.

"Thank you," I began, my voice steady and clear.

The crowd quieted as I spoke, listening intently.

Pausing for a moment, I started again. "Thank you all for being here today. Because today is the beginning of a new chapter for Lockersley. This tournament means so much to us all. It is not just a celebration; it is a testament to your strength, your unity, and your resilience. Together, we will overcome any challenge that comes our way. Together, we will build a brighter future for all."

The crowd erupted into cheers, and a sense of pride washed over me. Their applause might be from the excitement of the tournament and have nothing to do with me, but soon they will realize what I was willing to do for them.

My uncle stepped forward again. His hand rested on my shoulder and his fingers dug into my skin. "Let the tournament begin!" he declared, and the crowd's excitement surged once more.

As I stepped back from the dais and the crowd, Jane appeared at my side, slipping her arm around mine. Her gaze conveyed so many emotions, not the least, pride.

"You did it," she whispered. "You were amazing. I've never seen you like that."

I smiled, the weight of the crown feeling a little lighter now. "Thank you, Jane. I couldn't have done it without you."

Together, we moved to our seats, ready to watch the tournament unfold. The first day was filled with excitement and anticipation, but I couldn't focus; I needed to find a way to get away. My first match was this afternoon.

Finally, the ceremonies were over, and the competitors were announced. The crowd cheered as each name was called and they stood, recognizing the audience, including Master Robin. I'm not sure who it was, but someone stood and waved at the crowd in my place. I found myself glancing over at Milo and Will, who were standing together. Milo caught my eye and winked reassuringly.

As the last competitor was announced, my uncle leaned towards me. "You should mingle with the guests, meet some of the more promising contestants," he said. "Make sure they feel welcome."

"Of course, Uncle," I replied, bowing my head slightly. Relief washed over me as he provided the excuse I needed to leave his side and return to my other role. Little did I realize how intently he would watch me as I mingled with the contestants.

Jane and I moved through the crowd, greeting people and exchanging pleasantries as my uncle watched my every move. I had to be careful. I needed to leave, change into Robin, but I couldn't escape the suspicious eyes of my uncle. One wrong step and everything we had worked for could be in jeopardy.

Eventually, I made my way back to where Will and Milo were standing, Jane following behind me.

"Everything okay?" Milo asked quietly.

"Not really. My uncle is suspicious," I replied, glancing around to make sure no one was listening. "I need to change before my first match, but it feels like his eyes follow me wherever I go."

"That's easy enough to fix." Jane rubbed her hands together.

Will moved towards Jane. "What's going on in that devious mind of yours?"

Jane grinned, her eyes twinkling with mischief. "I figure we have two options here. One, we cause a distraction. There's enough going on here that we can cause some chaos to distract your uncle, and you can slip away. Or, two, you can be the distraction. Let your uncle know you aren't feeling well and excuse yourself from the rest of the day's events. Both have risks."

Milo raised an eyebrow. "And what type of distraction were you thinking of causing?"

Jane's smile widened. "Well, the event is in full swing. There's bound to be something we can capitalize on.

Maybe an argument or a small fire—something that will require your uncle's immediate attention."

Will nodded, catching on. "I like it. But it would have to be something that he would have to take care of himself. He can't send an underling."

I glanced around the square packed with people, trying to think of something that would meet all the elements required for it to work. "What about the jousting area? If something were to happen there, he'd have to investigate. It's the most important event of the competition. Uncle Jonathan wouldn't be able to ignore it." I stopped for a moment, deep in thought.

Milo nodded. "That could work. Maybe a fight between two competitors. No one needs to get injured or anything. Just something that would draw a crowd."

"Would it be better for me to fake illness?" I hadn't heard a word Milo said. "It would be a useful excuse for the rest of the event."

"You have a point, Rowan, but maybe this time we use the distraction and next time we go with the not-feeling-well plan. Today I think it's more important that you look strong and capable whenever it's you in public." Jane clapped her hands together. "Now, I'll handle the details. Make sure you're ready to move as soon as it's time. Your clothes are in the stables; it was closer than your room, and I didn't want you to get caught going in and out of the castle."

Will looked at me, his expression serious. "You sure you're up for this?"

I took a deep breath and winced. The crown was heavy and my head was aching. "I have to be. We decided on this path. It's not like I'm going to bail right as we might actually accomplish something."

Jane and Will both squeezed my hand, one after another, and left to put the plan into action, leaving Milo and me alone for a moment. He took my hands in his and brought them to his lips.

"You've got this," he whispered in my ear, sending a tingling sensation through my body. "Just remember why you're doing it."

I nodded. "For Lockersley," I whispered. "For my father."

I leaned on Milo, my head on his shoulder. There wasn't really time for this and if my uncle saw me with Milo, I didn't know what would happen. But I could feel his belief in me as I stood there in his arms. It gave me the strength I needed to continue. Especially since there was no turning back. The plan was in motion, and I had to play my part to perfection.

A few minutes later, the sound of angry voices reached my ears. I turned to see two burly men shoving each other near the jousting area, their faces red and their biceps bulging. A small crowd was gathering, and I turned to see my uncle storming towards the commotion, his expression thunderous.

"This is it," Milo whispered, giving me a nudge. "Go."

I disappeared into the crowd, moving towards the stables where Jane had left my bundle of clothes. Milo stood watch as I quickly donned my Robin attire. The transformation was almost complete when I heard footsteps approaching. I froze, afraid to move or even breathe. The footsteps stopped for a moment and I knew it was over. But then the footsteps started again, fading away in the distance.

"Hurry," Milo hissed, his eyes darting, taking in every nook and cranny of the stables.

I laced up my boots and pulled my cap over my hair. Feeling extra cautious, I wrapped a scarf around the bottom of my face, threw on a cloak, and pulled the hood up over my head, leaving only my eyes visible. With one last glance at Milo, I nodded. "I'm ready."

We moved quickly through the maze of tents, heading towards the hand-to-hand combat competition ring where the first match had just begun. I was in the next match. This was the competition I was the most nervous about. I struggled fighting Jane because of her height, and every man here was taller than me. How in the world was I going to win today? These thoughts continued to race through my head as we neared the edge of the crowd. I took a deep breath, trying to calm the nerves that were overwhelming me.

Milo stopped me, taking me by the shoulders. "You can do this, Robin. Jane wanted me to remind you to fight to your strengths instead of attacking their strengths. I want you to remember that you are not alone."

I nodded despite the fact that out in the ring I was alone. No one could do this for me. "Let's get this over with."

I don't know how I missed the end of the first fight. But the next thing I heard was my fake name being called out. I stepped into the ring, the roar of the crowd filling my ears. This was it. The moment we had been working towards. That's when I looked up into the honey-colored eyes of Prince Connor Blackwood.

CHAPTER TWENTY-FIVE

I stared up at Connor, fear coursing through my body. Not because I was afraid of him, rather I feared I wouldn't be able to do my best because I liked him. I didn't want to hurt him.

Connor's eyes met mine, his expression softening for a moment. "Master Robin," he said just loud enough for me to hear. "There's something about you . . . Someone you remind me of." He shook his head almost imperceptibly. "May the best man win."

I nodded, forcing a smile onto my face. "May the best man win."

We bumped fists before we circled each other, the roar of the crowd fading into the background. This wasn't just a match; it was the first test of my training and research. I had to stay focused and not let little things, like a soft spot for my competition, distract me. I reminded myself why I was here, a litany that rang through my head over and over again:

For Lockersley, for my father, and for my own future.

Connor struck first, jabbing with his left before coming around with a right hook. I moved back and then ducked, dodging his punches, each movement instinctive. Seeing a small opening, I countered with a quick jab. He blocked it, basically swatting my fist away. Through all of this, his eyes never left mine. We moved in a deadly dance, each blow met with a parry, each step calculated.

As the match continued, I gained confidence. Connor was good, surprisingly so for the son of a king, but so was I. Every time he pressed forward, I was able to dodge and respond, holding my ground. My fear disappeared. I was determined to win this fight. I couldn't let my feelings for him, the friendship I felt forming between us, interfere with what needed to be done.

A fierce exchange left us both panting, circling each other with our fists protecting our faces. Connor swung a left hook. "You're better than I expected, Master Robin. But the fun and games are over. It's time to end this."

With a move so quick I almost didn't see it, I realized Connor had been lulling me into a false sense of superiority. I stumbled but quickly regained my footing. I held my arms near my face, unable to do much against the blows he rained down on me, each one harder and faster than the previous one. He pressed his advantage more, his blows coming faster, more aggressively. I did everything I could to stay in the fight, but it didn't feel like it would be enough to win. Connor was outmatching me.

My green eyes met his, and he hesitated. His eyebrows shot up. "Rowan?"

The crowd's screams drowned out his words, but I heard him and nodded. He grabbed me in a headlock, shocking me. I fought back.

"What are you doing? Why are you here fighting? Do you know what would happen if you were caught?"

I realized he wasn't really fighting me anymore. It was an act to get more information. So, I played along while we spoke.

"I couldn't let my uncle give me away as a prize. Like I would ever sit around and be awarded to some man as a trophy to be won." I used a counterattack I learned at the nunnery and took control. "Not to mention the prize money would help Lockersley."

Connor was surprised at the sudden reversal of our positions. But it was so much more than that. My identity and conviction threw him off balance. For a moment, his grip slackened. It didn't take long for him to process the information, which was when our fight transformed into a choreographed dance of whispered words and fake combat.

"You could have told me, should have told me." He tightened his hold just enough to keep the crowd invested in our battle.

"Would you have let me compete?" I retorted, twisting to break free from his grasp. "This is the only way I can control my fate and help my people."

"It wasn't the only way. You could have married me," he retorted.

"I couldn't live here if I married you," I said with a grimace. But then I saw Milo in the crowd and felt myself smile. "It wouldn't be fair to you."

Connor's eyes followed mine, landing on my scientist. "I see."

He hesitated, and I seized the opportunity to slip out of his hold, spinning to face him. The crowd's cheers and jeers were a distant hum compared to the pounding of my heart. Connor's face was a mixture of frustration and admiration.

"Rowan." His eyes pleaded with me to stop this deception. "What you are doing is dangerous. If you're discovered—"

"You don't think I know that?" I interrupted, stepping back into a defensive stance. "I have to win this tournament. It's the only way."

He nodded slowly, understanding dawning in his eyes. "Okay, I understand. But I can't—I won't hold back because I'm fighting you, not as the prince."

"I understand, and would expect nothing less," I replied with determination. "Now let's get this over with so we can move on to our next opponents."

With renewed vigor, we resumed our fight. Connor's blows were measured, precise, but no longer held the same ferocity. He was testing me, pushing me to my limits without aiming to defeat me outright. I met him strike for strike, each clash of our hands echoing with the weight of unspoken words.

Then, with a move I'd practiced countless times, I saw an opening. Connor's guard dropped ever so slightly, and I lunged, my fist finding its mark. He stumbled and dropped to one knee, and the crowd erupted in a cacophony of noise.

Connor looked up at me, a wry smile playing on his lips. "Well fought, Robin. Or should I say, Lady Rowan?"

I extended my hand, helping him to his feet. "Thank you, Connor. You were a worthy opponent."

As we exited the arena, Milo and Jane rushed to my side, their faces alight with relief and pride. "You did it," Jane said, hugging me tightly. "You really did it."

Milo clapped me on the back. "I never doubted you for a second."

But as I glanced back at Connor, who was being tended to by the healers, a pang of guilt tugged at my heart. Despite the victory, the weight of my deception and the risks I was taking loomed large.

"We need to be careful," I whispered to Jane and Milo. "My uncle can't find out about any of this."

"We will," Jane assured me, her eyes scanning the crowd for any signs of trouble. "But for now, let's focus on the next round."

I nodded, pushing my worries aside. The fight was far from over, and I had a town to save.

CHAPTER TWENTY-SIX

"Rowan, we need to talk." Jane's eyes darted around, bouncing from the vendor tents to the arenas and back. "In private, as soon as possible."

I moved to hike up my skirts before I realized I was still dressed as Robin. It had been a long, exhausting day that didn't seem close to ending.

"You lead the way, I'll follow," I said, unable to make a decision about where to go. Too many options ran through my head and I wasn't capable of grabbing one and focusing on it long enough to convey it to Jane.

Jane paused for a moment, then nodded, leading the way into the keep. Instead of turning towards our rooms like I expected, she went into the bustling kitchen, making her way through it until we were in the room where mead and other beverages was stored.

"What's so important that you've dragged me away from the festivities?" I looked around our location. "And so secretive."

Jane pulled some papers out of her pouch. "I found your father's last nurse. The one that stuck around the longest."

"Why are you just now telling me this?" I reached for the papers.

Jane held them out of my reach. "I didn't want you distracted. But I sent her a letter, and she wrote me back. It's not going to make things better."

Jane's eyes were watery as she handed me the letter, the slight tremble in her hand exaggerated by the crinkling of papers extended in front of her. I took it and unfolded it with care, my breath unsteady as my heart felt like it was going to leap out of my chest. This was the first genuine lead we had. She could tell us something about what happened to my father, confirm whether or not my uncle had a hand in my father's death.

Dear Jane,

I remember Laird Richard well. He was a kind man and a gentle ruler. It broke my heart to see him wither away like he did. To watch his mind betray him. I knew there was something else going on when I took over as his nurse. His illness was sudden and severe, beginning soon after his brother arrived for a visit. It is my belief that he was poi-

soned, but I could never prove it. I was given the medicines to administer to him. However, I was never included in the mixing process. His symptoms were consistent with a toxin that is very rare and that leaves no trace. I started to give him the antidote, but the symptoms persisted until Laird Richard didn't know who he was or where he was. It is my greatest wish I was hired sooner and could have done more for him. I wish I could discuss this further, but now is not the best time. Hopefully soon, we can meet and talk more. Get everything out in the open.

Yours sincerely,

Nurse Eleanor

I read the letter once, then immediately read it again. As I read each word a second time, something seemed off with the nurse's words. Even though the letter echoed Tuck's suspicions, it was difficult to comprehend. How could my uncle be ruthless enough to kill his own brother, poison him? Watch someone that had cared for him his entire life lose their ability to remember who they were. It was so hard to believe. Poisoned. The word bounced through my thoughts, bringing a flood of images of my father from the healthy man I remembered to the man the nurse described. Anger, grief, and a burning desire for justice coursed through me, hardening my resolve. There was no way I could let my uncle get away with this.

"Poisoned," I whispered, looking up at Jane. "My father was poisoned."

Jane nodded, her eyes filled with sorrow. "I thought you should read the words yourself. I hope it's okay I didn't tell you sooner. My goal was to arrange to see her as well, but she's been steadfast in her refusal to meet during the tournament, in case your uncle finds out."

I nodded, feeling a new resolve harden within me. "Thank you, I understand and I know you weren't keeping it a secret. Did you notice anything strange about her words, though? She never actually said he was dead. Just that his symptoms continued."

Jane's eyes widened as she took the letter back and scanned it again. "You're right. She only mentioned the symptoms and her regret that she couldn't do more for him." A mix of relief and concern flitted across Jane's face. "I'll try to find the notebook you saw in your uncle's study while everyone is busy at the tournament tomorrow, but you need to stay focused on your task. We can't afford any slipups."

I tried to stop the surge of hope growing inside me. Could my father actually be alive somewhere? If he was, why hadn't he come forward? Did he not know what was happening in Lockersley or that I was back? So many questions ran through my mind, all of them a distraction that I did not have time for.

"We have to find him if he's still alive. If he's not, we're already on the path to seek justice for his murder."

Jane nodded, her lips pursed with the same determination I had. "We will figure it out. Right now, you need to stay focused on the tournament and your role as Robin. You have to do everything you can to subdue your uncle's suspicions."

So much of what needed to happen depended on me and my abilities. The weight of it was crushing, but the potential that my father might still be alive gave me strength. I hugged Jane, thankful she was here by my side even after nothing here was like I promised her. I don't know what I would do without her friendship.

"I'm ready," I said. Taking a deep breath, I rolled my shoulders and tugged my cap down. "Let's win this tournament, and then we'll figure out what really happened to my father."

Jane cracked open the door to the storeroom. "We'll meet again tonight in the forest after the festivities. Promise me you'll be careful."

"I will do what I can to protect myself." That wasn't what Jane had asked for, but it was the best I could do under the circumstances.

As we left the kitchens and made our way back to the crowd, the cacophony of noise and excitement of the tournament accosted my ears. The confirmation of my father's poisoning made it difficult to keep the smile on my face as I weaved through the merriment around me. I had to play my part in the tournament. My people were depending on me more than ever, whether they knew it or not. But my heart wanted to focus on another goal: uncovering the truth about my father and bringing those responsible to justice.

Today, we had taken the first step towards repairing the town of Lockersley and unraveling the mystery that had haunted me since my return, since Tuck had uttered his suspicions. I would do whatever it took to ensure that my father's legacy was honored and avenged.

The festivities continued around me, the sounds of music and laughter a stark contrast to the turmoil inside me. I knew I had to play my role convincingly and needed to win the tournament. However, the confirmation that my father's death, if he was truly dead, was no accident, changed everything. It made it incredibly difficult to focus on the task at hand. Instead of risking being seen in the mood I was in, I made my way to the forest early. I needed a place to sit and wallow in my emotions. If I didn't, I wasn't sure I could get my head on straight and finish what I needed to finish.

I slipped through the crowd, moving farther and farther away from the joyous atmosphere. I walked down to the beach, away from my uncle and his schemes and ultimatums. My plan had been to continue on to the forest and wait for Jane and the rest of my merry bandits there, but I found myself stripping down to nothing and running into the frigid waves. I dove in and swam until I couldn't handle the cold anymore. My swim couldn't have lasted more than fifteen minutes, but it was enough to bring my focus back to where it needed to be. I guess swimming had it's purpose. It still wasn't something I would call fun, but it helped focus my mind.

"Oh shit, I'm supposed to have dinner with my uncle." I threw on the clothes that I could in a hurry and gathered the rest. A string of curses escaped my lips as I made my way up the stairs to the keep. The fear of getting caught was the only thing that kept my legs climbing. The exhaustion from the competition and the constant fear of my uncle discovering me was kicking in, but I didn't have time for it. I had to keep going and change before dinner.

CHAPTER TWENTY-SEVEN

I finally reached the last step to the keep. The atmosphere that had been joyous and bright all day had melted into something messy and exhausted. Fatigue had become a palpable thing as I scurried through the stragglers and merchants until I was inside, racing down the hallway to my bedroom. As soon as I was through the door, my bed called to me. I wanted nothing more than to sleep, maybe for days. But first I had to attend dinner with my uncle and then I needed to recap with my friends. After everything that had happened today, from fighting Connor to discovering what potentially happened to my father, I was amazed. I managed to maintain my disguise and composure through the rest of the day, which had pushed me to my limits, at least mentally. Tomorrow would be physically harder because there were many more events happening. And I needed to win them all to get enough points to be crowned champion.

I ignored my bed and went to the dresses Jane and Erin had made for me. Every single one of them was stunning in their own way, but for tonight I put on a simple gown of blue-green wool with intricate knot work embroidered on the sleeves, neckline, and hem. It was easy to put on but detailed enough to satisfy my uncle while still being able to dress myself.

"Here, miss."

I jumped. "Oh . . . You startled me," I replied, giving her a tired smile. Winnie held out a belt for me to wear with the dress, her eyes shining with excitement and something else. "How do you move so quietly?"

"I'm sorry, miss. I can be louder." Winnie's expression changed from excitement to horror.

"Oh no, I'm just on edge. Please, you don't need to do anything differently." I tried to reassure her but wasn't sure if it had worked.

She nodded. "Of course you're on edge. I saw what you did today. It was inspiring to watch." Winnie fidgeted with my clothing. "You're such a small thing, and you beat the prince fair and all."

"It isn't anything really, just the use of tactics the nuns and Jane taught me." I shrugged, embarrassed by her admiration.

"Don't do that," Winnie said. "You're an inspiration, miss, whether you like it or not."

I stood there, staring at Winnie. "I don't know what to say, but I'm not doing this for admiration. I'm doing it because someone needs to help the people here, and I'm in a position to do so."

"Aye, miss." Winnie nodded. "You'd better finish getting dressed. Your uncle . . ."

"I know."

The maid helped me finish changing from Robin to Lady Rowan. Deep down, the question of whether I was losing myself in all the roles I was playing ran through my mind, especially since none of them were truly me. The tumultuous thoughts and feelings swirled around as I walked to the dining hall. The reality of my dual identity weighed heavily on me. I needed to switch back to Lady Rowan for the evening festivities and dinner with my uncle. The clothes I was wearing were easy to change in to, but my attitude—I was having a harder time shifting into the more docile version of myself. Unfortunately, I couldn't afford any mistakes, not with the stakes so high.

To my surprise, Jane was waiting outside the dining hall. She was supposed to be waiting for me in the woods.

"You look worn out, Rowan." Jane took me by the shoulders and stared into my eyes, checking to see how I was doing. "Are you okay to keep going?"

"I have to be," I replied, taking a deep breath. "My uncle is already suspicious. I was too . . ." I searched for the right word, not finding it. I settled on something close to what I was looking for. "Confident at the opening ceremonies. I need to show him that everything is normal."

Jane nodded, but I could see the worry in her eyes. "Just be careful."

"I will," I promised, giving her a reassuring smile.

As I entered the grand banquet hall, my gaze instantly went to where my uncle was seated at the head of the table. He was thrumming his fingers on the table, impatience radiating off him. When he saw me, he nodded, the only acknowledgement of my existence, but I could sense his lingering suspicion. I made my way to my seat, greeting the guests with a warm smile, doing my best to play the part of the gracious lady of the house.

Dinner was another tense affair. My uncle's gaze was constantly on me. Every word he spoke, every question he asked, felt like a test I didn't know the answers to. Throughout the dinner I stayed polite, my eyes cast down. I answered all his questions about the day and the tournament, mostly with lies. I tried to find some truth in my answers, but it was difficult considering my role in most of the day's events.

Despite my concern for getting caught, I couldn't stop myself from thinking about tomorrow: all the events that were planned, who I might be up against, and what preparations I needed to help me win. And then there was the murder of my father, something I was trying to push to the back of my brain until I could do something about it. Every piece of me wanted to scream at my uncle, accuse him of his wrongdoings. However, I knew I would regret it instantly because I couldn't act on any of those accusations, only hurl them at his face to see how he would react.

This overwhelming desire was the reason I excused myself as soon as the last dish was cleared. I claimed fatigue from the day's events, but I was unable to sit there in his presence a moment longer. Finally, I was able to go to my room and change back into me, and for a few hours I didn't have to worry about being anyone but my true self.

Back in the woods, Jane and Milo were waiting.

"How did it go?" Milo asked, concern written across his face.

"He's suspicious of me, but has no idea what I'm doing. He tested me throughout the night, but somehow I managed to play the part of a modest lady the entire time, even though I wanted to accuse him of my father's murder," I replied, sinking to the ground. "Tomorrow is going to be extremely stressful. I have multiple competitions and my uncle is not going to let his guard down now."

Jane handed me a flask, her expression serious. "You're going to need this. I know you need rest, but everyone wants to check in with you. Rest will have to wait."

I nodded, understanding how important it was for my friends to see I was holding up to all the pressure placed on me. I took a sip of the fiery drink. The liquid burned its way down to my stomach. The tension in my arms, neck, and back melted away as I took another sip from the flask.

Milo knelt beside me, taking my hands in his. Our eyes met, his filled with empathy . . . and something else. "You were unbelievable today, Rowan. I believe in you, we all do. I'm sure this feels like it's all resting on your shoulders, but we're all here for you, ready to do whatever we can to help."

I pulled him down so he sat beside me and rested my head on his shoulder. "Thank you, Milo. I needed to hear that. I just . . . I just need to get through this tournament. It's hard to focus on that knowing what I now know. I want to discover the truth." I soaked in his warmth and the feelings behind his words.

Jane sat down on my other side, placing a reassuring hand on my shoulder. "Let me help with that. I can find out more while you focus on the tourney."

I sat up. "Do you think you can find out more?"

"I can at least try while you're doing everything else."

Milo's arm dropped to my side, creating a disconnect I wasn't used to feeling.

"Are you okay?" I whispered.

"I've been working on . . ." He stopped himself from saying more. "It's nothing to concern yourself with, Rowan. You've got too much pressure on you right now."

A snap had my head popping up. What if the sheriff had followed me somehow?

"Rowan, today looked like it went splendidly!" Tuck exclaimed as he walked out from the trees with Will and Erin by his side.

I nodded. The adrenaline that had been keeping me going for so long was almost gone.

"Thanks, Tuck. At least it looked like it was going well. Switching between Lady Rowan and Master Robin was tough today," I said, trying to muster a smile. "And to-morrow is going to be even harder. I don't know where or when my uncle is going to demand my appearance."

Will's face filled with concern. "What can we do to help? The back-and-forth between the two is so much pressure. The more you can focus on the games, the better."

Erin nodded. "With Winnie's help, I can make sure your clothes are close and easy to change into tomorrow. That way you can focus on winning."

I sat up straight, the support of my friends filling me with the hope I had been losing just moments before. "Let's go through tomorrow's plan one more time so I can get some sleep. We can't afford any mistakes."

We huddled together for the next hour, working out our strategies for tomorrow and ensuring everyone knew their roles for the day. I did my best to stay focused and participate until we were done, but the day finally caught up with me and I woke up to everyone moving away from the fire to sleep for the night.

"Get some sleep, Rowan," Jane said softly. "We'll sleep here tonight instead of walking up and down those stairs."

I nodded, feeling exhaustion weigh on my eyelids. "Thank you." My voice sounded muffled. I wanted to tell them how much their support meant to me. Maybe I just thought it, or maybe I said it aloud, I wasn't sure.

Milo helped me to my feet and led me to a small tent with a makeshift bedroll. "We all know, Rowan."

As I settled into bed, exhaustion finally overtook me. The day had been long and grueling, but I had survived it. With thoughts of the tournament and the fate of Lockersley swirling in my mind, I drifted into a restless sleep, determined to face whatever came next with the same resolve and courage that had carried me through today.

CHAPTER TWENTY-EIGHT

Rubbing the sleep from my eyes, I looked around expecting to see my bedroom, but instead I was looking at the white canvas of a tent. I snuggled farther into my bedroll, the leaf-covered ground softer than I would have expected. Icy fingers of cold air slipped around the blankets I had tucked around my body as a shield against the autumnal chill, finding cracks in the woolen armor I didn't know were there. The cold settled into my already sore muscles, forcing me to accept my fate. I was not going to be able to sleep any longer.

As I left the cocoon of my tent, the soft hues of morning could be seen through the naked branches above me. My head tilted back as I took a deep breath, filling my lungs with fresh frigidness. The warm rays of the sun caressed my cheeks, and I opened my eyes to see the pinks of dawn were shifting to the golden light of morning. The sense of duty that had momentarily disappeared rushed back. I had to get back to the keep for breakfast with my uncle.

Gathering the few items I had brought with me last night, I dressed quickly, not bothering with binding my chest since I would have to change into Lady Rowan as soon as possible. A breeze ruffled through the red and orange leaves on the trees, causing my teeth to chatter uncontrollably as the cold air bit at my skin. Jane was still asleep, her form bundled tight in her bedroll. My eyes took in the rest of the camp. Funny, Milo was already gone. The thought flitted through my brain as quickly as it had come before I tiptoed out of the clearing and made my way through the forest with the ease born from familiarity. The path to the keep was serene, basking in the early morning light; the entire place was still, a stunning contrast to what the area would be in just a few hours after the day's activities began.

As I approached the heavy gate to the keep, I slowed my pace, looking around for anyone that might report me to my uncle. I didn't see anyone. The last thing I wanted to do was get caught sneaking back in. It would only raise unnecessary suspicions and garner attention I didn't want. I scurried along the side of the building and entered through a side door, then took the stairs two at a time until I could run down the hall to my chambers.

I breathed a sigh of relief when I saw Winnie there, waiting with a dress already laid out for me.

"You're cutting it awful close, miss. I was starting to worry you wouldn't make it to brekkie with your uncle," the maid scolded.

I smiled back at her as I made my way to the dressing screen. The unexpected support of my lady's maid warmed my heart, releasing some of the tension I had been carrying with me for the past few weeks. "I didn't mean to make you worry. I'll be sure to plan better from here on out." I shimmied out of my clothes from the night before and bent down to pet Rogue while I waited for my outfit. "What have you picked out for me today?"

"I thought the teal wool with the burnt orange overcoat looked ever so regal." She tossed the dress over the screen.

I slipped the dress on, appreciating the softness of the wool and its warmth. "I love this combination. Can you be sure to hide some of Master Robin's clothes for me? Somewhere near the stables. Erin will be around to show you exactly where."

"Of course Lady Rowan. Whatever you need." She moved about the room, picking up some of the disaster that I left in my wake.

I slid into the overcoat and put on the heavy jewelry and crown Winnie had picked out for me. Rogue's paws slapped the stone floor as she walked away and jumped onto the bed. The pup curled into a ball as I looked over my costume with a critical eye.

"What do you think?" I twirled. "Will it do?"

Winnie looked me over with a critical eye. "Your da would be so proud of you." She sniffed. "Now go, don't keep Laird Jonathan waiting."

I turned as my eyes filled with tears, not wanting Winnie to see the grief that suddenly overcame me at her thoughtful words. A few tears escaped before I wiped them away with the hem of my sleeve. I pushed thoughts of my father away as much as I could. Jane said she would look into the letter the nurse wrote and I believed her. Not only that, I needed to let someone else work through that mystery while I focused on my multiple personas and winning the tournament.

Standing outside the doors to the dining hall, a shiver coursed down my spine. I wanted to turn and run, do anything but sit through another meal waiting for my uncle to yell that he had figured it all out and was locking me up. Instead, I pushed open the doors.

My uncle, seated at his usual spot, looked at me with narrowed eyes as I entered. "Good morning, Rowan," he greeted, his tone neutral but his gaze sharp.

"Good morning, Uncle," I replied, my lips turning up into a smile that never reached my eyes. "I trust you slept well?"

"Well enough." His mustache twitched as he continued to watch my every move from underneath his bushy eyebrows. "And you?"

"I slept soundly." It was a good thing he didn't ask where I slept, just how. "The festival kept me busy yesterday. By the end of the day, I could barely stay awake."

He nodded, each word I said seeming to lessen the suspicion I saw in his eyes. "There's more going on today than yesterday. The competitors are very talented, and many eyes will be watching."

"I'm excited to see as many matches as I possibly can," I said with excitement as my mind wondered how I was going to balance being seen as Lady Rowan and as Master Robin.

"See that you do," he replied.

As breakfast continued, I played the part of the dutiful niece my uncle believed me to be, murmuring in agreement when it was necessary to do so while my mind ran through what events I had to win, how to score the most points, the events I would struggle with, and how I was going to appear as Lady Rowan throughout the day to keep my uncle's suspicions at bay. Every step mattered, and I couldn't afford any missteps.

"Did you see Prince Connor lost to some unknown yesterday?"

My hand twitched, knocking over the goblet in front of me. The amber liquid inside spilled over the table. I gulped. "I'm so sorry, I don't know what happened." I patted the table dry, waving away servers, while my uncle looked on, scorn written in every crease across his forehead. "I saw the match. It was an impressive fight."

"Interesting, I didn't see you there." My uncle's words worried me more than anything else that had happened at this table.

My opponent and I shook hands to signify the end of the sword event. As I walked off the field, I couldn't help but think about the match in my head. It didn't go as well as I had hoped, ending in a draw. It wasn't the worst outcome, but it still had me reliving every move, every missed opportunity. I knew I had to let it go so I could focus on the upcoming events. My disappointment clung to me, sticking to my soul like tree sap.

Milo was there, waiting for me. I hadn't seen him at all during the match, but there he was, ready to lift my spirits after what felt like letting down everyone depending on me.

He reached for my hands, then let them drop to his side as he remembered who I was right now. His eyes raked over me, the look he gave me a mixture of concern and encouragement. "You did well, Robin," he said, placing a reassuring hand on my shoulder. "A draw isn't a loss. You've still got this."

It was like he could read my thoughts. Maybe not all of them, but the ones that were currently racing through my head over and over again.

I nodded, forcing a smile. "I know. It's just . . . I need to win."

"And you will," he said firmly. "Don't let what you can't change affect your other events. You're an amazing archer and your quarterstaff skills are unmatched. Focus on those skills. Leave what's done behind you, especially since there's nothing you can do to change it."

Taking a deep breath, I listened to what he was saying, trying to take it in and let my loss . . . tie . . . roll off me. Milo was correct. I couldn't afford to dwell on what was done. I needed to focus on what came next and use every opportunity left to prove myself.

The archery event was next, but it wasn't for a couple of hours. With that much time in between events I had to change into Lady Rowan and make sure my uncle saw me at the tournament, interacting with the other competitors.

"I need to change into Lady Rowan, maybe even run into my uncle at some point." I increased my pace until I was almost running to the stables. "Or maybe I should sit with him during the joust."

I could feel Milo following me, even though he didn't say anything as we made our way through the crowd.

The stable doors loomed ahead and I wanted nothing more than to run the rest of the way. Milo's hand on my shoulder tempered my pace slightly.

"Easy, there's time." He walked next to me like there was nothing in the world that could make him move faster.

I sighed. As much as I hated to admit it, he was right: rushing would only draw more attention. I forced myself to slow down, concentrating on how my body moved as I put one foot in front of the other. Were my hips swaying too much or had I actually mastered the loping walk I enjoyed watching? Together, we entered the stables. Milo stood guard as I changed in Artie's stall. Thankfully, the horse was used to a bit of commotion.

My transformation was quick but meticulous. Gone was the rough, practical attire of Master Robin, replaced by the elegant, teal and burnt orange wool of Lady Rowan from this morning. Jane's handiwork was impeccable. She had somehow found time to embroider beautiful knot work on the overcoat. Details like that were something my uncle was sure to notice, and they helped me shift my demeanor. I could feel it happen as the dress settled on me.

The weight of the crown on my head also helped remind me of the role I was playing and the reason behind it.

Once I was ready, Milo let out a low whistle. His eyes sparkled with appreciation. "You are stunning, I wish I . . . Get out there and show everyone who you are. It won't be long until they all appreciate you as much as I do."

I took a deep breath, squaring my shoulders. Together, we made our way back to the tournament grounds, Milo walking half a step behind me. I couldn't tell if it was my imagination, but the crowd seemed to part in front of me, leaving a path directly to the arena where the joust was being held. The area was already buzzing with excitement, the crowd eagerly awaiting the next match. I spotted my uncle up in the grandstand sitting on his throne, his eyes scanning the crowd.

When the crowd noticed me walk towards the grandstand, they fell silent. It wasn't what I wanted, but I accepted the attention as if it was my due, waving to my people as I passed them.

The entire way, I could feel my uncle's eyes on me, following every single movement. I forced a smile, nodding slightly as I made my way to his side. "Hello, Uncle. The tournament is quite the spectacle. There are so many events to watch. How do you choose?"

He bowed his head ever so slightly, his expression a mix of suspicion and something akin to pride, which was shocking, to say the least. "Indeed, it is. And you, my dear niece, seem to be enjoying yourself."

"I am," I replied, keeping my tone light. "It's a wonderful opportunity to meet so many skilled competitors."

His eyes narrowed slightly, but he said nothing more. I took a seat next to him, engaging in small talk and observing the joust. My heart raced with each passing moment, but I maintained my composure. For the next event the competitors were Jocelin Montfort and . . . Milo? Why hadn't he told me he was competing today?

I scootched forward in my seat, completely forgetting about the man next to me watching my every movement. Will held the reins as Milo mounted his horse, weighed down by his armor. Or so he should have been. Instead, he mounted as if there was no extra weight holding him down. The thought that he had invented something lighter skitted through my brain as the first squire stepped into the field.

Introductions were made, and the white flag dropped. I held my breath until the first round was over. Both competitors were still on their horses, but Milo's lance had glanced off Montfort's armor, giving him the point for this round. For the next two rounds, I could barely breathe as I watched the event unfold. Montfort's lance broke, almost knocking Milo off his horse. But Milo held on for dear life. It gave Montfort the upper hand going into the final round. I waited for the last round, barely able to breathe as the white flag dropped and the mounted men raced towards each other. Milo's form looked good until his shoulder dropped back ever so slightly. I hoped the sheriff wouldn't notice, but my hope was in vain. Montfort broke his lance again, sending Milo flying off his horse. I wanted to run down to him; I would have, but my uncle's hand was on my shoulder, pressing me back into my seat. His fingers dug into my skin in a way that I knew would leave a mark.

Montfort stopped in front of the grandstand. Raising his visor, he smiled at me. It felt more like a threat than a welcoming gesture.

"This win is for you, Lady Rowan, and the honor of becoming your husband."

I stared at him, not acknowledging his words. Over my dead body would he become my husband. I would marry, whether it was for love or duty, but my husband would be of my choice. I refused to be a trophy.

CHAPTER TWENTY-NINE

I sat through the next set of competitors, seeing nothing that was happening before my eyes. The only thing I could focus on was Milo. I needed to know that he was okay so I could kill him. I know he said he was entering the tournament, but I never expected him to joust. He was an inventor. He made things to make life less dangerous. He did not run headfirst into a big wooden stick that would knock him off his horse and get himself injured, that was something I would do without even thinking about it.

I excused myself, making my way back to the changing area. Milo was waiting. I breathed a sigh of relief to see him standing there, ready to help me switch back to Robin.

"What were you thinking? You could have got yourself killed!" I hissed at him while maintaining the smile pasted on my face as I walked over to the stables.

Milo shrugged. "I told you I had entered."

"I know, but I don't want to have to worry about you while I'm trying to win." I stormed away, needing to become Master Robin and having zero time to focus on what I thought Milo should or shouldn't be doing.

As I changed, the nervous energy transformed into focused determination. This was my chance to prove myself. Archery was my best event, after all.

Pulling my cap down over my hair, I sauntered out of the stables, only to hear the incessant whistle of the sheriff. I turned to run back, but thought that might look suspicious. So I turned again to continue on my path, knowing I was going to have to interact with Montfort.

"Master Robin!" Montfort called out. "I've wanted to speak with you."

"You have?" I asked with a gulp.

He clapped me on the back, full of jovial camaraderie, something I would have never associated with my uncle's henchman.

"I want to congratulate you on your win against Prince Connor. Not many would have been brave enough to continue fighting once they knew it was the prince. You seemed to have no issues at all." His weasel-like smile was something that would haunt my dreams.

I cleared my throat, remembering to drop my voice an octave or so. "I'm sorry I didn't get your name. Do we know each other?"

"Jocelin Montfort, Sheriff of Nottinghamshire, at your service." He bowed. "I'm Laird Jonathan's right-hand man."

"How nice," I muttered. "Jocelin, what a unique name. Where did it come from?"

Montfort's face turned red. "It's a family name, on my mother's side. I'll see you at the archery range." He tossed his last words over his shoulder as he walked away.

I followed Montfort to the archery range, arrows in my quiver and my bow resting on my shoulder as I made my way through the crowd. This event was different from the rest. Every other event was one-on-one, but the archery competition was done in heats. Thankfully, I was in the first heat and would have time to show up as Lady Rowan before the competition was over.

As I took my place next to the other competitors, I grabbed my bow. The weight of it reminded me of everything I cherished in life, from my father teaching me how to shoot, to the days at the nunnery on the practice field, and finally, to the special tools Milo had created to aid in my endeavors. Standing there, the bow became an extension of my arm. My lungs filled with the chilly air of the day as the familiar rush of adrenaline mixed with a deep sense of calm came over me. I exhaled. This was my arena, my home. I could do this.

Each contestant had targets set at varying distances in front of them, each shot required precision and control. I drew my first arrow, focusing on the center of the closest target. The world around me faded as I released the string, the arrow flying true. I didn't even watch to see if it hit the bullseye before moving to the next target. As soon as the arrow left the bow, I knew exactly where it would land.

The cheer from the crowd confirmed what I already knew, but it was still gratifying to hear. From that moment on, my focus was on the next target, and then the next. Arrow after arrow, I hit the targets with unerring accuracy. By the time the final target was in my sight, my confidence was soaring. I released the last arrow and walked away from the center of the arena. The roar of the crowd had me releasing my breath. The screams, clapping, and stomping of those watching let me know I was accurate in my assessment of the arrow's path straight for the center of the bullseye.

I turned back to the crowd as I reached the exit of the arena. I thrust my bow above my head. The roar of the crowd was deafening as I lowered my bow and left to change once again.

It felt like mere moments before I was back at the archery arena as Lady Rowan taking a seat by my uncle's side.

"Where have you been? You just missed one of the most impressive displays of archery I've ever seen." My uncle didn't even look at me. His eyes were fixed on the next round of competitors. This heat had both Prince Connor and Montfort in it.

I tried to hide my smile. Little did my uncle know that I was the one he was admiring. "I'm sorry, Uncle, I needed some quiet."

At my words, he glanced over. "Where's your crown?"

I clenched my hands in my lap to prevent them from flying to my head. "My head ached. I left it in my room."

"Rowan." The muscles in his jaw twitched as he clenched his teeth. "That is unacceptable. After the event is over, get your crown and ignore the pain."

I nodded, thankful for an excuse to run as soon as the event was over.

Connor had gone. His aim was quite good, not as good as mine, but he almost challenged my score by hitting the bullseye on all but the last target. Montfort was next. I tried not to hold my breath as he fired his first shot and it hit right outside the center. It went on like this until the last arrow hit the outside ring of the target.

His miss meant I had won. I wanted to jump up and down as the excitement of winning coursed through me. Instead, I stood sedately.

"Uncle, I'm going to go retrieve my crown. I want to make sure I have it for tonight's festivities." I didn't wait for his reply but walked off, my pace sedate, until I knew my uncle could no longer see me. Then I hurried to the stables to once again change who I was, replacing the luxurious fabric of Lady Rowan with the scratchy clothes of Master Robin. The exhilaration of winning had erased my exhaustion as I made my way to the quarterstaff competition.

It was the only event left for today. Tomorrow, the final challenge for me would be the joust, the only event that had me truly worried. For now, I pushed aside my concern as I entered the arena to face the competitor in front of me right now, my head and my muscles still buzzing with energy from the archery win. This was a different kind of challenge. Archery required concentration, patience, and skill; the quarterstaff required both strength and agility. I rolled my shoulders back as I let out a deep breath, centering myself before I stepped into the ring and the competition began.

My opponent was huge and I had never seen him before, but the research Jane and I had gathered meant I was prepared, at least mentally. We circled each other, setting the tone of our intricate dance, staffs at the ready. He struck first. The power of his blow sent vibrations up my arms and through my fingers. I almost lost my grip on the staff, but I dug my fingers into the wood, grasping it as if my life depended on it. At this point, all I could do was counter his moves.

The fight was the most intense battle I had ever been a part of, a flurry of strikes and parries. I was in awe that a man so large could move so quickly. My muscles screamed at me, begging for me to end this, but I pushed through. I fell back on my training and Jane's words to fight my fight, not my opponent's. I crouched down, swung the staff out, and swept the legs of my opponent out from under him. He landed with a thud, his staff flying from his hands and rolling to the edge of the ring.

The crowd erupted in applause, its cheers washing over me. I had won, taking down someone almost twice my size. This morning had been a rough start, but I had redeemed myself and was even closer to winning the entire tournament.

As I left the ring, Jane was there to greet me, her face alight with joy. "That was amazing! You were amazing!" Jane pulled me into a hug.

Milo's smile was warm and proud. "I knew you could do it."

I smiled back. "I'm still mad at you for this morning, though," I said before shifting over so he could join our hug.

CHAPTER THIRTY

I couldn't sleep. It wasn't because I wasn't tired. Exhaustion had taken up residence in every part of my body except my brain. I tossed and turned, thoughts racing through my head faster than a galloping horse. One thought kept coming back: why was Milo so insistent on participating in the tournament? At first, I believed that it was to help me out. Maybe he would try to position himself as my opponent and let me win, but that hadn't happened. Instead, I watched him have his ass handed to him in the joust and him struggle, winning by the smallest margin in almost every other event. He had managed to stay in the top five contestants, barely.

In a fit, I threw off the covers. There was no reason for me to lay here in bed with all these questions when I could just go ask him. Especially if it would ease my mind so I could finally get some sleep.

I changed into my favorite black pants and tunic, for once leaving my room feeling like myself instead of someone else. I crept through the hall, once again sticking to the shadows until I was standing outside of the keep and in front of Milo's lab.

I stood in front of his door wondering what I was doing there, if I should turn around and go back to my room. I took a deep breath, the chilled night air filling my lungs, and raised my hand to knock. My hand stopped and hovered there, inches away from the door. I wasn't sure if this was a good idea, but after everything, shouldn't I be allowed to ask him questions and get honest answers? I rapped on the door a few times and waited.

The only sound to reach my ears was silence, at least at first. After a few moments, I could hear footsteps approaching. The door opened with a deafening creak that pierced the quiet of the night. I looked around, worried someone would hear the noise, investigate, and find me standing alone at night in front of a man's home. That's how nervous I was.

From behind the door, Milo's face appeared. His eyes widened in surprise. "Rowan? It's late. What are you doing here?"

I glanced around yet again, this feeling of being constantly on edge, waiting to be caught, wearing on my psyche. "I need to talk to you. Can I come in?"

He opened the door wider, stepping to the side so I could get through. Upon entering, I was hit with an array of scents from various herbal concoctions. I always forgot that he did more than invent things, that he was always looking for herbal remedies, better ways to grow food, and so much more. Milo's lab was a chaotic smattering of beakers, scrolls, and other devices. The cluttered space, so much like my room, helped to put me at ease.

He cleaned off a stool so I could sit.

"So, what did you want to talk about?" Milo leaned against his workbench, knocking a few things over as he did so. He tried to catch them, but they only ricocheted off his hands. He bent down to pick them up and his glasses slipped off the top of his head and clattered on the ground. "For fuck's sake. Really?" He put the items down, grabbed his glasses from the floor, and shoved them on his face.

I stood and looked around at the table and all the papers on it, pausing when I saw drawings of some buildings. "I don't understand why you're taking part in the tournament. I thought it was to help me win, take the loss if you had to, but after today, I know there's some other reason. I need to know what it is."

Milo's expression was unreadable as we stared at each other, and he sighed. "I knew you would ask, eventually. I even tried to tell you the other day, but you were so tired. I have plans for something that I think will be great here in Lockersley."

"So you entered to try to win me, like I'm some sort of trophy instead of a human being?" I turned to leave. Did I really need to hear any more?

Milo grabbed my hand, preventing me from walking out the door.

"No, it's not like that at all. There's something I want to do for the town, but I don't have the funds for it. There's a monetary prize for the runners' up. I was hoping I could at least place and get some prize money for my project. And if I did win, I would give you the choice of marrying me or not. I would never assume you would choose me and I would always want you to feel in control of the outcome in your life. You're not a trophy or a prize."

I frowned, trying to reconcile his constant support with what he was saying right now. It felt like he had been lying to me this entire time. "But why now? While I'm risking everything to win this for Lockersley? You've become my actual competition."

He met my gaze and grimaced upon seeing something in my eyes he didn't like. "It really wasn't ever like that. I believe in you and what you're doing. I never believed I would beat you. I couldn't when we were teenagers. Why would it be different now? But if I could just reach the top three, everything would have worked out perfectly. I could have continued carrying out my plan, and you and Lockersley would get everything you need. But after today, it doesn't look like I'll finish in the top three."

"What do you need the money for? What is your plan? You know all of mine. Why are you hiding yours? I want to know what you want for yourself, for Lockersley." My voice was soft, disguising the anger I was trying to contain. I needed to know more because his answers had so far left a huge gap in reasoning. Something wasn't adding up, and it felt like the betrayal was growing because of the unknown.

He hesitated for a moment, then nodded and grabbed the drawings I noticed earlier. He pushed them towards me. "It all has to do with that."

I raised an eyebrow, still very unsure of what I was looking at.

"I want to open a school. Not one for children to learn how to read and write, but something that will have more of an effect on the area. I could teach advanced farming techniques, the mixing of herbs for medicinal purposes, how to build something that's just an idea in your head. I've been working on it since before your father passed." Milo paused for a moment, shoving his hand through his hair and pinching the bridge of his nose. "He was going to sponsor it. But then everything changed. I know there's no use going to your uncle."

"Is this why you're always late? You're working on these plans." I looked down at the drawings. It would be a wonderful addition to the town.

"Yes and no, I'm late because I've already started tutoring some people. The stable boy, Thomas, is one. His mind is very mechanical, a lot like mine. When we're working, I'm always losing track of time." Milo's eyes lit up as he spoke, and excitement danced across his face.

I felt betrayed. We had been working together since I had formulated my first plan for Lockersley, and he had kept this all to himself. Did he think I wouldn't care about the things he wanted to do, that I only cared about myself and my goals?

"Why didn't you come to me? I could have helped . . . No, I would have helped. All that gold we stole from my uncle's room—some of it could have been set aside."

His head snapped towards mine as he heard the hurt laced through my words. "I wasn't intentionally keeping things from you. You were dealing with enough. Some would say, too much."

He reached for me, but I backed away, not ready for physical contact because I knew it would only confuse me.

I looked at him as he shifted from one foot to another, his hands twisting some tool of his. "You should have let me in. Given me the opportunity to support you the way you've been supporting me."

"But . . ." He started to say something that would defend his choices.

"No buts. I've always thought of us as partners. Even before I left. We support each other. It's never a one-way thing, and it never should be," I explained.

"You're right. It just didn't seem important, and you had so much weighing you down. I didn't want to be another thing dragging you down when I could lift you up, or at least shoulder some of your burden."

I shook my head. "As chivalrous as that sounds, it's only taking away my ability to make choices for myself. Maybe I would have told you I couldn't help with the school just yet. That I had other things I needed to focus on, or maybe I would have jumped in and been right beside you trying to get it built. But you will never know because you chose for me. Don't ever do that again." It was impossible for me to put into words how I was feeling. I wasn't angry with him, but there was something else . . .betrayal, untrustworthy . . . like I wasn't worth confiding in.

I wrapped my arms around him and laid my head on his chest. "Thank you for telling me, even though you should have told me sooner. As often as you tell me I'm not alone, you should know that you have my support as well. And if you weren't sure of that, I'm sorry."

Milo was stiff in my embrace at first, but as I spoke, he leaned into me, his arms encircling me. "It's not that at all. I didn't want to burden you. You came home to find out your father had died and your uncle was driving your hometown into poverty. Then you were so determined to fix it all— I couldn't give you anything else to worry about."

I looked up at him but didn't let go. "I get to decide what I'm capable of doing, not you or anyone else." I laid my head back on his chest before I got a crick in my neck. "And if I haven't said it before, thank you for believing in me. Just . . . be careful, okay?"

He nodded before he kissed my forehead. I could feel the small smile on his lips. "I will. And you get some rest, alright? You've got a big day tomorrow."

I stood on my toes and pressed my lips to his. "You too. Goodnight, Milo. I'll see you in the morning."

As I left his lab and made my way back to my room, I couldn't help but think about our conversation. We were all fighting our own battles, struggling to reach our own goals. It was important that we work together, because together we would find a way to win.

CHAPTER THIRTY-ONE

"M aster Robin, stop!" Connor hollered at me.

I halted mid-step and turned towards him. The joust was starting soon. My uncle's machinations with the competition schedule had me in three matches today. He somehow had used my score from the other events to push me up into a higher bracket—meaning I started jousting with the top eight competitors. Up until now, my arm had been thanking me for the respite, but today, knowing I was going up against the best after two days of competition, my arm was not as happy.

Standing there, it was easy to admire the handsome man walking towards me. The fact that he was a prince didn't hurt anything either.

When Connor caught up to me, we started walking. "You don't have to do this, you know. In fact, I wish you wouldn't. The joust is dangerous. Men have died while participating in this sport. In fact, it happens more often than I would like."

"Are you going to compete?" I asked, not bothering to change the timbre of my voice.

Connor looked back at me in surprise. "Of course I am."

"Why? What purpose does this tournament serve for you?"

His pace slowed as he thought about my question. "Not much, other than to prove to my people I'm who they want me to be."

"Shouldn't they already know that based on everything you do?" I watched my feet take one step in front of the other.

"They should, but I feel like I constantly have to prove it." He paused, then quietly muttered, "To myself and to them."

My eyes shot up to look at Connor from beneath the brim of my cap. "I have to finish this tournament. Maybe if I win, I'll feel like I'm enough to save my home and my people."

"Of course you're enough, but you don't have to do it alone. I'm still an option if you need me to be one." Connor put his arm around me, but it didn't make me feel the way Milo's touch did. "We both love our home country and feel a deep connection to the people that depend on us. I think we would get on just fine."

I studied his eyes, trying to gauge his emotions. There was a genuine kindness, but also a sadness. "Connor, you've been so good to me, and I value our friendship deeply. But don't you think I deserve more than just fine? Don't you deserve more?"

He gave a small rueful smile and shook his head. "Just fine would be an improvement over all the other potential wives I've met. You and I would have fun together."

My heart ached for him. He was a good man that deserved to be loved. A small part of me wished I harbored romantic feelings for him. It would make some things easier. My eyes drifted over the crowd, falling on the swashbuckling scientist that I had way too many feelings for at the moment, not all of them good. Even with my mixed emotions, I felt myself smile.

Connor followed my gaze and saw who I was looking at. "I see. I'm not surprised that your heart is otherwise engaged. But the offer still stands and will until one of us marries."

"I don't deserve your friendship," I said, bumping his shoulder.

"True, but you have it anyway. Now let's hope I don't have to go up against you in the joust." He smiled. It even reached his eyes.

Connor's subtle sadness stayed with me as we walked towards the festivities. Feelings of gratitude and guilt mixed as I thought about what a wonderful man he was, but my heart belonged to another. Just the thought of Milo made my heart race in a way the thought of Connor never could.

The prince looked in Milo's direction. "I'll leave you to go talk to him." He nodded towards one of the vendor stalls.

I turned to look and saw Milo there, talking with Jane. I turned back to thank Connor, but he was already making his way to the grandstand. Milo looked up as I approached, and a smile spread across his face. "Hey, what did Prince Connor want?"

"He was worried about me competing today," I replied, glancing back at where Connor had been. "He's very kind and a good friend. Too bad he's not the person I want to spend my life with."

Milo's eyes softened, and he took my hand in his. "Oh really? And who would that person be?"

Jane cleared her throat, breaking the moment. "Alright, you two, we still have a lot to do. The tournament isn't over and the joust is the hardest event."

I nodded, squeezing Milo's hand before letting go. "She's right. I need to stay focused."

The armor I had made was acting like a furnace instead of protection against a lance. I was sweating so profusely the heavy metal was more likely to rust on me than save my life. There was nothing I wanted more than to take off the helmet and let my hair catch in the slight breeze, but I couldn't without giving away my identity. Jousting in this get-up was a necessity, but I wasn't looking forward to it.

My uncle was sitting in the grandstand, and the chair next to him—the one I should be sitting in—was empty. Jane had made my excuses, intimating I was having "female problems." My uncle's face had creased in disgust before he dismissed her. I smiled at his reaction, a small victory, as it freed me for the day.

The jousting arena was buzzing with activity. Competitors mounted their horses, squires adjusted armor, and the crowd's excitement grew with each passing moment. I took a deep breath as a droplet of sweat raced down my back, drawing my attention to the oppressive heat of my armor once again.

Trumpets blared to signal the start of the joust. This morning I was participating in one of the first competitions, going up against one of the few people I didn't know in the top eight. I mounted my horse for the day, a beautiful dappled grey stallion, with the help of my squire. The crowd cheered, waving flags with colors that represented their favorite competitor, their painted faces a blur as I focused on my opponent across from me at the far end of the list. He was a formidable knight, his armor gleaming in the sunlight, astride a black stallion that stood a couple hands taller than the one I rode. Fear slid down my spine, following the droplet of sweat from earlier. Just like the droplet, I ignored it. There was no room for distracting emotions. After all, this was for Lockersley.

With a final nod to the squire, I lowered my visor and took up the lance. I held it with my hand underneath it like I had done in practice. The flag was dropped, our visors clicked down, and we spurred our horses forward. The world narrowed to the pounding of the horses' hooves, the rush of wind finding its way through the slits in the armor, and the man barreling down on me. I lifted the lance, set it in the lance rest Milo had added to my armor, lowered it, and aimed. The immediate impact was so jarring my teeth rattled; a clash of metal and wood reverberated through my body and into my bones. When the dust settled, I was still seated, but my opponent was on the ground on his back. How I managed to stay atop my horse was unknown, a surprise and a relief.

The crowd erupted in cheers as I rode out of the arena, my uncle's gaze fixed on me until I was out of sight. As soon as it was safe to do so, I dismounted and removed my helmet, tilting my head up to feel the cool air on my face and in my drenched hair. I felt like I had just stepped out of a bath. My clothing was so wet.

I made my way back to the stables, where Milo and Jane were waiting. Milo wrapped his arms around me. "You did it, Rowan. You've made it to the final four."

I stepped out of his embrace, needing the metal contraption off me more than anything. "Aren't you tilting soon? Shouldn't you be getting ready?"

"Yes," he said carefully. "But I needed you to know how happy I'm for you."

"Go. You can't be distracted if you want to stay on your horse this time. I expect to see you in the final four with me." I turned and started to remove my armor.

Before he left, I caught a glimpse of Milo. His expression pained, as if something I said had hurt him. That hadn't been my intention, but I needed to focus and he needed to do what he could so I wouldn't worry about him.

Jane handed me a flask, her expression serious. "You'll need this. There are three matches, then they will announce who will go up against who in the next round. You'll have to be at your best. I have a feeling you're jousting either Milo or Connor."

I nodded, taking a sip of the fiery liquid. Her prediction matched mine. It wasn't ideal, but it was better than someone I didn't know. I took another small sip from her flask, letting the liquid ease the tension in my muscles ever so slightly. Too bad it couldn't lessen the weight of my responsibilities. "I need to change into Lady Rowan, make an appearance with my uncle. He'll be expecting me. 'Lady problems' will only excuse me for so long."

Jane placed a hand on my shoulder. "It's easier if you remember why you're doing this."

With a deep breath, I made my way to Artie's stable to change. I peeled off my wet clothes and put on a blue dress with copper trim.

"Jane, I'm going to need something else to wear under my armor in the next round. I can't put those back on." I looked back at the pile of wet garments with disgust.

Jane nodded. It was like I could see her mind working, already thinking of solutions. "I'll find something. Remember, you're Lady Rowan now. You have to keep up the act."

I twisted my wet hair and pinned it up before placing the crown on. Jane handed me a mirror and I saw Lady Rowan staring back at me, poised and determined. Taking another steadying breath, I left the stables, heading towards the grandstand where my uncle awaited.

The crowd's eyes turned towards me as I entered the grandstand. These past few days, I had captured their attention both as Lady Rowan and Master Robin, both characters becoming crowd favorites. I straightened my posture, projecting the grace and confidence expected of the woman I was pretending to be.

My uncle looked up as I neared, a mixture of jealousy and suspicion in his eyes. "There you are, Rowan. Feeling better?"

I forced a smile. "A little better, thank you. I didn't want to miss the excitement even if I'm not feeling quite myself."

He nodded. "Good. Join me, then. The next round of jousting is about to begin."

I took my seat, my mind already racing with the challenges ahead. The winner of the next joust would be my next opponent.

I watched as Connor rode up to the entrance. He winked at me before flipping his visor down.

"He seems to have developed a tendre for you," my uncle said, his tone distant.

"Mm-hmm," I agreed without saying anything. Maybe it wasn't the wisest idea for me to watch the joust. My palms were sweating just thinking about what was ahead of me. My stomach flip-flopped with nerves.

I looked to the other side of the arena and gasped. His opponent was huge. If I had to compete against him in the next round, I would end up on the ground.

The thundering of the horses running towards each other rolled over me. The only thing separating the horses was a small wooden fence. It was low enough to the ground either animal could jump over it without a single thought. As the men on their great steads got closer, I could barely watch. My eyes were focused on what was happening, but my mind was unable to see the events occurring right in front of me.

The screams of the crowd brought me back to the present. My eyes focused on Connor still on his horse, while the giant of a man was being dragged off by the healers. Everyone loved the prince, and the excitement at his success was overwhelming.

My uncle's eyes rested on me, watching my reaction. "It would seem our young prince is quite impressive, a formidable opponent."

I nodded, forcing my lips to turn up in a smile. "Yes, he has always been very impressive."

The crowd continued to cheer for the prince, taking to their feet, the noise overwhelming. The thought of facing him caused a pit to form in my stomach; whether it was nerves, anxiety, or fear, I didn't know. I was relieved to see Connor succeed, but the thought of facing him tied me into knots.

Connor stopped in front of me and my uncle, his visor raised so we could all see his eyes. He smiled at me and nodded.

My uncle leaned towards me, his hand blocking his mouth, his voice low. "Maybe I was wrong before. An alliance with the prince could be . . . beneficial."

The pounding in my heart drowned out the crowd's cheering, and I tried to sound noncommittal. "Perhaps."

Once the crowd settled down for the next match, I excused myself, claiming I needed a moment. My uncle barely noticed me leaving, already engrossed in the next set of competitors, probably because his choice, Jocelin Montfort, was in the next round.

I kept my head down as I left the grandstand, my steps hurried as I made my way through the individuals that had decided not to watch the joust, towards the stables where Milo and Jane were waiting. As I entered the stables, Milo was adjusting the saddle on his horse, preparing for his own joust.

I stopped at the entrance and stared. Milo was handsome in his disarray as a scientist. I loved him like that. But looking like a knight ready for a quest—it was something else, a type of handsome I didn't expect to see in him. It fit Connor like a glove, but on Milo, it both fit and didn't fit. Like he could be a knight in shining armor if I let him, but that's not what I wanted or needed him to be.

"Rowan, how are you holding up?" Jane scanned my face, looking for a sign that I wasn't keeping it together.

"I'm doing my best," I said with more confidence than I actually felt. "Connor won his match. His opponent was massive, but he took him down."

Milo's jaw tightened. "And now you have to face him."

I nodded, the weight of the situation settling heavily on my shoulders. "And now my uncle is suggesting I try to form an alliance with him. Little does he know, Connor and I have already formed a friendship. It would be an alliance if I let it."

Jane's eyes widened. "Rowan, we don't know if he's trustworthy."

"I know he is," I replied, frustration lacing my voice. "He's known about me since our hand-to-hand combat match. After our talk earlier, I'm pretty sure he'll let me win."

Milo placed a reassuring hand on my shoulder. "I don't think you'll need his help, but you need to do what you feel is right."

Taking a deep breath, I nodded. "You're right. I can do this with his help or without. I would just rather have his help."

Jane smiled and handed me a bundle of clothes. "Here, this should help keep you cooler under the armor."

"Thank you." I took the bundle and headed to Artie's stall. I slipped on the garments, thankful for the new set of clothing, hoping it would make the event easier. At least there would be less sweat.

Emerging from the stables, I spotted Connor talking to a group of nobles. His eyes flicked towards me, and for a moment, our gazes locked. There was something in his expression—concern, perhaps?—that made me wonder what he was planning for our match.

Pushing the thought aside, I focused on the task at hand. I needed to win two more matches and it would all be over. Everything depended on it.

CHAPTER THIRTY-TWO

The crowd was going wild. They wanted this battle more than any other one that would happen today. The people loved their prince, and they loved the potential rags-to-riches story of Master Robin. The energy in the air felt like the moment after lightning strikes, and I could feel it buzzing through me as I waited to be announced.

Connor dismounted, basking in the crowd's adoration, his easy smile and confident demeanor only causing everyone to love him more. Meanwhile, my hands were shaking at the thought of the next match, my nerves making it impossible for me to focus.

Milo, still fully geared up after his win, approached me with a knowing look in his eyes. "They're about to call you, Rowan. Are you ready?"

Taking a deep breath, I nodded. "I am. I have to be."

As the herald's voice boomed through the arena, calling the next competitor, calling me, I felt a surge of adrenaline. It mixed with my nerves, making it feel like I was going to jump out of my skin.

Connor was already mounted and ready, his horse pawing at the ground, eager to begin. My dappled grey stallion stood waiting for me as I mounted and adjusted my helmet. The weight of the armor and the lance the squire placed in my hand felt more oppressive than before, but I forced myself to focus.

"Master Robin!" the herald called. "Are you ready?"

I nodded. I tried to lessen my nerves with a deep breath. It didn't work. I looked across the arena to Connor, and the world slowed down and came into focus. It was just the two of us and the field. The flag dropped, and we both spurred our horses into motion.

We charged across the arena, the short railing the only thing preventing us from running into each other head-on. Like before, I secured my lance in the lance rest and aimed it. I could barely keep my focus on Connor's shield, but I did. The impact, when it came, was jarring. My lance struck his shield, breaking, but he managed to stay in his saddle. That blow earned me two points. At the same time, his lance glanced off my shield, not breaking but still making my bones rattle at the force of the impact. However, it wasn't enough to unseat me. Connor's blow earned him a point.

I yelled for a new lance as I turned for the next pass, my heart was in my throat, beating faster than it ever had before. The crowd was forgotten as I homed in on my opponent. This time, Connor's lance struck harder, hitting my shield with a force that made me see stars. But I held on, refusing to be unseated. My lance only managed to graze his shield. We were tied.

On the third pass, everything seemed to move in slow motion. I watched as the look on his face changed as we charged at each other once more. In fact, I swore he winked at me right before our lances met. I saw him as he stood slightly in his stirrups and pushed himself backwards at the same moment I felt the impact of his lance's graze reverberate off the side of my shield instead of the center. Mine looked like it was going to strike the center, but skimmed the surface as Connor threw himself off his horse.

He landed on the ground with the crashing sound of his armor. The crowd erupted in a deafening roar as I rode past the grandstand, confused by his sudden willingness to let me win.

I dismounted, remembering to leave my helmet on at the last moment, unable to feel the cool air against my sweat-drenched everything. I walked over to Connor, who was already getting to his feet, and extended a hand to help him up.

"Well fought," he said, clasping my hand firmly. "You truly are a worthy opponent."

"Thank you," I replied, feeling a mix of relief and exhaustion. "But that last round, you . . ."

"Ensured the right man won. You won't be so lucky in the last match." He winked. What was with all his winking?

He walked away, leaving me alone in the middle of the arena.

As we walked back past the grandstand, I caught sight of my uncle, his expression inscrutable. Jane and Milo were waiting for me just out of sight of my uncle, their faces a mix of pride and concern.

"You did it," Jane said, handing me a flask. "Now rest. You have another round ahead."

I nodded, taking a sip of the liquid. It burned as it went down, warming me in ways I didn't mind at the moment. The next round would be even tougher, but I was ready; at least I was as ready as I could be. Hopefully, it would be enough.

Milo grabbed my hand as I left to hide in the stables. "I'm up against Montfort next. Maybe I'll luck out and win this time." Milo's low score in the other events meant he had to climb the ranks to get to the final set.

"Good luck," I said, not knowing whether it would be worse to face Milo or Montfort in the last joust.

For what felt like the hundredth time, I made my way back to the stables to rest out of sight until it was time for the last event of the tournament. I sat back in a corner of Artie's stall, trying to let the scents and sounds wash over me, luring me into a meditative state.

Instead, the muffled sounds of the tournament continued outside, invading my thoughts. The cheers and jeers of the crowd blended into a distant hum that kept me distracted. The exhaustion from the day's events made it almost impossible to move my arms, especially the one that held the lance. Ignoring the pain of sore muscles, I let myself close my eyes for a moment, trying to relax.

My eyelids were so heavy it was impossible to stay awake—but then the stable door creaked open, and I tensed. My muscles screamed, but I was ready to spring to my feet if it was necessary. It was just Jane, her expression filled with concern.

"I know you're supposed to be resting." She handed me a waterskin. "But I figured you would be in your own head by now."

I smiled, taking a sip of the cool water. She knew me so well. "That does sound like me, if I wasn't so exhausted, I probably would have been."

She sat on the ground beside me, and her being here next to me helped slow the thoughts in my head. She was one of the few people that understood how much I questioned everything.

She wrapped her arm around me. "You've done more than anyone could have expected, Rowan. You just have one more round, that's it."

"One more round," I echoed. They were just words, but they felt so heavy. "I can't afford to lose now. Montfort or Milo . . . I thought this would be fun, but now I just want it to be over."

Jane nodded. "You've got this. It's what you've trained for. Now is the time to trust in yourself and your abilities."

I rolled my shoulders, every move made a different muscle angry with pain. "Thank you, Jane. I needed to hear that."

The two of us sat in the stable until we heard the end of Milo's match against Montfort. It was impossible for me not to worry about the outcome.

"Let's go." I stood. My body was so tired. "Let's see who I'm up against next."

Jane and I walked back to the grandstand for the last time today. She stood back while I walked through the entrance. Montfort was waving to the crowd while Milo was standing on the outskirts, holding the reins to his horse. He must have lost, but at least he was alive and uninjured. Hopefully, I could say the same after the joust with Montfort.

I nodded to Milo before letting my squire know I was back and ready for the final match. He waited for me, my lance and helmet ready, his eyes wide with excitement.

"You've got this, Master Robin," he said. His confidence in me was overwhelming.

I smiled at him. "Thank you. You've been the best squire I could ask for."

I mounted my horse, then took my helmet and lance from him. Adjusting my grip, I felt the weight of the moment settle over me. I took my place, ready to start. The only thing louder than the roar of the crowd was the pounding of my heart. Jocelin Montfort stared at me from across the arena. He smiled his weasely smile as he sat proudly on his horse, exuding confidence.

The flag was dropped, and we charged towards each other. The thunder of hooves pounding against the dirt echoed in my ears as I focused on my target. Montfort's lance was aimed directly at me, and I adjusted my seat and prepared for impact.

Everything was blurred together, every color and every sound melded together. Both of our lances found our targets. Both lances shattered. Both of us stayed on our horses. A collective gasp worked its way through the crowd before the cheering began again.

The two of us wheeled our horses around for the second pass, determination fueling my every move. It was like an intricate dance—our squires tossing us a new lance, the white flag dropping, the galloping of the horses; and we were once again running towards each other. I aimed lower, with the goal to unseat Montfort. The impact of my lance struck true, shaking me all the way to my bones. Montfort fell back in his saddle but managed to stay mounted, and his expression darkened with frustration because his lance didn't even make contact.

The third and final pass approached. I was in the lead but not enough to guarantee a victory. This was my last chance to get the win I needed so badly. I gripped my lance tightly, ignoring the ache in my arms, in my back, and in my legs. Then there was the sweat dripping down my face, attempting to blind me. None of that mattered as we charged towards each other. When I locked eyes with Montfort, there was a flicker of doubt in his gaze.

With the last bit of strength I had, I thrust my lance. The impact was teeth rattling, but it was enough. I watched as Montfort went crashing to the ground with a resounding thud. I dropped my lance, raising my fist in triumph. The crowd responded by erupting with noise: screaming, clapping, stomping their feet.

I dismounted and made my way over to Montfort, offering him a hand. "Well fought," I said, my voice steady despite the adrenaline coursing through me.

He ignored my hand, stood, and walked away. Montfort glanced up towards my uncle as he left.

As the crowd continued to cheer, I followed Montfort's gaze over to the grandstand. My uncle's expression was inscrutable, but I could see the wheels turning in his mind.

I had done it. I had won the tournament. Now I just had to prove my father was murdered. But for tonight, I would allow myself a moment of victory.

CHAPTER THIRTY-THREE

"Come on, Rowan, it's time to go celebrate." Lady Jane grabbed my foot and pulled me in an attempt to get me out of bed.

"Don't make me get out of bed," I groaned, reluctant to do anything that required effort. "Everything hurts. I just want to lie in bed for the next five years," I mumbled, burying my face deeper into my pillow. "Do I have to?"

"Of course you do! You won the tournament, and everyone that has done everything they can to help you along the way is waiting to congratulate you," Jane insisted, her tone playful but firm. "Besides, this will be the first time in a long time you just get to be you."

"I'm perfectly capable of just being me in this bed. And look, I'm celebrating. Woooo!" I moved one finger on my left hand in a circle. "Dammit, even that hurt to do."

Jane tugged on my other foot. "Rowan, you're not getting out of this. Besides, once you're there, it'll be fun."

I sighed and eased my way up to a sitting position. "Fine, I'll go. But if I thought for a second you would let me stay here, I wouldn't be moving from this spot."

Jane laughed as she helped me get out of bed. "See, that wasn't so hard, was it? Do you need my help to get dressed, or can you handle it yourself?"

I dressed quickly, opting for one of the outfits I had brought back with me from the nunnery. They were the clothing I felt most like myself when wearing. As we walked near Lockersley on our way to the clearing in the woods, I could hear the sounds of laughter and music growing louder. The entire town was in high spirits after the tournament and the success it had brought the town.

Jane and I arrived at the clearing, and all of our friends were there already. Will and Erin were dancing as she sang. Tuck was clapping along with Erin's song. And Milo, he was sitting on the outskirts of the opening, waiting.

Milo jumped to his feet as soon as he saw me. The smile on his face made my heart flip-flop. "Here she is, our champion! How are you feeling?"

"Exhausted," I sighed. "And in so much pain. But the hard part is done. Tomorrow, my uncle will hand out the awards and I'll finally be able to reveal my true identity. This is all almost over, finally."

He pressed his forehead against mine. "You did it, Rowan."

"I did."

Our eyes met. I was tired of keeping my distance from Milo, so I reached up on my toes as he lowered his head.

"I've been waiting to do this again," he whispered, his lips inches from mine.

"To Lady Rowan, the fiercest competitor and the heart of Lockersley!" Tuck handed me a goblet of wine, raising his own in a toast.

Milo and I jumped apart, embarrassed that we were caught almost kissing.

My friends all cheered for me, for my success. I raised the goblet Tuck had thrust into my hand in response, feeling so many emotions that my eyes filled with unshed tears.

My victory was more than just winning the tournament. It was the first step to restoring Lockersley. Now I could focus on my father and what happened to him, then take the place my father wanted me to have.

I watched from the sidelines as everyone sang and danced in our secret meeting place. Their merriment lifted my spirits even though I didn't have enough energy to move, much less dance.

Milo sat beside me. "Why aren't you out there? This celebration is for you."

"I'm too tired and all I want is a bath. The armor was hot, and I spent the day sweating." I sighed. "But I don't want to spoil everyone's fun."

Milo stood and held his hand out to me. "Let's go."

"But the party . . ." I grabbed his hand despite my protest.

"No one will notice. And I have something to show you." He pulled me to my feet.

Our bodies met, pressing together. I looked up into his blue eyes and saw his concern.

"Rowan, I'm sorry. I should have told you about the school and my tutoring sooner."

I put my fingers to his mouth. "It's okay. I wish you had told me earlier, before I became preoccupied with the tournament. But I understand why you didn't."

"Does that mean you forgive me?" he asked, his expression hopeful.

I took a step back and shrugged. "It depends. Do you promise to never make a decision like that for me again?"

He wrapped his arms around me and pulled me close. "I will try. Is that enough?"

"I guess we'll have to see how many times you mess up to know." I kissed his cheek. "Now, what did you want to show me?"

He dragged me through the trees, away from our friends. When I could barely hear the music and laughter, he stopped. A campfire lit the area and next to the fire was a large copper tub almost filled to the brim with water.

"Please tell me that's for me and the water is hot." My eyes lit up at the thought of soaking in a tub. My muscles sang at the thought of something that would ease the pain.

"I knew you would be sore. I have everything you need to help. It's a salt bath with arnica and birch oils. That should help."

I threw my arms around his neck and instantly winced at the pain. "This is one of the nicest things anyone has ever done for me." I was already taking off my clothes to get into the tub.

Milo turned around, his back towards me and the bath. "I'll leave you to relax. If you need anything, just holler. I won't be far."

I climbed into the tub and slipped down into the warm water. How did I miss Milo disappearing long enough to heat water and fill a bath for me? That didn't matter; what did matter was the combination of warm water, salt, and oils easing my aching muscles as I soaked. I sighed, letting the stress of the past few weeks melt away as I relaxed for the first time since arriving home.

I piled my hair on top of my head, droplets of water cascading down my face and neck. Listening to the fire crackle, I watched as the flickering of the campfire caused

the shadows to dance, casting a warm glow in the sanctuary Milo had created for me.

I leaned back and closed my eyes as I let the sounds of
nature and distant celebration wash over me. This was the
closest I had been to feeling at peace—it was like I forgot
what it felt like.

Knowing Milo was out there making sure I wasn't disturbed, I whispered, "Thank you."

"You deserve so much more," he said.

I shifted in the water. The cold air of the autumn night
hit my wet skin and my teeth were chattering. "Can you
get me something to wrap myself in? The water's turning
cold."

"Of course."

Moments later, Milo walked into the area from behind
some trees. He kept his eyes averted. I was going to say
something, but he was trying so hard to be a gentleman I
didn't want to ruin it. He grabbed a robe that was hanging
on a nearby branch. I giggled. It was so close to the tub, and
I hadn't seen it there at all. Blinded by the idea of soaking
away my pain, I guess.

Milo walked backwards towards me with the arm holding the robe outstretched. He was almost close enough for
me to grab it when he tripped and stumbled. His arms
flailed around him as he tried to find his balance. He let go
of the robe, and it somehow got stuck in the tree above the
bath. I was looking at that, wondering what the likelihood

of that happening really was, when Milo stumbled into the tub. The rim of the copper hit the back of his knees and he fell backwards. He splashed me and everything around us when his ass landed in the water.

"I'm so sorry." He twisted back and forth, trying to find some sort of purchase to get out of the tub.

I burst into laughter as water sloshed over the rim, soaking his shirt, kilt, boots—really everything he was wearing was now soaked. His arm brushed against my leg as he attempted to push himself out of the tub. Instead, I grabbed it and pulled him in on top of me.

"Rowan, what are you doing?" His blue gaze was questioning and something else, something much more mischievous.

Instead of using words to answer him, I melded my mouth to his until I felt his tongue swipe across my lips. I opened my lips, letting him invade as I did the same. I kissed him until I needed air. My lips moved from his lips to his neck, all while we both panted.

"This isn't why I did this. I wanted . . ." The fabric of his kilt shifted in the water and I stroked the length of him, eliciting a groan.

I smiled, my lips pressed to his skin directly under his ear. "What did you want?" I shifted so I was straddling him.

"This, this is what I wanted. But it's not why I did any of this." His hands ran up and down my body like he was trying to touch every inch of me all at once.

"As long as you want this too, I don't see that your intentions matter much now. Because I've wanted this for a while."

My words broke whatever restraint he was holding on to. He lifted me up and turned me so my back was pressed against his chest. I could feel the hard length of him between my legs. He moved my hair and kissed my neck, his other hand massaging one breast and then the other, pinching my nipples before moving his hand lower, slipping it between my legs, and caressing me there before slipping inside me.

I turned my head back to him, searching for his lips, my fingers tangled in his hair as our tongues sparred while he brought me to the edge of ecstasy. Pulling away from our kiss, I whispered, "I want you inside me."

He groaned his response into my ear, then took the lobe into his mouth and bit it as he thrust inside me. My gasp disappeared with the breeze. Both his hands came to my shoulders, squeezing them before he shifted to his knees, pushing me forward until I was holding on to the rim of the tub.

"Is this okay? You're so beautiful," he asked as his fingers stroked down my back, settling on my hips that I had always thought were too wide. He held me there as he pulled out, then buried himself inside me.

I cried out in pleasure, "Please! Don't stop." My fingers held on to the tub as I lost sense of everything around me.

The pleasure in my body built until I burst into a million tiny pieces at the same moment Milo collapsed on top of me.

We stayed there for a moment, until the world around us came back into focus and I remembered that the water had grown cold. Once again, my teeth chattered.

"Here, let me get you a blanket." He stepped out of the tub, the firelight dancing over his sinewy muscles as he moved around looking for something. "Here it is."

He grabbed a large towel, gesturing for me to stand. I did. He wrapped the fabric around me, then swept his arm behind my knees, picking me up.

"You need a blanket too," I said as he carried me to a rock near the fire.

"Who needs a blanket when I have you to keep me warm?" He buried his face in my neck.

I giggled. "That might be so, but you don't have any dry clothes. What are you going to wear?"

The breeze picked up, and the robe that had been stuck in the tree fell into my lap. "Well, that seems awfully suspicious." I stared at the trees, wondering why it had fallen at that moment.

"It seems we have the forest sprites' approval." He kissed me before setting me down to put on the robe. "You should get dressed. It sounds like the revelries are ending. Everyone will want to say goodbye."

It didn't take long for me to throw on my clothes and make my way back to the clearing. Milo stayed on the outskirts, looking out of place wearing my dressing gown. They must have heard me coming because they all looked towards me, pride and excitement on their smiling faces.

"What's next, Rowan?" Jane asked. The look she gave me when she noticed my wet hair made me want to laugh.

I rolled my shoulders back as I took a deep breath, looking at my friends, my allies. "We keep pushing, fighting. We won this round, but I need to prove my father was poisoned and bring the man responsible to justice. But that's a concern for tomorrow. Tonight, we celebrate."

I felt Milo move closer to me. I looked over towards him.

Milo nodded, raising his glass. "To tomorrow and facing it together."

I raised the glass that had been pressed into my hand. "Together," I whispered. In this moment, with my friends surrounding me, it felt like I could accomplish anything, including making my uncle pay for his crimes.

CHAPTER THIRTY-FOUR

Why is there always incessant pounding on my door at a god-awful time in the morning? I covered my head with my pillow, willing whoever was at my door to disappear.

"Whatever it is, it can wait until I've slept for a few weeks," I hollered at the door, cursing whoever was there under my breath.

"Rowan, if you don't open this door, I'm going to get Winnie. And I promise you, you will not like how I get you out of bed," Jane hissed, each word sounding more and more like a threat she would follow through on.

"Fine!" I threw everything I had used to block out the noise to the floor before climbing out of bed. My body protested every single movement I forced it to make as I hobbled to the door.

I unlocked the door, stepping out of the way as Jane barreled through, holding parchment and an old journal in her hand.

"What is so important that you couldn't let me sleep?" I folded my arms across my chest. The cold was seeping into my sore muscles that were no longer under the blankets I had been enjoying thoroughly.

"This." She shoved what she was holding into my hands, then walked out the door.

I stared at the open door. "What . . ." Did she really just come in here, thrust papers at me, and leave?

I went to rub the sleep from my eyes, forgetting that my hands were full, and hit my head with the journal. It was too early for any of this.

"I ordered you a bath." Jane walked through the door, talking like I was supposed to be paying attention to her already. "The nurse wrote again, and I relieved your uncle of some of his journals. That one has all the information we need."

"What . . ." My brain finally caught up to the present and what Jane had said. "You found proof? Where? What does the nurse have to say? Can we go see her?"

Jane smiled; she was used to these moments. "Eleanor is coming here. She told us the name of the poison, antidote, and some of the effects of both, which include loss of memory and the melancholia."

I sat on the edge of my bed. "What causes such a thing?"

"Well, Eleanor thought it was some combination of amnesic shellfish poisoning and Henbane. She started giving him an antidote that's supposed to be good for everything. That's where her letter ends. But I found the journals you were talking about. Better yet, I found *ledgers*."

We sat with our heads together, poring over the evidence she found. I barely noticed the tub come in and the servants filing in, bringing the hot water. The ledgers enthralled me. Who would write down what they were actually buying when they had such nefarious purposes? Apparently, my uncle.

"Lady Rowan, I'm sorry to interrupt, but your bath is ready." Winnie dipped in a slight curtsy.

My squeal of joy turned into a groan as I moved before my body was ready. "I'm getting in; it's the only way I'm leaving the room today. But let's continue going through what you've found. There's no time to waste."

This was especially true now. My uncle was hosting the awards ceremony for the tournament this afternoon. Which meant the charade ended today.

My emerald green gown swirled around my feet as I walked beside my uncle on to the dais. It was time to announce the winner of the tournament and my hand in marriage. I couldn't help but giggle at the thought. My uncle turned and glared at me.

"This is no time for levity, Rowan. You're about to meet your future husband." He spat out the words, turning away from me as he sat. "And in an unexpected twist, it is a peasant. I should have banned them from the contest completely."

I rolled my eyes behind his back. "It's too late to change the rules now."

His head whipped around. "You don't think I know that? Now I'm stuck giving my gold to some nobody. I don't know who he is or where his loyalty lies. I can't believe Montfort lost to that slip of a man." He turned back to the arena in front of him, his brow furrowed, and his fingers steepled in front of him.

I watched my uncle until he appeared completely absorbed with the ceremony, awarding prizes for individual events. I watched as Erin, dressed as Robin, stepped to accept the quarterstaff prize. The only thing we had in common was our height, but she wore the same clothing I had been in all week, including the cloak with the hood up. I hoped it was enough to fool everyone watching until I could take her place.

Jane squeezed my shoulder, our sign that everything was in place. I slipped away, and she sat in my chair wearing the same color as me. No one would confuse us if they actually looked, but we were in the background at the moment. It was my belief that my uncle would only see the color of her dress, not that she was tall and willowy while I was short and curvy. I really hoped I was right.

Will was waiting with my clothes, an exact duplicate of what Erin was wearing right now. I stepped out of one costume to put on another, pulling the cap low on my head to hide my hair, then covering that with the hood of the cloak. By the time I was done, only my green eyes could be seen.

I passed Milo, whose eyes were filled with concern. This next part was necessary, but also pretty risky considering what I was going to do during the ceremony. I nodded towards him and he took off to let Erin know I was ready for the switch to happen.

Erin filed in behind the other competitors, leaving the arena to make room for the archery event contestants. I looked back to see Erin take off the cloak and cap, her curls bouncing in every direction as it was freed. She shoved the items behind a hay bale before passing the trophy to Tuck, who scurried off to hide it in our agreed upon spot.

Inhaling, I rolled my shoulders back and stepped into the arena. The colorful flags moved with the breeze as the crowd's cheers grew louder until I could barely hear myself think. Who would have thought so many people would arrive to watch other people be given prizes?

The archery contestants made their way to line up in front of my uncle. His gaze passed over us, but I don't think he truly saw anyone. He called up Prince Connor who had taken third in the event, then Montfort, and finally Master Robin. I stepped forward and my uncle's eyes locked with mine. I couldn't be sure, but I thought I saw a gleam of some sort in his eye.

"Thank you." I kept my eyes down as I took the proffered item.

The group of archers made their way out of the arena.

I kept my eye on my uncle. He was so absorbed in what was going on in front of him he hadn't noticed I was no longer sitting beside him, watching him watch me and the other competitors file back into the arena. It was time to announce the winner of the tournament.

Excitement coursed through me, running up my spine and causing me to shiver. It was finally time to reveal myself and take control of my life. Removing my uncle's power to marry me off to the person of his choice would allow me to focus on taking my rightful place here, and punish my uncle for poisoning my father.

I held my head high as the competitors approached the dais. My uncle called out Milo's name first; his success with the staff had barely edged out Connor in the final score. The crowd clapped politely as he received his award. I hoped it was enough to finance the school he wanted to open. To my dismay, Jocelin Montfort, the Sheriff of Nottinghamshire, was called up next. His smile sent a different type of shiver up my back, and it wasn't pleasant at all. When he made eye contact with me as he walked back, I tried to smile, instead of shuddering under his smug gaze. As much as I wished it didn't, his presence unsettled me. I rolled my shoulders back in an attempt to settle my nerves, reminding myself that right now was my moment.

My uncle raised his hands to quiet the crowd, insisting on the attention of everyone in the arena. "And now, in a shocking turn of events, the champion of the tournament, the winner of the grand prize and my niece's hand in marriage, a veritable unknown, Master Robin!"

The crowd's cheers made it impossible to hear anything else, their excitement contagious. I strode forward as Robin, attempting to convey confidence in every step. In reality, my palms were clammy and my heart was trying to pound its way out of my chest, but I kept my face composed. This was it, the last step in this part of the plan.

"Master Robin"—my uncle's deep baritone quieted the crowd—"step forward and claim your prizes." There was an edge to his tone that I wasn't used to hearing.

I stepped up, feeling the weight and the thrill of the moment. My hands shook with anticipation of the reveal.

My uncle tossed the gold at my feet. "And of course, Lady . . ." Uncle Jonathan looked back towards my chair for the first time. "Where is my niece?"

I removed my cap and shook free my long red hair. Gasps echoed through the crowd as they recognized me.

"Lady Rowan?" My uncle's voice shook with a mix of shock and fury. "What have you done?"

I met his gaze, no longer willing to cast my eyes down when he spoke to me. "What I've done is win this tournament fair and square, and I'm claiming this prize money to support the people of Lockersley." I picked up the sack of gold. "More than that, I reclaim my right to decide not only who I marry, but my future."

Whispers ran through the crowd as they processed what was happening in front of them. Then the cheers started and spread like wildfire. I stared at my uncle as he turned the most unnatural shade of red I had ever seen.

"What you've done is outrageous!" he shouted.

CHAPTER THIRTY-FIVE

"Guards!" My uncle gestured for them to move towards me.

Next thing I knew, my uncle's men surrounded me. Montfort held me in place with my arms behind my back. His grip on my wrists was like manacles as he held me there.

"Unhand me!" I fought to set myself free against Montfort's grip. "You have no right to arrest me!"

"Enough!" My uncle took a step forward.

Instantly, the cheers stopped, as did the murmurs of those who couldn't figure out what was happening. For a moment it was so silent I was positive everyone could hear my heart racing as my carefully planned reveal fell apart.

Uncle Jonathan stood over me on the dais. "You've lied to us all, made a mockery of the tournament, of Lockersley, of each and every one of us. I cannot let that go unpunished. Take her to the tower."

The crowd's cheers turned from murmurs of confusion to whispers of dismay. My heart pounded as the sheriff pulled me towards the exit of the arena. My eyes darted around, searching for an ally, a friend, someone to speak up for me. I saw Milo and Jane standing at the edge of the crowd, shock and horror written across their faces. I caught Milo's eye, begging him to do something, anything to stop this from happening.

"You cannot do this! Arresting someone because they embarrassed you is not justice, it is tyranny," Milo shouted, stepping forward. "Lady Rowan won the tournament. She should not be punished for that."

"Shut your mouth, scientist!" Montfort spat, tightening his grip on me. "This is beyond your concern. It is a matter for the nobility."

"That's exactly why it is my concern," Milo responded. "In fact, I believe I have more of a say in what's happening than you do."

"For now, maybe, but not for much longer," the sheriff sneered.

"I wouldn't be so sure about that. You claim this is a matter for the nobility. My lineage can be traced back further than most people here," Jane added, her voice strong and unwavering. "And I say Lady Rowan has every right to claim her prize and her freedom. You cannot take that from her because you don't approve of the outcome."

"I suggest you keep your mouth shut before I have the guards put you in the tower as well. My niece didn't do this on her own. I'll lock you in the tower with her as accomplices." He turned back to the crowd, rubbing his hands together as he plotted out my demise. "Since the tournament prize was won through trickery, my niece's hand in marriage will go to the runner-up, Jocelin Mont-fort."

My screams of denial echoed throughout the arena, almost drowning out the sound of my uncle's villainous laughter.

Montfort tossed me into the tower room so hard I tumbled until I crashed into the wall, causing pain to burst in my shoulder and ricochet down my arm. The pain intensified as I pushed myself off the cold floor and ran to the door, trying to get there before I was locked in.

I failed. The clang of the lock snapping into place, along with the laughter of the sheriff, only intensified my failure.

"Enjoy your last night of solitude," Montfort said through the barred opening on the door. "Tomorrow, you'll find out what it really means to defy your uncle, and you'll wish you'd never done something so outrageous."

"I will never marry you, Montfort," I yelled after his retreating form. "Never, you hear me?"

His laughter bounced off the stone walls as I leaned against the door to my prison. I sank to the floor, every movement I made causing some part of my body to flare up in pain, whether it was from today, or the events of the tournament, it didn't matter. I was battered and bruised and now I was locked in this cold, dimly lit, sparsely furnished room with a window so high I doubted I could reach it even if I climbed on the chair or bed. Maybe I could reach it if I put the chair on the table. But even then, it wouldn't be easy.

It wasn't long before the last dregs of sunlight filtered in through that small window, but soon there would only be darkness. With that last thought, I struggled to breathe; the walls felt like they were closing in on me.

I shut my eyes and took measured breaths in an attempt to stop the panic creeping up my spine because it was making me lose my ability to think my situation through. It wasn't easy, as frustration weaved with my failure and physical discomfort. My hands trembled as I sat there staring at the tiny bed with its threadbare covering. Even if I could reach the window, there was no way the fabric would hold my weight if I used it to climb down. I was truly trapped in here.

I stood and paced the length of the room. Desperation chased me, nipping at my heels as I walked five steps one way, turned, and walked five steps the opposite way. Every time I reached the wall, I thought of something I could do to escape. I knew how to climb the walls of the castle. It wasn't hard, but I was much higher than the two stories I normally climbed.

I stacked the chair on top of the table. Holding my breath, I climbed the teetering ladder I'd created. Standing on my tiptoes, I looked down to see the ocean crashing against the base of the tower below me.

"Shit." I climbed down carefully, and the entire thing wobbled underneath me. By the time I jumped to the ground, my legs trembled from the nerve-racking descent. "That's barely an escape route," I muttered under my breath.

I let my legs collapse underneath me and sat on the floor again, feeling even more helpless. My mind ran through a thousand scenarios, each one worse than the last. If I had some of Milo's inventions, maybe I could get out of here. But I had nothing with me, just my wit, and that wasn't enough to get me out of here.

What would my father do if he was in this situation? And it hit me—my dad had been in a similar situation and he hadn't found a way out. If he couldn't find a way out, how was I supposed to find one?

The cold of the floor seeped into my body as my thoughts swirled in my head. I pushed myself off the floor and climbed into the hard bed and under the thin cover. My teeth chattered as I curled into a ball, trying to preserve whatever heat I could. At some point, I must have fallen asleep because, for once, my brain was silent. That was until I heard the soft knocking on the door.

"Rowan, are you in there?" Jane whispered.

I saw dark curls and blue eyes peer through the barred window in the door. "She has to be in this room. It's the only one left in the tower." Milo banged on the door in frustration.

I jumped at the noise and sat straight up on the uncomfortable bed.

"How can we rescue her if we can't find her?"

Even through the haze of sleep, I could hear the frustration in his words. I grunted as I attempted to let my friends know they had found the correct room. But the dregs of sleep were making it impossible for me to form a coherent thought, much less a coherent sentence.

"This is the room they are keeping her in," Winnie whispered. "At least that's what the other servants told me."

I cleared my throat. "I'm in here."

Milo's head popped into the window. "I'm so happy to see you. Are you okay?"

I sat up, and the cracking as I straightened my spine had me wincing. I rolled my shoulders back, causing every single one of my muscles to scream in protest. The cold weather and the hard bed hadn't done me any favors. "I could be better." When I spoke, my voice was hoarse from sleep and disuse. "I'm okay. I take it you three have a plan to help me escape?"

Milo's clenched jaw relaxed with relief. "Of course, we have a plan: get you out of here."

"That's more of a goal than a plan," I muttered.

Jane's eyes popped up in the window. "Unfortunately, we're going to need your help to get out of here. Can you move?"

I swung my legs over the side of the bed, grimacing as I felt pain all the way into my toes. "Yeah, but not fast. I'm not injured, but I'm sore and banged up."

"That's okay, as long as you can walk," Milo said. "Once the door is open, Jane and Winnie are going to get you out of here while I distract the guards."

I heard Winnie speak on the other side. "One of the guards told me about a secret exit. Just hold on a little longer, Lady Rowan. Milo's going to get you out of here."

I heard shuffling around the door, metal hitting metal, and then silence. Sleep clung to me and no matter how hard I tried to shake it away, it would not let go. Everything that had happened over the last few days pressed down on me in the silent room. I shook my head, pushing away my feelings. Now was not the time for self-pity or regret.

"Milo? Jane? Are you there?" I whispered.

No one responded. I knew they would be back but the wait felt like it lasted for hours; every moment spent in the tower chipped away at my confidence, replacing it with fear. I was trapped without someone here to help me escape. Then, faintly, I heard sounds again.

Suddenly, the door opened on the hinge's side. In the doorway stood Milo. I tried to run towards him and stumbled right into his arms.

"Thank you." The words caught in my throat as tears sprung in my eyes.

He wrapped his arms around me. "I just opened a door."

Sounds of a scuffle and raised voices reached our ears. It was only a few seconds before Winnie and Jane came around the corner.

"It's time to move now." Milo's hands trailed down my arm, and he took my hand in his. "While the guards are distracted."

We lurked in the shadows as we made our way down the corridor and another set of winding stairs. I couldn't help but jump at every creak of the floorboards and each distant shout, but we pressed on together. I swore I smelled freedom, and the scent grew stronger with every step we made.

A group of guards stood just inside the tower's exit, causing my heart to plummet. We were so close. Milo stepped forward, brandishing a book. "Keep going," he urged. "I'll keep them distracted."

"No," I said, wanting to throw myself on the floor in a tantrum. "We stay together." Why did he pull out a book? Was he going to lecture the guards to sleep?

Jane grabbed my arm, pulling me towards an area of the tower I didn't recognize. "Milo's right, Rowan. We can't all fight them and win. He has a plan that should work . . . and it will allow you to escape. You need to get out of here before you end up married to Montfort."

I hated that she was right. The last thing I wanted to do was get someone else into trouble. With one last look at Milo, I turned and fled with Jane and Winnie. I followed them into a room I had never seen before. Winnie moved a tall wardrobe to reveal a narrow opening. She gestured for us to follow before she disappeared into the darkness. I stepped through the opening, Jane right behind me, and was blinded when Winnie lit a torch.

"Damn, that's bright after running around in the dark for so long." I couldn't keep the thought to myself. I glanced around to see a dank hall that seemed to head downward for an indeterminable distance.

"I'm sorry. I probably should have said something, but this is my first prison break," Winnie said with more sass than I expected from her.

I threw my head back and laughed. "We need the light. I'm just being a whiny damsel. My apologies."

"Can you wait until we're farther away from the tower before making noise?" Jane hissed. "And you may be whiny, but I don't think anyone would ever describe you as a damsel."

"Fine. I'll be quiet. But just for you, Jane."

Winnie giggled but didn't add to our nervous banter.

The hall turned into a tunnel, and the walls a solid stone instead of the pieces that lined every wall of the castle. It grew colder and wetter the farther we went until we started walking uphill instead of down. The uphill portion was much steeper. By the time Winnie opened the storm doors that led to the fresh air of outside, the three of us were panting and sweating despite how chilly it had been below ground.

I took a moment to gulp in the fresh air, trying to breathe it in as it seemed sweeter after being imprisoned. Is this what freedom smelled like? Had I taken it for granted before? Then we ran, and we ran some more. We didn't stop in the normal clearing, or even in the town of Lockersley. Instead, we ran until the castle was a distant silhouette against the light of the rising sun somewhere on the outskirts of Sherewood, far enough from those that followed my uncle, far enough that we did not fear getting caught.

"We did it," Jane said, a note of disbelief in her voice.

"Thank you for breaking me out," I replied, determination hardening within me. "But it's not over. I'm going to take down my uncle and vindicate my father. Did you plan a signal to alert the others where we are for tonight? We need to plan our next steps. Whatever we do has to be foolproof. He's never going to lock me up again."

"I don't like it," Milo mumbled as he sat on a rock near the campfire.

I had spent the entire night awake trying to figure out the best way to take Lockersley back. My father had intended for me to take his place, and I was going to make it happen. By morning, I knew what had to be done. But I had waited for my fellow bandits to arrive before laying it out.

I looked over at Milo and raised an eyebrow. "Do you not like it because you think it's a bad plan, or because you're jealous of Prince Connor?"

He swiped his hand through his hair before answering. "The latter, I know it's not a good look on me, but he could be the solution to all your problems." He rested his arms on his knees, clasping his hands together.

I stopped my pacing in front of him and took his hands. "That may be true, but he isn't who I want."

"I can't figure that one out—have you not looked at him, Rowan?" Erin sighed wistfully.

The look I gave her would have withered a lesser soul. "Not helping."

She shrugged. "What? You would have to be . . . I don't know what you would have to be. I'm pretty sure creatures large and small fall in love with his beauty."

"I'm even willing to admit he looks like a golden god." Will shrugged before stretching out next to a thick tree trunk.

Jane stood. "Okay, so you're going to take proof of your uncle's treachery to Connor in the hopes he follows your father's wishes and convinces the king to let you have the land and the keep."

"That's it. After a night of stewing over what to do, that's what I came up with. If anyone has any better ideas, I'm up for suggestions." I stood and crossed my arms, defiance emanating off me.

Tuck made his way over to me. He put his arm around me and escorted me to a flat rock to sit on. "If you think we can trust him, I can't think of a better plan." He sat next to me. "Having the royals on your side will strengthen your claim more than anything else."

Milo looked at Tuck and then me, resignation written all over his face, but there was acceptance behind his own self-doubt. "You're right. I hate putting our trust in someone we don't really know all that well."

Tuck patted Milo on the shoulder. "We have to work with what we have in front of us, my friend. And right now, Prince Connor is our strongest option."

"I know him better than anyone here, and I trust him. He kept my secret even after I said no to his proposal." I stood and looked around at my friends, my merry band. "We've faced worse odds since the beginning. This will work because we're in it together."

Jane nodded, a determined glint in her eye. "I have all the proof of your uncle's wrongdoings. Let's organize it and you can present it to him. Your uncle will pay for what he did to your father."

Erin sighed, but smiled. "I can't believe you turned down Prince Connor. Sorry, Milo, but have you seen him? I'm still with you, even if you have questionable taste in men." She winked at me to let me know she was teasing.

We huddled around the fire to stay warm while we spent the next few hours organizing the evidence we had: letters from the nurse, receipts for ingredients the nurse believed were in the poison, everything we could find that proved my uncle's treachery. As the sun set, we were ready. Fear and hope raced through me. Connor might be our best hope, but his father was an unknown.

Milo, ever supportive despite his reservations, wrapped his arms around me and whispered in my ear. "Let's go get your land back."

I stared at the imposing castle rising in front of me, my cloak pulled tight around me, the hood covering my hair, hiding my identity from anyone who could see us. Knowing what I needed to do wasn't the same as actually doing it. Now that I was here, about to turn to the prince for help, I wasn't sure it was the right thing to do. What if I didn't get the help I expected, needed? Unfortunately, there was nothing left for me to do but move forward and trust that everything would work out if I leaned on someone else.

I clicked my tongue to let Artie know I was ready to continue on. My mare whinnied before continuing forward. The sound of her hooves crunching on the gravel path leading to the castle gates added to the tension I carried in every part of my body. The towering stone walls seemed to close in on me as I approached the grand entrance, which amplified the sound of my ragged breath and the pounding of my heart until it was the only thing I could hear. I took a deep breath as I steeled myself for what was to come. It was never easy for me to ask for a favor, but this was the only way I was going to be able to claim my rightful place in Lockersley.

Milo's presence as he rode beside me was the comfort I needed to keep moving forward. The others followed closely, each of them determined to help me in any way they could. When we reached the gate, the guards eyed our little band with suspicion. I maneuvered Artie until we were in front of everyone.

"I'm Lady Rowan of Lockersley." I threw my hood back. "I need an audience with Prince Connor."

The guards looked at each other before their inspection turned back to us. One gestured towards the keep. His partner took off, the metal of his armor clanking as he disappeared from view. After that, we waited. I hated waiting. It felt like doing nothing, or worse, being denied. But eventually the doors opened, and we were let through.

A stable boy took our horses before we were escorted into the keep. The inside was grand without being ostentatious, very different from what my uncle had done to my home. We walked into the great hall where the prince stood waiting for our arrival.

Prince Connor's honey-colored eyes were filled with concern as he approached. "Lady Rowan," he said warmly, extending his hand. "I see your uncle's prison couldn't hold you for long. I've been working on getting you released, but there were roadblocks I still had to overcome."

"Your attempt to have me freed means the world to me." I took his outstretched hand. "I hope it means you won't deny my request without hearing everything first."

Connor's expression grew serious as he listened. "Come to my office," he said, motioning for us to follow. "We'll discuss this in a more private setting."

We followed him up two flights of stairs into a cozy room with a view of the surrounding land. For such a small room, there was an abundance of seating, from a sofa that looked like it would envelope anyone that sat there, to a variety of chairs, ones you could just perch on, and a cozy armchair perfect for reading a book. The best spot was where the desk was, close to the window, with a cozy chair right behind it.

"Let's get down to business. I know you must have escaped, and I don't want to do anything that could jeopardize your freedom." Connor sat in the chair behind his desk.

Jane laid our proof on the desk. "Here's proof that Jonathan poisoned Rowan's father." She pointed to the letters, the receipts for medication, and the journals.

Milo stepped up. "And here's what I could find that backed what Rowan's father had told me personally. He wanted her to rule Lockersley after him. It's why he sent her to the nunnery for all those years. To learn things he couldn't teach her."

I stepped in front of my friends. "Will you help me—I mean, us—restore Lockersley to the leader my father wanted? I know it is not how things would normally work. But it was his will, and he should have a say as to who will continue his legacy."

"Leave this with me and I will see what I can do." Connor stood. "We will meet at your camp in two days. Until then, stay out of trouble and away from your uncle."

CHAPTER THIRTY-SIX

Two days had passed in a blink of an eye. Spending time in the forest with my friends was easy, even if there was the constant reminder of why we were waiting and the importance of what we were doing. But that didn't stop us from sitting around the fire and telling stories about our pasts, the parts we spent together and the times we were apart. The lull in our mission was a necessary respite that allowed us to reconnect in ways that had been missing until now.

That didn't mean we weren't all on edge, jumping at every little sound the forest made, especially the rustling sounds of wild animals walking through the woods. I was ready for Connor to be there at the end of the second day. I just hoped it was with good news.

"Rowan?" A whisper filtered through the sounds of our camp.

I turned towards the sound, my hand on the hilt of my dagger. The shadows around our campsite flickered, and out of the darkness, a familiar figure stepped forward.

"Connor." Relief washed over me. "You're actually here."

He nodded, the creases on his forehead a sign of his concern. "It's time for us to talk."

I motioned for him to sit by the fire, where the others were already gathered. The lighthearted mood we had maintained for two days had gone as we waited for whatever news the prince brought with him. Connor sat on a log, resting his elbows on his knees, as the firelight caused shadows to dance across his face.

"I have spoken with my father, the king." His voice was low. "He has agreed to listen to the evidence against your uncle. My father and your uncle have never liked each other. The allegations against your uncle disturbed him. He was unaware of the level your uncle was willing to go to gain control."

It wasn't the same as condemning my uncle, but it was one step closer. "Is what we showed you enough? The notebooks, the ledgers, the letters?"

Connor's eyes flickered to Milo, then came back to me. "It's not that my father doesn't believe you, but he needs more to depose your uncle. He's sent his men to Lockersley to investigate and, if necessary, arrest your uncle."

I wanted more, something more definitive, but at least they were willing to help. "This means the world to me, Connor. Thank you."

He smiled as he broke eye contact. "It's not just for you, Rowan. What your uncle's done threatens the stability of the entire region. The betrayal is something the king cannot let go unpunished."

Tuck leaned forward, his brow furrowed. "How long will it take for the king's men to get to Lockersley?"

"Within a week," Connor replied. "While you wait, get everyone in town ready to testify, especially anyone that has knowledge of what happened to Rowan's father, and anyone who supports her in taking his place."

Will nodded. "Erin and I will rally the town."

Connor stood, his eyes clouded with the weight I had put on his shoulders. "I have to get back, but I'll let you know if there are any changes. Stay safe, all of you, and especially you, Rowan."

I watched as Connor disappeared into the night. The next week would be crucial to completing my mission. My uncle was going to be brought to justice all because of the fortitude of my friends.

I looked at my merry band of bandits, the crackling campfire illuminating their faces. "One more week and everything will be set right. We're almost there."

"It's time, Rowan," Jane said as she pushed her way through the brush we had left in place to hide where our camp was located.

I jumped to my feet. The last few days had been unbearable. I'd been stuck in the forest, unable to do anything to work towards my goals. My friends all agreed it was too dangerous for me to go anywhere near Lockersley. So, I had been stuck in the woods while everyone else did something to get justice for my father.

Finally, it was time for me to do something, to say my part against my uncle.

I stood and brushed the wrinkles out of my clothes and took a deep breath, steeling myself for the day in front of me. The forest, once a place that felt safe surrounded by my friends, now felt like another prison I had to break free from.

As soon as I stood, Milo was at my side. He could tell how much of a toll the last few days had taken out of me.

He wrapped his arms around me. "I'll be with you every step of the way. But first I have something to remind you of everything you accomplished," he whispered in my ear before stepping back and slipping a necklace over my head.

I looked down at the pendant, a delicate bow and arrow. It was some of the finest metalwork I had ever seen. I gently wrapped my hand around it, finding strength and solace in his gift to me. I stood on my tiptoes and let my lips graze his, grateful for his unwavering support. "Thank you, I will cherish it always." I turned to the rest of my friends. "Let's go. It's time to take back Lockersley."

The rustling of leaves and the chirping of birds cheered us on as we moved through the forest. At the edge of Sherewood, I could see the silhouette of Lockersley Castle resplendent against the pink morning sky. Its presence was both a beacon of hope and a symbol of what I had lost, what I had been fighting to get back. I shook my head—how could one place mean so many things to me? For a moment, I questioned whether or not I really wanted it. But then we walked into town, reminding me that this battle was for each and every one of them, not just for me.

The town was bustling as we arrived, so different from when I had returned from the nunnery. Everyone must have heard that the king was coming. They nodded as they watched us walk by, supporting us in the only way that was safe. But it gave me hope, I felt unstoppable with their backing.

In the town square, a platform had been built for this hearing, and a small contingent of royal guards had already arrived, their uniforms pristine, kilts perfectly pleated. Prince Connor watched from the front, his presence commanding and reassuring, signs he would make a great king one day. His eyes swept over the crowd until he saw me. Then he nodded, an acknowledgment of me and the task in front of us.

My uncle's eyes bored into the crowd, his face a mask of anger and hate. Beside him, Montfort saw me in the crowd and sneered, his eyes cold and calculating. It would seem he had picked my uncle and was not being swayed from his choice.

Connor raised his hand, and the crowd fell silent. "People of Lockersley, we are gathered today to seek justice. Lady Rowan of Lockersley has come to my father and me with grave accusations against her uncle, which we present to you to ensure that the proceedings are fair and unbiased."

I stepped forward, removing my hood, my heart pounding in my chest. "I, Rowan of Lockersley, accuse my uncle of poisoning my father, Laird Richard, and usurping his rightful place as lord of this land. I have evidence and witnesses to support my claim."

I paused as a murmur ran through the crowd, allowing everyone to let my accusations sink in before I continued. Taking a deep breath, I painted a damning picture as I went through each piece of evidence we had gathered: letters, testimonies from servants, and accounts of my uncle's suspicious behavior.

As I weaved the story together based on the facts we had found, I could see the townsfolk's interest shift from looking forward to a potentially prosperous day to outright anger at my uncle's villainy. Those that had suspected foul play but had been too afraid to come forward stood beside me. Especially since I had the backing of the prince, and potentially, the king.

My uncle's face turned an unbecoming shade of red. "This is preposterous! These are lies, all lies!" he spluttered, so angry he was practically foaming at the mouth. "I demand you call a halt to these preposterous proceedings."

Connor stepped forward, his voice firm. "The investigation will continue. However, if you are innocent, you should have nothing to worry about."

Montfort's sneer faltered, and a flicker of doubt in his eyes betrayed him.

A booming voice interrupted the proceedings. "There is no need for an investigation. I can confirm that everything my daughter has said is the truth, except for my death. I fear that has been greatly exaggerated." He smiled down at the woman by his side. "But it would have been true if not for this lovely woman that not only got me out of the castle but nursed me back to health."

"Father . . ."

CHAPTER THIRTY-SEVEN

I leapt from the platform and ran to the man I had been grieving. As soon as I was close enough, I threw my arms around him. Tears streamed down my face. I couldn't control them, not that I wanted to. I was so happy to see my father standing in Lockersley, alive.

"How?" I took a step back. "Everyone thought you were dead. I was told you were dead."

He took my hands in his. "I know, and I'm so sorry. At first I couldn't remember who I was, and when I did, I fell in to a deep melancholy. I believed I had failed you, failed everyone." Tears welled up in his eyes, but only one escaped. "If it wasn't for Eleanor, I wouldn't have made my way back here. Truth be told, if it wasn't for her, I wouldn't have survived."

"Eleanor?" I was both bewildered and grateful by this turn of events. "The nurse who wrote to me and Lady Jane?"

Before my father could respond, a woman stepped from behind him. Everything about her, from her warm brown eyes to her soft curves, radiated kindness and compassion. "I am Eleanor." Her gaze met mine. "I was hired by your uncle to 'care' for your father, but he really intended for me to continue to administer the poison that was killing him. It took months for his body to heal, even longer for his memory to return."

My father squeezed my hands. "Eleanor risked every-thing to save my life, Rowan. She got me out of your uncle's clutches, nursed me back to health both mentally and physically. Once I recovered, I knew I had to come back. It was the only way to set things right."

I looked at Eleanor. I wanted to throw my arms around her, let my embrace show just how grateful I was. Instead, I used words, even though words would never be enough. "Thank you," I said, my voice trembling. "Thank you for keeping my father safe and bringing him back to me."

She nodded, a gentle smile on her lips. "It was the right thing to do. Your father spoke of you often, even when his memories were fragmented. His love for you was always clear."

The murmur of the crowd got louder as the news of my father's return spread from everyone near the platform towards those that couldn't see or hear what was happening. I climbed back on to the platform. "My father, Laird Richard of Lockersley, has returned! Together, we will bring Lockersley back to the place it used to be. And we will punish those that plotted to do us harm."

The crowd erupted, cheering for the return of my father. Their love for my father filled my heart. Prince Connor stepped forward, his arms extended in an attempt to quiet the crowd. Once there was silence, he spoke. "With Laird Richard's return, Jonathan's treachery has been confirmed. He will be punished for his acts."

I watched as my uncle turned as white as a ghost, his confidence gone as his deceit was exposed. Montfort looked equally scared, his sneer replaced by the slack jaw of disbelief.

"My uncle will pay for his crimes. Not just those against my father, but those against the people of this town," I declared, my voice strong. "Lockersley will be rebuilt. It will be the town I left behind, but better, stronger." I nodded to the guards.

The guards apprehended my uncle. He struggled and shouted his lies, but there was no way for him to escape the truth. Not with the victim of his foul deeds here as living proof of his guilt. Montfort was taken into custody for his complicity in my uncle's crimes, as well as his role in my false imprisonment—an end to his time as sheriff.

I turned towards my father as the crowd dispersed, embracing him again, unable to believe he was really here in front of me.

"I'm so proud of you, Rowan," he whispered. "What you've done has taken courage, strength, and so much more."

"I wasn't alone. If it wasn't for my friends, I could've never seen this through to the end," I replied, glancing at Milo, Jane, and the others who had stood by me. "We did this together."

Eleanor wrapped her arms around both of us, smiling. "Now is the time to focus on healing, both as a family and as a town. You're lucky to have the support of the royal family."

As if he knew we were talking about him, Prince Connor approached. His respect for me shone in his eyes. He took my hands as I extricated myself from my father's and Eleanor's embrace. "You proved to my father and myself that you are a true leader, Lady Rowan. Your determination and capacity to care for your people have earned you the admiration of many, including myself."

I felt a blush rise to my cheeks. "Thank you, Prince Connor. I can't put into words how much your support has meant to me."

He nodded. "Let's work together to rebuild Lockersley." He held up his hand to stop me from interrupting. "Not as partners in marriage—I know your heart has been given to another—but as friends. With your father's return, I have no doubt that there are brighter days ahead."

My father stepped forward. "About that: I had always planned on you taking my place, Rowan. After my time away, I think now is as good a time as any. I'll be around to support you, but you would be the one everyone turns to, the Lady of Lockersley."

Milo stepped beside me, his arm around my waist. "You're ready. And you have all of us supporting you."

"You were meant for this, Rowan." Jane squeezed my shoulder. "All the time in the nunnery, the training you've done since getting here. This is what it's all been for. You've been preparing your entire life, whether or not you knew it."

I looked at everyone around me—my father, Milo, Jane, and Prince Connor—and suddenly everything felt right in this moment. Their belief in me was the last push I needed to believe in myself. I was ready for this role because it wasn't just a part I was playing, it was my true self.

I looked down at the ground and took a deep breath. I nodded. "Thank you, all of you. Because of you standing by my side, I can take the mantle of responsibility my father is passing on to me. Your support has allowed me to succeed, and it will help me lead Lockersley into the future. And the first thing we will do is build the school Milo has diligently designed."

Milo stood there, frozen. The words sank in, and he swept me off my feet and spun around.

My father cleared his throat, smiling, his expression filled with pride. "That's exactly what I was planning before . . . everything—I know you can do this, Rowan. You've proven your strength and wisdom in secret. Now it's time for everyone to see exactly who you are."

Prince Connor clasped his hands behind his back. "I've already said you have our support. Lockersley will become a symbol of resilience and unity. Your clan's recovery will strengthen the kingdom."

I took Milo's hand in mine. Everything that I'd done, I succeeded at because of the people on my side. Jane, Tuck, Will, and Erin, my merry band of friends—they had all been so important in helping me finish my mission. I knew they would be integral to the future.

I turned towards my father. "Let's plan our next steps."

He nodded. "There is much to be done, but with you leading the way, things can only get better."

As we discussed our plans, Jane leaned over and whispered, "So, are you ready to play a lady for the rest of your life?"

I couldn't help but laugh. "No one here expects me to be a lady. I think the entire town would rather I continue to be a bandit, or some form of it."

Her laughter shook her entire body. "You're probably right, Rowan, although I would guess everyone here wants you to just be yourself. That's who we all love best."

Milo leaned in and whispered, "I'm so proud of you, Rowan."

Looking up at him, I smiled. "I couldn't have done it without you." I stood on my toes and pressed my lips to his before wrapping my arms around him and resting my head on his chest.

We looked at the castle. With my friends and family around us, it would become a symbol of our strength and determination. This was the start of a new chapter for Lockersley, and I was ready to lead my people into a bright and hopeful future, surrounded by the people I loved and that loved me.

Content with the knowledge I was the Lady and the Bandit of Lockersley.

EPILOGUE

"I suppose it's time," I muttered, glancing toward Lady Jane with a reluctant sigh.

Our eyes met; a resigned smile danced across her lips. "We have to tell them at some point. If we don't, they'll never stop asking. "Her voice was its usual calm, but I could hear the undercurrent of amusement she was trying to suppress.

Expectations hung in the air as I sank down into my favorite old, worn leather chair. I took a deep breath; the smell of parchment and ink filled my nose. The comforting scents were only one thing I loved about the library, the other was how the flicker of firelight cast dancing shadows across every surface in the room, from the books to the eager faces of my friends. I wasn't excited to tell this particular story, but with everyone's eyes fixed on me, it was clear there was no escape this time. Even Milo's blue eyes were fixed on me, his expression expectant. He was supposed to be on my side—curse him for siding with our friends. He could have helped me out, but no, he'd joined their ranks, eagerly waiting for the story that had become the stuff of whispered legends.

Tuck leaned forward in his chair, his fingers steepled under his chin, his eyes glittering with curiosity. "Come now, Rowan. Most of us in this room have known you since you were a child. Whatever this 'Incident' is, it can't possibly be worse than some of the other things you got up to growing up."

A familiar, deep laugh sounded from behind me, and I turned to see my father enter the room, a wry smile on his face. "You'd be surprised what Rowan and Jane managed at the nunnery," he said, settling onto a nearby bench. He reached for Eleanor, gently guiding her to sit beside him, his arm wrapped around her protectively. The love between them was clear—soft and unspoken, but undeniably there for all to see.

I smiled at the sight before turning to meet Jane's eyes. A mischievous glint danced between us and I winked. "Perhaps you should start," I teased.

Jane's lips curled into a grin. "I don't know, Rowan. You've always been the better storyteller." She winked back, clearly enjoying the suspense we were weaving.

Erin, impatient as always, crossed her arms and stomped her feet, her face scrunched up in frustration. "Someone tell us something already! We've waited forever to hear what happened!"

A loud chuckle erupted from my father, clearly reminiscing. "Is the 'Incident' the time you two decided to sneak a deer into the dormitory because you missed having a pet?" His voice was full of humor a she thought back to the letter he'd received from the headmistress, detailing the chaos of finding a fawn hidden in my room. I'd named her Clover. Jane and I had nursed her for weeks after hunters killed her mother and we had done our best to keep her hidden.

I shook my head, suppressing my own laughter at the memory. "No, Father, though Jane and I went to great lengths to keep Clover alive and well, *that* wasn't the Incident."

Will, seated beside me, nudged my chair with his knee. "Stop stalling, Rowan. You're not getting out of this. You're telling us, whether you like it or not."

With a resigned breath, I straightened in my seat, glancing around the room, catching the eager faces of our friends. "Alright, fine," I said, leaning forward, my voice lowering as if sharing a dangerous secret. "It all started the day Jane arrived . . ."

The headmistress's sharp clap echoed through the hall, silencing the low murmur of young ladies conversing about things I found mundane. I tried to sit still; my gaze cast forward as she spoke. I might have been looking right at the headmistress, but I didn't see her as all my focus was on being still, but the urge to fidget overcame my good intentions before long. My fingers tugged at the lacing of my tunic, twisting the fabric as I struggled to keep my restlessness at bay. The nun seated next to me noticed, her hand suddenly covering mine with a firm, silent reprimand. Startled by her touch, I forced my hands not to move, but now the need to do something, anything, always simmered under the surface, making it impossible to focus on the headmistress's words.

Something about a new student—those were the only words that penetrated my wandering thoughts. I blinked and looked up, a new student could be interesting, maybe she would care about something I actually liked, instead of all the boring things the other girls talked about here. That's when I caught sight of a young lady walking toward the front. She looked to be my age, though it was hard to be certain because she was tall, taller than everyone she passed on her path towards the headmistress. She moved with an elegant stride, it was almost like she was floating, commanding attention without uttering a word. I couldn't help but wonder what it must be like to be so tall and to move so elegantly. At fifteen, I had come to accept that I was small for my age and would never be tall. It didn't stop me from wondering what it would be like if things were different.

I couldn't look away from her as she greeted the headmistress. Who was she? And why did I feel that her arrival was about to change everything?

As soon as the nuns excused us, I darted out of my seat, unable to contain my excitement. I weaved my way through the others, determined to reach the new student. The other girls meandered around me, drifting out of my path and away from the headmistress and the newcomer, their disinterest baffled me. How could they not be curious? Anew face was something to be excited about. But they didn't seem to care.

Maybe it was because they had already found their friends here, comfortable in their little groups, something

I had not experienced at the nunnery. For some reason most of the girls avoided me, or worse, tolerated my presence. It was probably because I was always getting in trouble, pushing boundaries. But I couldn't change who I was, after months spent trying to make friends, only to feel more isolated, I had stopped trying. But this girl was someone who might not know of my reputation, someone who might actually want to be my friend.

My heart thudded as I approached her, the thought flickering in my mind: maybe she was different. Maybe I wouldn't be alone anymore.

I pushed through the last cluster of girls and found myself standing just a few feet from the new student. She towered over me, her dark hair tied in a simple braid. She wore the nunnery's uniform with ease, as though she'd been here for ages, even though I knew she hadn't. I didn't understand how she could have an air of calm about her, as if she didn't mind the whispers following her arrival, but she did, and I found it refreshing.

I cleared my throat before I took a step forward. "Hi! I'm Rowan," I blurted, faking confidence as my heart raced in my chest. "Welcome to the nunnery." I gestured to the almost empty room.

She looked down at me, her face inscrutable. I began to worry I'd overstepped, but then, to my relief, her lips curved into a small smile.

"Jane," she said, her voice low but warm. "It's actually Lady Jane but I don't care much for titles."

"Oh!" I smiled. "Well, it's nice to meet you, Jane. I'm actually Lady Rowan, but titles don't really mean much around here so it's a good thing you don't care for them. Do you need help with anything? I can show you around, if you want." The words tumbled out one after another with an eagerness I could not hide.

Jane's eyes flickered with something—amusement, maybe? She glanced around the empty hall; the other girls had drifted away like leaves in the wind. "I suppose that would be helpful," she said, her tone light but thoughtful. "Though, I imagine it won't take me long to figure it out on my own."

The way she said it reminded me, of me, determined to do everything on her own, an independent streak I recognized. Still, I was going to make a good impression. "I'd be happy to show you the dorms," I said, searching for something that would interest a newcomer. "Or we could go to the pub—celebrate your arrival."

Jane's smile widened just a bit, and she nodded. "Now that sounds interesting and like something that's more fun with someone else along."

The pub was dimly lit, smoke and stale ale filled the stagnant air while patrons sat at tables talking among themselves, ignoring anyone that entered. It was still too early for the raucous crowd that filled the room every night. Jane and I had slipped away from the nunnery for the afternoon, right after she was shown her room. The public house was nestled just outside the town's border, an easy walk through the old woods from the nunnery. We found a small corner table so we could keep to ourselves.

Jane leaned back in her chair, her eyes scanning the room with casual interest. "I can't believe you actually brought me here," she muttered, her tone more amused than anything else. "Do the nuns know their rebellious student has a taste for pub life?"

I smirked, taking a sip of my drink. "They'd be shocked, wouldn't they? But sometimes you need a bit of fun. How do you know I'm a rebellious student?"

Before Jane could respond, a pair of men entered, talking as they made their way to an empty table, their voices low and rough. There was something about their furtive glances and mismatched attire that caught my attention. One man was clearly noble, even the cloak he was trying to hidebehind cost more than what most people spent on food in a year. The other man was most likely a highwayman with a dramatic, but rough costume.

I nudged Jane. "Look." I nodded toward the two men.

She followed my gaze, eyes narrowing when she laid eyes on the mismatched men. "What do you think they're up to?"

I shrugged, not from lack of interest, but because I had no clue what was happening. I couldn't shake the feeling that something wasn't right. The two men didn't notice two women sitting in the corner. It wasn't much of a surprise when the nobleman sat with his back to us, the highwayman sat directly across from him. Jane and I exchanged a glance that spoke volumes without saying a word. At first, I wasn't sure we truly understood each other, but then we simultaneously slid our chairs closer, just enough to catch bits and pieces of their conversation.

". . . need . . .end of the week," the highwayman said. ". . .sabotage . . . trade routes . . . delay . . ."

The nobleman shifted, his eyes darted from one table to another, ignoring where Jane and I sat. "The nuns are well-armed," his tone hushed. " They've got a store of black powder hidden away for their defense. That's the only place to find enough black locally."

Jane and I froze, our reason for being at the pub forgotten. My mind processed the men's words. Black powder?

The nunnery's black powder? My heart raced thinking about someone attacking my home.

The highwayman leaned in, continuing on in the loudest whisper I'd ever heard. "Once the roads are gone, it'll take weeks, maybe even months to rebuild. Everything will come to a halt, and we'll bleed them all dry. No one will dare defy us—not even the king."

My eyes found Jane's. Her eyes locked onto mine. Her face had gone white with fear. We both knew this was something that would cripple the region if they succeeded. Not to mention they were planning to steal from the very place we currently called home.

"We need to do something." I clenched my fist, ready for action.

Jane nodded, her expression resolute. "But what and how? I'm pretty sure those men will kill anyone that gets in their way."

"We have to tell the headmistress. Let the nuns know everyone is in danger," I said. "Before those two can do any real damage."

Jane's jaw tightened as she glanced toward the door. "We need to get out of here—quietly."

I dragged my feet, the sound of my boots scuffing against the path emphasized as I followed Jane toward the head-mistress's office. With each step, the knots in my stomach tightened. Maybe going to the headmistress wasn't the best idea. It wasn't just that we rarely saw eye to eye—she didn't appreciate my habit of bending the rules.

I bit my lip as doubts swirled in my head. Would she even believe us? The tale sounded ludicrous, even to my own ears—*a nobleman and a highwayman plotting together to steal black powder from the nuns and destroy the trade routes*? It sounded like something out of a badly written ballad, just add a verse about them doing it to help save local merchants and it would make for a good story.

"Jane." My feet slowed to a stop. "Maybe we should take care of this ourselves. I don't have the best relationship with the headmistress. I don't think she's going to believe me."

Jane halted as she heard my words. She turned to face me, her expression unreadable. "Wouldn't it be better to let them handle it? How do you plan to stop those two from blowing the roads to pieces?"

I knew she was trying to be practical, but I had been thinking through the situation from all different angles since we left the pub. "Well .. ." I tapped my chin, acting like I was still thinking about what to do, even though I had been working on a plan the entire walk.

Jane's expression was a mix of exasperation and curiosity. "Rowan, don't tell me you're planning to single-handedly fight off a group of highwaymen?"

I folded my arms. "No . . . of course not." I smirked as I pictured taking them on in a fist fight and succeeding. "We don't have to fight them. We just need to keep them from getting their hands on the nun's black powder."

She raised an eyebrow. "And how are we going to do that?"

I pretended to think it over for a moment, but the truth was, I'd been mulling it over the entire walk. "We could move the black powder, hide it where no one would think to look. We set a trap then, when the highwayman and his noble friend show up to steal it, the trap is triggered, and we catch them in the act."

Jane's eyebrows shot up, her skepticism changed into something else, like she was intrigued. "How are the two of us going to move a stock pile of black powder without anyone noticing? Where exactly do you plan to hide the barrels? It's not like we can tuck them under our beds."

A grin spread across my face as the plan clicked into place. "What about the root cellar near the vegetable gardens? It's filled with crates of corn and tomatoes. No one's going to question a few extra barrels hidden among the produce. And we can do it at night, no one pays attention once they've done bed check and seen we're in bed."

Jane blinked, then let out a laugh tinged with disbelief. "You want to hide the black powder with corn and tomatoes?"

"Why not?" I said, shrugging. "No one would ever think to look for black powder there."

She rubbed her chin thoughtfully. "And what sort of trap were you thinking of?"

"We can put together some kind of alarm—maybe one of the old warning bells the nuns use for emergencies," I suggested, my excitement building. "Then we'll know the moment they try to break in, and we can trap them."

Jane stood there silently, staring at me as if she was trying to decide if I'd completely lost my mind. But then, she smiled—a small, mischievous smile that mirrored mine. "Alright," she said, her voice firm. "Let's do it. But if this plan backfires, we'll both be peeling potatoes for a month."

I nodded, already imagining the barrels of black powder nestled safely among crates of corn and tomatoes. "It won't. Trust me."

The night was still, there wasn't even a breeze to ruffle the leaves, the only sound was the occasional hoot of an owl. Jane and I crouched behind a stack of barrels near the nunnery's storage barn, our breaths shallow. We'd moved the black powder a few nights ago, carefully tucking the barrels behind and between crates of corn and tomatoes. Now, all we had to do was wait, just like we had the last couple of nights waiting for the highwayman to show up.

"I can't believe we're doing this again." Jane's breath was visible in the cold night air. "What if they abandoned their plan? How many nights are we going to sit out here in the cold?"

I grinned, tapping my fingers on my leg as excitement coursed through my body. "Trust me, they'll show, and we'll catch them. Our plan is foolproof."

She gave me a sidelong glance, clearly, she was less confident in my definition of 'foolproof.'

Before I could respond, a shadowy movement caught my eye. Someone was near the entrance to the nunnery's grounds. The figure stepped into the moonlight. I recognized the highwayman from the pub. I watched as he crept toward the munition's storage, his lantern flickered in the darkness. I held my breath; my palms were clammy and my heart raced as he approached the door.

The highwayman paused, glancing over his shoulder as if he expected to see someone before he slipped inside. Jane and I exchanged a quick look, silently communicating that it was time. She reached for the cord that would trigger our makeshift trap—a set of bells strung near the entrance. The moment he went for the decoy barrels, we'd know.

Seconds later the bells rang, the sharp sound piercing in the quiet night. The highwayman froze as he realized he had been caught by a couple of teenage girls.

I stood up, a triumphant smile spreading across my face. "Gotcha."

The highwayman dropped his lantern as he turned towards me.

But before I could take another step, I heard it—the unmistakable hiss of a spark. My smile vanished as I turned toward the barn.

"Rowan, what's that—?" Jane started, but she didn't get a chance to finish.

"Run!" Whatever was about to happen wasn't going to be good.

A crackling sound filled the air, followed by a burst of light. The spark had somehow found its way to the barrels, igniting the black powder we had so carefully hidden among the food stores. For a split second, there was silence—then the barn exploded in a loud bang, followed by quieter pops bursting one after another.

The blast sent popped corn flying in every direction, bits of white fluff rained down like snow covering the ground. Tomatoes splattered against the walls, the ground, even our faces as the juice sprayed everywhere, leaving the area looking macabre.

I ducked, shielding my head as kernels of popcorn flew towards us, mixing with the squished tomato guts. It was absolute chaos—an explosion of food and fire. I bit my lip trying not to laugh.

Jane was covered in tomato pulp. She turned towards me with wide eyes. "This . . ." she gestured to herself, before wiping a chunk of tomato from her cheek, "was *not* part of the plan."

I couldn't help it—I burst out laughing. Popped corn continued to fall like a bizarre hailstorm around us. "Who knew black powder could make such a mess?"

The highwayman, now thoroughly coated in popped corn and tomato bits, scrambled for the exit, his face a mix of shock and horror. Jane and I watched, helpless with laughter, as he bolted into the night, tripping over crates in his attempt to flee the scene only to be stopped by the headmistress and several other nuns.

When the chaos finally settled, we stood in the wreckage—popcorn still drifting lazily through the air, tomatoes splattered across every surface. The barn smelled like a strange mix of smoke, black powder, and a failed kitchen experiment.

Jane wiped her face again, her expression caught somewhere between exasperation and amusement. "Well, I suppose we did stop him."

I grinned, brushing a piece of popped corn from my hair. "And we made a snack in the process."

Dawn broke over the nunnery. The rising sun cast a soft glow outside the window of the kitchen where Jane and I sat, peeling what was an endless pile of potatoes. My hands were already cramping, and the smell of earth and raw potatoes assaulted my nose and clung to my fingers. I glanced over at Jane, who worked diligently beside me, her expression unreadable as she methodically scraped another peel off.

"This is your fault, you know," she didn't even look up, her tone too calm for comfort.

I raised an eyebrow, stifling a grin. "My fault? How was this my fault?"

She glanced sideways at me, a smile tugging at her lips. "It was your brilliant idea to set a trap that nearly blew up half the nunnery."

I couldn't help but laugh. "My hands may be sore now, and I might always smell like potatoes, but at least we stopped the highwayman—and gave everyone a bit of a show."

Jane chuckled, finally setting down her knife. "I don't think the nuns found the explosion of corn and tomatoes quite as entertaining as we did."

"No, they definitely were not amused." I agreed, shaking my head with a sigh. "But in our defense, it was a good plan."

"A good plan we executed terribly," Jane corrected with a shrug.

I shook my head. "It wasn't that we executed terribly, we just didn't take into account that barrels of black powder could leak. If that trail of black powder hadn't been there when the highwayman dropped the lantern the explosion would have never happened."

We sat in silence, both of us peeling away, the memory of last night's chaos still fresh in our minds. Somehow, despite the punishment, despite the mess, and the scolding from the headmistress; I couldn't help but feel . . . triumphant. We had done something to stop a bad guy. It may have been reckless, but we did something, on our own, that no one else would have dared to do. Together the two of us had faced danger and survived, even if we were covered in tomato guts and popped corn when all was said and done.

"This . . ." I paused, "is going to be one of those stories we tell when we're old, isn't it?" I looked over at Jane hoping she understood what I was really asking.

She threw her head back and laughed. "Oh, definitely. 'The Incident,' as we'll forever call it. The day we nearly set the nunnery ablaze and the first time we ended up peeling potatoes for a week as punishment."

"Worth it." I grinned, my days at the nunnery looked brighter than they had not too long ago.

She looked at me with a smile that matched mine. "Absolutely."

And in that moment, as we sat side-by-side in the nunnery's kitchen, surrounded by piles of potatoes, I knew something had shifted. The Incident had done more than just earn us a week of peeling duty—it had bonded us. Jane and I, against all odds, were friends for life.

"That's quite the story, you two wouldn't happen to be exaggerating, would you?" Tuck looked at us as if he expected us to break down and admit we had told a tall tale. It was like he had forgotten just how much trouble I was capable of causing on my own.

My father cleared his throat. "I'm afraid it's all true. The letter I received from the headmistress after this was rather illuminating, to say the least. She was not pleased."

"You mean it's all true?" Milo gulped. "Maybe we should have a couple lessons on the properties of black powder. Just in case."

"You needn't worry Milo it's been months since Rowan and I have started a fire or caused anything to explode." Jane patted him on the shoulder."

"Just months? That's not as comforting as you think it is." Milo muttered.

I snuggled into his arms. "But now Jane and I can count on all of you to be there for us. No need to figure it out all on our own when there's people like all of you on our side."

ACKNOWLEDGEMENTS

If you've read my other books and the acknowledgements I probably sound like a broken record. However, I have a wonderful support system that I can't help but thank every time I write a book. This time I have to start with my dad, who drove two hours one way on Scottish roads because I wanted to see Dunnottar Castle because I saw a picture on Facebook and wanted to see it in real life. This became the inspiration for Lockersley Castle and the waterfall. It wouldn't be my acknowledgements if I didn't mention my mom, she put up with my constant questions regarding Rowan's character struggles and was one of the eyes that edited my book. Then, there's always Charlotte, who gets to hear a lot of it and is constantly trying to help me with my social media. It's an upward battle but it helps to have the encouragement.

It wouldn't be a book if I didn't thank Sarah, my editor, who manages to build me up as she corrects my work. Her excitement at the little things I do in my book always make me smile. In fact, I save a draft that has all her comments in it because they make me feel clever when I'm not feeling all that clever,

And then there was Jamie, Adalynd, Trish and the other authors in the set who were always willing to help me work through my struggles. I enjoyed working with them immensely and can't wait to work with them again.

The final thanks goes to my readers. Thank you so much for picking up my books. I hope they always make you smile.

Thank you everyone!

ABOUT THE AUTHOR

Stephanie K Clemens is known for many things: an author, photographer, dog mom, instagrammer, adventurer, teacher, lawyer, and more. When she's not sitting behind her laptop she can be found on some adventure. Most of the time it's a road trip with her two doggos, but recently it has been in the pages of a book.

To subscribe to her newsletter go to www.stephanie kclemens.com or follow her on Instagram or TikTok at @bookishstephaniek

ALSO BY

Ladies of WACK Series
A Study in Steam
A Practicum in Perjury
A History in Horticulture – Coming Soon
Ladies of WACK Prequels
The Daring Adventures of Honoria Porter: Volume 1
Wynterfell Romances
For the Love of Hot Cocoa
Villain Rehab – Coming 2025
Fantasy Books
Stripped Away
Cursed by Bandits
Dangerous Days and Enchanted Evenings – Coming 2025

Children's Book by S.K. Clemens

Frankie Wants to be a Sled Dog

Made in the USA
Middletown, DE
03 November 2024

63462697R00203